P9-AGL-800

A TRAIL OF BLOOD

The search for princes, 'tis a trail of blood
Winding among the smirch'd and spatter'd scrolls
Of unrelenting time.

O sov'reignty,
Beneath the dark-dyed robes of time gone by,
How many crimes, how many strangled truths
Lie hid at thy command?

King Edward V
(fragments of Prologue from the *Harleian Miscellany*)

A TRAIL OF BLOOD

Jeremy Potter

The McCall Publishing Company

NEW YORK

AUTHOR'S NOTE

This is a work of fiction, based on historical fact. The information concerning Richard III I owe mainly to Paul Murray Kendall's biography. Josephine Tey's novel *The Daughter of Time* was an inspiration. Ever since their supposed murder the princes in the Tower have haunted English history. The question of Richard III's guilt has been debated for nearly five hundred years. All I claim for my version of events is that it is as plausible as the one circulated by three earlier practitioners of the art of crime fiction: H. Tudor, T. More and W. Shakespeare.

Family Tree of the Plantagenet Houses of York and Lancaster appears on page 282.

FIRST AMERICAN EDITION 1971

Library of Congress Catalog Card Number: 74-139526

SBN 8415-0063-0

The McCall Publishing Company

230 Park Avenue, New York, N.Y. 10017

PRINTED IN THE UNITED STATES OF AMERICA

CONTENTS

Part One

THE ABBEY

I

'You speak of treason,' said the abbot.

'Not so,' the chancellor replied. He was coarse-featured, boar-snouted.

They were old enemies and the abbot chose not to heed the contradiction.

'Treason,' he repeated. 'You would have me hung on the gallows and cut down alive. You would have my entrails drawn from my body and burnt before my living eyes. You would have quarters of my naked flesh displayed to public view.' He spoke evenly, without evident reproach.

'God forbid!' The chancellor bared his blackened stumps in a Judas smile.

'It happened to our brother in God, Prior Houghton of the London Charterhouse.'

'The prior sought martyrdom. You, my lord abbot, are too wise.'

Provocation and flattery; incitement to treason. The abbot sighed to himself. On his return home from affairs of church and state in London, two unwelcome visitors had been waiting to disturb his well-earned peace: John Rayne, chancellor and vicar-general of the diocese of Lincoln, and Robert Aske, a pert young lawyer from the north.

Home was Croyland. It was fifteen hundred and thirty-six years since God had sent His only Son to redeem the sins of all mankind, and for more than eight hundred of them the abbey in the fens had served His cause in an ever more sinful world. John Wells's reign as abbot had lasted a mere twenty-four of these, but the weight of the centuries lay on his shoulders. If any could bear it in these dangerous times, his could. They were broad and unstooping. Past sixty now, he was still tall and fresh-countenanced, with a nobleman's bearing. Handsome, tranquil and worldly.

These words could be used of his parlour too, where he sat with his guests and prior. The beams were of oak from the Rockingham forest. Brightly-coloured hangings woven with peasant scenes in Flanders served as a shield from draughts. An oriel window displayed the modern marvel of truly transparent glass. The fire warmed them from a new hearth, and its stone was the finest in Christendom – a gift from the Conqueror's abbey at Caen.

Abbots were not as other monks. The fur-trimmed velvet gown bore witness to that. They had a foot in each world. Their apartments stood outside the enclosed heart of the monastery. Here at Croyland they abutted the south wall of the abbey church but turned their back on the seclusion of the cloisters, choosing to face the bustle of the outer court.

In these lodgings the abbots played host to important travellers who sought their hospitality. No one would put up at an inn who could find accommodation at an abbey. Abbey food was better, abbey beds were softer, and payment was optional. Travellers were sufferers, like the sick, and received due charity. Even kings had been pleased to lodge at Croyland: from Ethelbald of Mercia in the eighth century to the saintly Lancastrian Henry and the far from saintly Yorkist Edward in more recent years.

King Henry had come in Lent to fast and pray. He had announced that he would like to take the cowl and spend the rest of his days as one of the brethren. Edward had complained of the cold and scandalously demanded the gatekeeper's pretty daughter to keep him warm in bed. When he left he gave the abbey one gold noble and the porter a fistful. By way of entrance money, he had said.

Here, too, the abbots ran an establishment to rival any secular lord's. They supervised the upbringing of the local gentry's sons, who were entrusted to their household to learn letters and seemly behaviour and the social graces. Here the business of the abbey was conducted, the administration of its estates arranged, its accounts balanced. Here men came in times of war and plague and uncertainty to leave their most precious treasures in the safe custody of a house of God. Often the times were so uncertain that they never returned to reclaim them.

Looking through the glass in his window, the abbot could see rain falling steadily. Damp to damp. The district was so waterlogged that men called it Holland. The name Croyland itself meant 'muddy earth'. When St Guthlac had chosen it for his hermit's cell so long ago, it had been a deserted island. Now, even at the zenith of the abbey's power and glory, it seemed still to attract God's particular disfavour. The previous summer had been as sunless as men could remember, the winter as bitter as the news it brought from London. May had come at last, but February's weather had still not gone.

Perhaps God had decided to turn His back on all of England. With the king behaving as he was, could one blame Him? Whatever one might think of the cardinal archbishop, he had run the country's affairs well while the king devoted himself to pleasure. Now that he was disgraced and dead, an upstart tradesman had become the chosen instrument of government. The king had declared himself Supreme Head of the Church in England and appointed Thomas Cromwell his vicar-general.

This was the man who presided at the convocation the abbot had attended in London. The very presence of a low-born layman was an insult and they had exchanged high words over the Act dissolving the smaller of the monasteries. During the summer months these houses of God would be closed, their possessions seized, their buildings destroyed, the monks expelled.

The king was a spendthrift. Even debasing the coinage hadn't saved him. He needed money and the religious houses had it. That was the kernel of the matter, and Master Cromwell was the maggot in the kernel. He had been elevated above all the ecclesiastical dignitaries of the realm so that he could plunder them. His greedy eyes were on their monastic estates and the jewelled shrines of their saints.

The abbot barely suppressed a malediction. Croyland was safe – for the moment. At Christmastide Cromwell had sent an agent armed with the powers of a royal commissioner, but the abbot had worsted him. Now had come the quarrel in London. Worse trouble must be expected, but he had not foreseen its coming so speedily or in the bloated shape of Chancellor Rayne. With his customary cunning Cromwell had selected an enemy from within.

The abbot's clear blue eyes wandered from window to hearth. Above it hung the sword of St Guthlac. Formerly a holy relic in the church, it had suffered demotion to the parlour. He had felt obliged to take note of the undoubted Norman workmanship on the chasing of the blade. It could not be reconciled with the fact that the founding saint was a Saxon who had died some centuries before the Normans came. He found comfort in its presence nonetheless.

'You call me wise,' he said, 'but in these days wisdom may not suffice.'

'Is that the reason you keep the saint's sword so bright?'

The chancellor had been watching, patient as a huntsman waiting for his quarry to make a false move.

'And sharp too,' replied the abbot easily. 'My body-servant Gervase sees to that.'

'You would scruple to use it,' suggested the chancellor less easily. 'We are men of peace – at least I trust so. That is our vocation.'

'I came not to send peace but a sword,' said the abbot. 'St Matthew chapter ten verse thirty-four. He that hath no sword let him buy one. St Luke chapter twenty-two verse thirty-six. These are the words of our Lord.'

'Then you are a warrior and will not hesitate to do what we have come to ask of you in Christ's name.'

This time it was the young man who spoke. His face was flushed, the skin tight over his cheek-bones. He had only one eye, the other lid drawn down over the blindness of an empty socket. But one was enough for the abbot to glimpse the fire within.

'Seeking a rightful king cannot be treasonable,' the young man went on. His voice trembled with the passion of a fanatic.

A dangerous ally, thought the abbot. A peril to himself and others.

'Who but God can judge the rightfulness of kings?' he asked.

'The law,' said the young man, who was a lawyer.

'And God's representatives here below,' added the chancellor, who was both lawyer and cleric. 'But let there be no talk of treason. We wish you, my lord abbot, to authorise an investigation. Nothing more.'

'Who will undertake it?' the abbot demanded.

The prior coughed nervously and spoke for the first time. 'Brother Thomas, if it pleases you, my lord,' he said.

2

At the mention of Brother Thomas the abbot stirred and his buttocks winced with pain. That morning on the last stage of his journey from London he had ridden along a sodden track which was unfit for man or horse. Hoping to conceal the alarm he felt at the proposed inquiry, he made a show of burrowing his tender rump gingerly into the depths of his cushioned chair.

The sharp-tongued Aske spoke again. 'After half a century of Tudor misrule, who are the surviving Plantagenets? Where are they now? That is what we seek to discover.'

'To what purpose?' the abbot asked softly.

The chancellor opened his mouth, but the young man was first.

'The chancellor speaks for himself. For my part I mean no treason either. Since I am among churchmen and friends, let me state my opinion that the traitors are those who support Henry, without the grace of God unlawfully king of England, unlawfully king of France, unlawfully lord of Ireland, formerly Defender of our Faith, self-styled Supreme Head of our Church – a heretic, an adulterer, a usurper.'

'Spare us your abuse,' the chancellor demanded, shocked to the soles of his fleece-lined slippers. 'Remember, I pray you, that Henry is our crowned and anointed sovereign lord – our undoubted king.'

'Unless there exists a better claimant.'

'Even then your words would not become excusable. You must guard your tongue, Master Aske, or I cannot continue to keep you company.'

'Go then. You have brought me here. Your mission is accomplished.'

The fiery eye challenged him. The chancellor averted his gaze and did not stir.

Watching them, the abbot weighed Chancellor Rayne in the balance of his mind. Aske he dismissed as too rash for this world, a man moreover without consequence or support. The chancellor was another matter. As vicar-general to the bishop of Lincoln he represented episcopal authority throughout a see which spread from the Humber to the Thames, from the sheep-rich wolds of Lincolnshire to Oxford and beyond.

The diocese cut a swathe across the heart of England. It contained more religious houses than any other. The black monks were at Croyland, Peterborough and Ramsey. The black canons were at Leicester, Dunstable and Oseney. Such powers as the bishop had over these and many others were exercised for him by his chancellor. In Croyland and all its domains the abbot's own authority was absolute. Except during visitations. Nearly ten years ago there had been such a visitation, an episcopal investigation into moral lapses and financial malpractices in the monasteries. John Rayne had come to Croyland armed with powers which temporarily overruled the abbot's. Their enmity dated from that occasion.

Not that any scandals had been uncovered, the abbot was thankful to remember. The rule of the order was being faithfully observed. There was no laxness in the choir's performance of its duties. No loose women were living within the walls; no meat being eaten in the refectory. Proper accounts were kept.

In other houses matters had been very different. At Peterborough the chancellor had found the abbey gate unlocked all night and monks enjoying the pleasures of the flesh. The dormitory roof leaked and no grammar master was employed to instruct the younger brethren. At Humberstone the monks had dispensed with discipline altogether and not taken kindly to the chancellor's interference. He had stopped them playing tennis in the village and dicing for money in the taverns.

Without doubt he would dearly have loved to report such goings-on at Croyland, the most important of the abbeys. But he had to content himself with a charge of engrossment of the office of cellarer against the abbot and a tart comment about the head porter, who was accused of maliciously misdirecting pilgrims inquiring the way to Our Lady's shrine at Walsingham.

These were pinpricks. The substance of the quarrel between abbot and visitor had concerned the abbey's records. These included *Historia Croylandensis*, the famous Croyland chronicle, begun by Abbot Ingulph at the time of the Conqueror and carried forward unbroken into the present century. Sometimes the chronicler was a scholarly monk like the learned Peter of Blois. Sometimes the pen passed to men who had played an active part in the events they chronicled, men who retired or fled from government to record the truth for posterity.

Croyland kept such treasures close. When the chancellor ruled that they should be 'lent' to the bishop's library at Lincoln, all the chronicles and deeds and charters unaccountably disappeared. In vain he reminded the abbot of the authority of a visitor. The abbot referred him to the precentor, who had charge of the documents, but this good man had (with the abbot's permission) prudently taken a vow of silence. In the chapter house the brethren made it plain that their obedience was due not to the bishop but to the rule of St Benedict and their father in God, Abbot John.

The abbot had no doubt who it was who wanted the

records and why. Rumour had escaped that they contained evidence which could topple the house of Tudor from the throne. After Chancellor Rayne's failure he had doggedly awaited the next attempt. Only someone armed with powers greater than his own could hope to succeed.

At last another visitation was ordained. This time a royal one. The man who had supplanted the Pope would make his own investigation. The riches and morals of the so-called religious houses would be pried into and publicly recorded. There were nearly six hundred of them in all, and between them they were believed to own one-third of the realm. This wealth was what the king coveted, but the visitation offered other opportunities. Master Cromwell, the king's creature, who promised to make him the richest king that ever ruled England, had not forgotten Croyland's secrets.

The royal commissioner arrived one dark day during the long winter. He had been selected with royal venom.

Thomas Bedyll had served as counsel to the king in the great divorce suit which led to the cardinal's downfall and Cromwell's rise and the assault on the monasteries. The assignment of extracting the Oath of Supremacy from the most orthodox of the religious had gone to him. He had been the interrogator of Chancellor More and the bishop of Rochester before their executions.

Normally a visitation followed prescribed canonical procedure. Each member of the community underwent individual examination. But Master Bedyll was in a hurry. He galloped up the road from Bury at the head of his retinue, bringing with him in his saddle-bag the most precious relics from the abbey of St Edmund the martyr. In his infamy and impiety he had stolen their lumps of coal left over from the fire which toasted St Lawrence.

So far from showing shame, he had juggled with them in the outer court and announced that he had little time to spare for Croyland. He was anxious to press on to Walsingham, attracted by a crystal phial containing drops of the milk of the Mother of God. He was thirsty, he said, for Virgin's suck.

This coarse, blunt man tried the abbot's compassion sorely. Financial and scandalous information was what he demanded. Religion did not concern him except for what he called superstitious practices. The financial information was supplied. Scandals there were none. The abbot confessed to the superstitious practice of worshipping God. Then came the long-awaited moment. Where were the records of whose fame the commissioner had heard reports?

Precautions had been taken. The aumbry in the cloisters was empty of every document of value. The direst threats left abbot, prior and precentor unmoved: they would not lie, but they could not be brought to tell the truth. Given time, the interrogator of More and Fisher might have worn them down, but Walsingham beckoned and a long itinerary of abbeys and priories stretched beyond.

So Bedyll left Croyland empty-handed. He was not the man to suffer frustration unavenged. Before going he invited the brethren to petition for dispensation from their vows, which he was empowered to grant. When none responded he rounded on the two youngest and summarily dismissed them as being below the age when they could take vows with full understanding.

His parting gift to the abbot was a list of unpalatable injunctions for the future conduct of the abbey's affairs. In exchange for this he took the abbot's fool. The royal jester was past his prime and he hoped to curry favour by presenting the king with a successor. The abbot, who kept his fool to amuse his guests not himself, counted this a small price to pay. The injunctions he quietly ignored.

That was five months ago. Now Bedyll had reported to Cromwell, and Chancellor Rayne, using some passing pretext, had returned for the records and his revenge. This time everything was at stake – the abbot's life, the abbey's life, the Faith itself.

3

Though the chancellor's three score years and ten were run, God, in His inscrutable wisdom, gave no sign of wishing to take him to His bosom. The old man's cheeks, weatherbeaten from travel, were brown and tough as tanned leather. Age had impaired neither his health nor his subtlety of mind. Eyeing him across the parlous table, the abbot felt his confidence ebb. Old grudges grew deep roots and the tide of events was flowing the chancellor's way.

Aske was a puzzle. His search for another king seemed genuine. The sentiments he expressed were shared by many. In London the abbot had heard such words whispered in corners even while the formal speeches of loyalty to the crown were being delivered. But to be so forthright, so trusting of a representative of the established order as the bishop's vicar-general – this was carrying rashness to the bounds of sanity. Contact with Robert Aske could be as fatal as contact with the plague. Which was no doubt why he had been brought to Croyland.

Another complication was the prior, sitting beside him now, discreetly silent: as old as the chancellor, but frail, unsubtle, dedicated to God and the religious life.

Unhappily, during the abbot's frequent absences, conduct of the abbey's business descended on the prior's other-worldly shoulders. When he returned home the abbot's first concern was invariably to unmake unwise decisions and undo much of what had been done with so much good intent and bad effect. Into what folly of indiscretion and commitment had this pair of visitors lured the poor innocent prior? The call, no doubt, had been carefully timed to coincide with a period of his stewardship. Even so, little harm could have been done if Brother Thomas stood firm. It was the news of his involvement which caused the abbot most anxiety.

'The chancellor is right,' he said, deciding to make a show of loyalty. 'We owe allegiance and obedience to King Henry. He is our temporal and spiritual ruler, our king and the only Protector and Supreme Head of the Church and clergy of England.'

'And you are the leader of the abbots' party!' exclaimed Aske in disbelief. 'His Holiness the Pope—'

'—is bishop of Rome,' interrupted the abbot, 'and has no jurisdiction in this realm now. I have sworn to it. The prior and all the other brethren here have sworn to it. Every member of our order and of every other order has sworn to it.'

The prior showed his distress. 'Not in our hearts,' he protested. 'The outward man submitted, but the inward man did not consent.'

'An oath taken under duress is not binding,' said Aske.

'Where was the duress?' the chancellor demanded. 'The lord abbot is right, my friend. If you will not listen to my views, at least respect his.' He smiled his crooked smile.

The abbot inclined his head, not so much to acknowledge the compliment as to hide his distrust. 'An oath taken before witnesses in the name of God is binding indeed,' he said. 'No unspoken reservation can loose the bond of the spoken word. The Oath of Supremacy was administered in proper form. Those who searched their consciences and believed that they could not subscribe to it should have refused it and followed Prior Houghton to Tyburn.'

'May God rest his soul in eternal peace.' The prior crossed himself and knelt in prayer.

'Amen to that,' said the young man. He leaned forward and focussed his single eye accusingly on the abbot. 'Do nothing, my lord, and this house which you hold in trust for God will be destroyed. Eternal peace will reign here where we sit. Croyland will be dissolved for ever by the Devil's representatives here on earth.'

'So be it,' said the abbot, 'if such be the will of God.'

The prior moaned, his words stifled by the vow of obedience to his superior. The abbey was his world. He had come to Croyland sixty years before. His priorship went back for nearly thirty. On the death of Abbot Richard there were those who thought he should have succeeded. In the election of Father John, his junior, he often found it hard to discern the hand of God.

He found it especially so now. 'Quantum per Christi leges licet,' he murmured to himself.

So far as the laws of Christ permit. That was the reservation in the clergy's acceptance of the Oath of Supremacy, and it was a spoken not a silent one.

The abbot heard him and felt the breach between them widen. The prior led the true monastic life. He observed the rule with fervour and punished with severity any shortcomings among the brethren. Poverty and chastity came easily to him, but the abbot was well aware what an effort the duty of obedience sometimes cost him.

They were each other's earthly cross. While the prior struggled with himself to achieve complete subservience to the abbot, his worldly bungling ran the abbot's reserves of forgiveness dangerously low. The abbey's continuing prosperity depended on the abbot's skill in administration and diplomacy. The guardianship of the spirit of its many-centuried life of worship rested with the prior. The abbot ruled but the prior took precedence in piety.

This feeling the abbot detected not only in himself and the prior, but among the brethren at large. It was bad enough that he could not free the depths of his own conscience from it. But the prior's moaning and muttering expressed the lack of confidence of others. When the crisis came, Croyland's prior would gladly offer his body for torture and suffer the pain which only faith could make bearable. If it would save the abbey he would joyfully consent to be tied to a hurdle and dragged to the gallows. But – for all his acknowledged leadership of the Church's opposition to the royal will – would the abbot?

There was plenty to save. Once again his thoughts rested on the community he cherished and commanded. Croyland had come a long way since St Guthlac. It had survived sacking by the Danes, two conflagrations and an earthquake. With God's blessing and the gifts of the faithful, it had risen again four times.

Not only risen, but prospered. The brethren on this swampy islet, the despised but fertile 'cru land', had come to own not only everything in sight – and one could see for many miles across the fens – but plenty more besides. Of all the wealthy monasteries of England no more than a handful were wealthier. Westminster and St Alban's probably. St Edmund's Bury and the Priory at Canterbury possibly. Glastonbury in the west perhaps. This was the company Croyland kept.

In the surrounding countryside the abbot ruled like a

secular overlord. He owned some fifty estates or more, sprawling across five counties – the shires of Lincoln and Northampton, Cambridge and Huntingdon, and as far away as Leicester. In these parts it was his writ which ran, not the king's; his authority which was undisputed. For weeks at a stretch he would journey in state, administering summary justice in his domains. Other abbots delegated such matters to stewards, but not Abbot John. Sometimes he travelled by horse, more often by boat along the winding waterways of his private kingdom. Each night one of his own manor houses would be ready to receive him. Each morning bailiffs would be summoned for examination so that he could satisfy himself that the abbey was not being cheated of its dues by slothful tenants or faithless servants. He resolved disputes. He punished. He rewarded. He represented God.

In the management of the country's affairs too the abbot played a central part. He was mitred, taking his place with the bishops as one of the spiritual lords of the realm. When the king called a parliament, summoning the most eminent of his subjects for consultation, the abbot of Croyland was always among them. He would leave his own territory and ride away to wider responsibilities and more dangerous deliberations. In London he learned to practise the ways of the courtly world, to sway with the breeze, to manoeuvre and manipulate, to flatter and intrigue. Only thus did the endless law suits with neighbouring potentates reach a favourable judgment and prevent encroachment on his lands and rights.

After two dozen years of experience in such manoeuvrings the abbot knew well that the safety and welfare of his house rested on him and him alone. The prior in his seclusion knew nothing except the forms of worship and prayer. Had Prior Houghton's disembowelment helped the London

Charterhouse? Far from it. Croyland would do better with its abbot's bowels where they belonged.

He glanced up above the little door which led to his private chapel. There on a shelf rested the skull of one of his predecessors. A more authentic relic than St Guthlac's sword, it served to remind successive abbots of their duty even unto death.

Abbot Theodore had been head of the community when the Danes came to Croyland pillaging and slaughtering. All the most precious relics, including St Guthlac's body and his scourge and psalter, had been loaded on a boat and taken by the younger monks into hiding. The gold plates and chalices and patens, even the table of the high altar, were thrown into the well. Everyone fled except Theodore and one or two elderly brethren. They continued to perform the regular hours of their holy office, celebrating mass and singing steadfastly through the psalms until the pagans burst in.

The leader of these wild enemies of God had stabbed Abbot Theodore to death while he knelt at the altar praying for their souls. That was seven hundred years ago, but from where he sat Abbot John could see the gash of the dagger-thrust in the back of the skull.

At least it had been a more merciful end than living disembowelment.

4

The clatter of a falling chair broke the chain of his meditation. It was Aske rising in a fever of indignation to harangue him.

'The king quarrelled with the Pope because he wished to set aside his lawful wife and wed his whore. His Holiness forbade it, so the king – a man not even in holy orders – has declared himself head of the Church. How can you, an abbot, claim to recognise this absurdity as a legal fact, as pleasing to God, as an article of faith for all men to swear to?'

'Let me remind you,' the abbot replied, 'that two years ago the king asked convocation at Canterbury whether in this realm of England the Roman pontiff has any greater jurisdiction bestowed on him by God in the holy scripture than any other foreign bishop. The answer was no, with no more than four dissenting votes. The same question was asked of the convocation at York and the same answer received, without dissent.'

'Your brother in Christ, the lord bishop of Rochester, dissented. He refused the oath like a true Christian and died for it.'

'He will be numbered among the saints,' muttered the prior.

'His head was hacked from his body before it could wear the cardinal's hat sent him by the Pope. A man seventy-four years of age, devoted to the service of God and the state. I wonder the weak-stomached brethren among his fellow prelates do not lie down and die of shame at not following his example.'

The instincts of the abbot's long-past boyhood urged him to seize the sword from the wall and run this one-eyed ranter through the ribs. Who was he to lecture his betters on matters of conscience? The third son of an unimportant Yorkshire squire, so the abbot had been told; with a small practice at Gray's Inn and a small estate in Hampshire, which had gone to his head. A man in his thirties, too young for wisdom yet too old not to have learned manners and discretion.

'Your timidity, my lord abbot, does not become your high office.'

The man was sneering at him, insolently goading him to act or lose his temper and his self-respect. The chancellor's ugly face was alight with unmasked glee. The prior cried out against the offensive words but in his heart he would agree with them. So this was his reward, the abbot thought bitterly, for agreeing to become the Church's spokesman when even his peers from Westminster and St Alban's hung back.

He sat impassively, a seasoned campaigner in the craft of concealment. His anger he appeased by sinfully allowing his imagination to picture the young man lying on the floor with his life's blood staining the rushes. This was no time for emotion. Abbot Theodore's abbey had been of wattle and reed; its rebuilding was undertaken without difficulty in an age of rising faith. His own buildings were of stone, and he lived at a time when faith was receding at the speed of the tide in the Wash. A disaster now could mean the end of the community for ever.

He was conscious of it all, spreading around him like an ancient township. The cloisters, the chapter house, the refectory, the dorters, the infirmary, his own lodgings – these were merely the core of a community of hundreds who were somehow employed or tended or who clung on like leeches inside the long walls and great gatehouse of the brethren.

At the very heart, rising above it all, stood the abbey church. In this bare flat district the soaring tower was a source of wonder for miles around. Two lower towers flanked the west front, dwarfing the village outside the gates. Inside, the church boasted three aisles, the side ones broad enough for any ordinary church. One, indeed, was lent to the villagers for parish services and the abbot could spare it without noticing the loss. He could have supplied two more churches from the transepts and still have left himself space enough for a cathedral. The choir, which the brethren kept to themselves, ran to full ninety feet in length, and if the whole population of Lincolnshire had flocked to worship, there would have been standing and kneeling room for all in the vastness of the nave.

But nothing on earth was indestructible. One false move by one man and it could all collapse like a house on sand. Too much timidity or too much boldness, and desolation would descend. It would fall on the community and on the surrounding countryside. Every man, woman and child within sight of the tower depended on the abbey for their livelihood. Employment for the healthy, alms for the poor, care of the sick – these were provided by the abbey, and the abbey alone. Even lepers found a home under Croyland's protection. In a ramshackle cluster of huts on the far side of the river, poor blotched outcasts from the world were provided with food and shelter in accordance with the precepts of St Benedict.

The abbot permitted himself another quiet sigh. To protect all this and these was his responsibility. Had he the strength of mind and faith to overcome his adversaries?

The two who faced him were puppets. Forerunners of menace, no more. The chancellor was the creature of the bishop and the bishop, like Thomas Cromwell, was the creature of the king. That Cromwell was behind this visit the abbot had little doubt. Master Aske was being allowed enough rope to hang himself and the abbot too.

Was the king himself privy to the plot? That was the question. At court the abbot kept his distance where he could, but he knew the king – had known him since he inherited the crown more than a quarter of a century before. His private name for Henry was Ichabod, for the glory had departed. The tall fair youth who had excelled at scholarship and sport and good fellowship was gone, replaced by a stout, shifty reprobate. The abbot had chosen the path of discipline for body and will. The king had taken the opposite road, choosing the flesh and all forms of self-indulgence. Now, freed from the rein of Wolsey's guiding hand, his wilfulness had run away with him.

Some said that the king lurked behind every move made by Cromwell. Others believed that the Lord Privy Seal had a free hand and the king would have his head as soon as he overreached himself. To dissolve the smaller monasteries was one thing: Wolsey himself had suppressed a few. But a move against the Croylands and the Walsinghams – that surely would mean the dissolution of Thomas Cromwell.

The abbot inclined to the first and gloomier view. If Chancellor Rayne could find a pretext for riding back to Lincoln or on to London with a tale of high treason, it would be all over with Croyland. With himself ritually hanged, drawn and quartered, the way would be open for the appointment of a royal nominee to the abbacy. Once the brethren had sworn obedience to him – and they would have no choice – the abbey's property could be transferred to the crown without resistance and all its secrets prised open.

'Sit down, Master Aske,' he said in the voice he reserved for back-sliding members of his flock, 'or you will make me forget that hospitality is a rule of our order. And you, chancellor, what have you to say of this? You keep strange company for a loyal subject. Master Aske invited you to leave if you differed from him.'

'I accept no responsibility for his words.' The chancellor stared at each of them in turn, as though enrolling witnesses.

'Nor do I desire you to,' said Aske, 'and I will sit down when I have an answer. Even as I speak, sacrilege is being committed. What is God's is being seized in the name of the king. What does my lord abbot propose to do about it? Sit in his comfortable chair before the warmth of his hearth and say, So be it, it is the will of God?'

'Now you misquote me. I said, *if* it be the will of God.'

'How can it be? How can the theft of church property be the will of God? How can the suppression of communities dedicated to His praise and worship be in accordance with His will? Answer me that, my lord. Are you frightened to defend God's cause? Do you wish to survive in the ruins of your abbey?'

'God's ways are beyond human understanding,' said the abbot, stung to tartness, 'but I venture to believe that if He decided to convey His will to me He would not employ you as His messenger.'

'At least I represent men who are prepared to die for their faith. Where I come from, Englishmen are ready to rise against the royal anti-Christ. In Yorkshire, and in Durham and Cumberland too, there are men who love their Church. Here in Lincolnshire as well. Men who care sufficiently to give their lives. Men of courage. And abbots among them.'

'Then why do you have need of me?'

'We lack a leader.'

'You will not find him here.' The abbot spoke sharply.

'My lord, if I may speak. Brother Thomas—' The prior began hesitantly and broke off as his lord swung round, the abbatical brow furrowed in anger.

Under his breath the abbot cursed his prior for a muddle-headed fool. The old man's innocence and fervour might already have placed the whole abbey in jeopardy. As for Brother Thomas, the abbot reserved judgment only until the size of his iniquity became apparent. There could be no excuse of muddleheadedness in his case.

Since the prior did not dare to continue, Aske resumed.

'The chancellor has told me that you have the means of tracing a leader for us. We want an authentic claimant to the throne. We need a member of the royal house of York, whose kings were loved and revered. The passing of their rule is still lamented in the north. In Yorkshire today the ferment of unrest is rising. The archbishop's men from whom I made inquiry sent me on to Lincoln to speak to the bishop, and it is his chancellor, as you see, who has brought me here. If we can find someone whom the people will accept, the Church can be saved. Your Church and mine.'

'Then your undertaking has episcopal sanction? Their graces of York and Lincoln are asking me to aid you?'

It was the chancellor who answered, as the abbot intended he should.

'The archbishop personally knows nothing of this. The bishop did grant Master Aske an interview, and ordered me to accompany him here in view of the importance of the matter. But as an observer only. Master Aske has no authority to speak in his name. Let that be clearly understood.'

The abbot thanked him. 'In such circumstances I have no choice but to withhold my authority from any investigation and to request your companion to remove himself from my house and my domains. You, I trust, will honour us as our guest for a few days.'

He watched the dismay on all their faces. His contempt for the chancellor had grown. His anger with the prior had not abated. But despite the order of expulsion his feelings towards Master Aske were already melting into reluctant admiration.

'I trust that your refusal is not irrevocable,' pleaded the chancellor. 'It may be that I misled you about the bishop. Although he cannot but deplore Master Aske's views he is interested in the investigation. In fact, it was he who suggested it. Croyland's records have lain buried long enough. You kept them to you unlawfully during my visitation. Master Bedyll, although armed with the king's authority, has reported a similar reticence and disobedience. At Lincoln we too have records, and they lead us to suppose what your secrecy confirms: that yours contain information which could affect the wellbeing of all England. I am here as vicar-general of the diocese to request your co-operation with the bishop.'

'It would give me much pleasure to oblige you,' said the abbot, 'and the bishop no less, of course. This puts a different complexion on the matter. But I fear—'

'My lord—' It was the prior again, trembling to proceed.

'Your prior is trying to tell you,' said Aske, 'that as your deputy he has anticipated your consent and set the inquiry afoot. Your refusal comes too late.'

'Is this true?' The abbot spoke like Jehovah Himself.

The prior bowed his head. 'Brother Thomas is already at work,' he confessed.

5

Prior and chancellor. The old men made a contrasting pair, but the abbot cursed them impartially. Simplicity and deviousness. Piety and devilish tricks. One pale from a lifetime of worship in stone-chilled church and cell, the other hale from years in the saddle on his diocesan rounds. Aske he now re-appraised without rancour – as someone worthy of attention in his own right, not merely the chance pretext for the chancellor's visit he had first appeared to be.

The young man had made plain his knowledge that all bishops were not men of God as John Fisher had been. He would know the truth, therefore, about John Longland, the present incumbent of the see of Lincoln. A bishopric was a reward for service to the crown; a rich see the reward for outstanding service. Bishop Longland had earned the plum of Lincoln, as he had earned the handsome deanery of Salisbury before. He had been the king's own confessor, keeper of the royal conscience: an exacting task. He it was who had initiated the divorce proceedings which caused the breach between England and Rome.

The prior might plead ignorance of such considerations, but Aske must be well aware what trust he could place in Bishop Longland's vicar-general in the matter of finding England a new king. He was a London barrister, not the blunt simpleton from remote parts he chose to seem. His foolhardiness must be settled policy. A man of real courage, then. The abbot raised his glance to meet the hostility of that single burning eye.

'It is best that I should go to Lincoln,' he said, 'and speak to the bishop myself.'

He had no intention of going. Their rare meetings were a burden to both. Such obedience as the abbots of Croyland owed they owed to the Provincial of their order. For centuries they had been at pains not to recognise the spiritual sovereignty of Lincoln. The bishops for their part resented the extra-territorial rights of the abbots and their equality as fellow peers of the realm. It was half a century since the abbot had been in Lincoln or a bishop of Lincoln had come to Croyland.

'That will not be necessary, my lord.' A self-announced plenipotentiary, the chancellor bridled at the suggestion.

'Whatever steps the prior may have taken in my absence, I cannot consider revoking my decision and committing the abbey to such a delicate course without the bishop's personal and unequivocal request.'

'The bishop is not at Lincoln now, and he has left this affair in my hands.'

The chancellor laid a letter on the table, and the prior carried it to the abbot.

It was signed and sealed in due form. Not until he had checked that did the abbot's eye run up to what was written. The bishop sent greetings in love and friendship to his brother in God. The proposed inquiry had his blessing. His brother in God could rest assured that in this matter as in all others it was the bishop's own words which fell from his trusted and much-loved chancellor's lips.

Hurrying through the fulsome tribute to the episcopal vice-regent, the abbot was left in little doubt who had drafted the letter. He put it carefully away. At least it provided him with some defence against a charge of treason.

His other protection must be to avoid private conversation with the chancellor, who in Croyland was neither trusted nor much-loved. What fell from those fleshy lips might not always be the truth. Their evidence could only be refuted if he never allowed them within earshot except in the presence of witnesses. They were opening now like the mouth of a trap.

'It is many years since we had the pleasure of seeing you at Lincoln, my lord abbot. Not since the days of Bishop Russell I believe.'

'That is true.'

'Bishop Russell, Master Aske, visited this abbey in his last years. He was the lord abbot's sponsor, if I am not mistaken.'

'It was fifty years ago,' said the prior, 'but I remember it more vividly than yesterday. He was a great and gracious prelate. He came twice, once with a retinue of twenty. He even refused the abbey's hospitality and insisted on a weekly bill from the cellarer.'

'He made a long and unusual visit,' persisted the chancellor. 'I suspect that it may be pertinent to our investigation. The bishop was a high personage in his time. But you will surely remember him better than the prior, my lord?'

The abbot remembered. He had come to Croyland in the bishop's train. Here in this room Bishop Russell had presented him to Abbot Lambert – old Lambert Fosdyke, who could hardly rise from his chair and had died within the month. The dampness of the air had stiffened the old man's bones. But before they carried him into the church for the last time and left him there to lie till Judgment Day between Abbot Joffrid of Orleans and Abbot Osketul, 'Father of the Poor', he had accepted the bishop's nominee, young John Wells, for the almonry school.

When he left to return to the world, the bishop had sent for the boy, taken his hand and solemnly bowed over it as he called on God to watch over him. He laid a similar charge on the new head of the community, who had replied none too graciously that he watched over all his flock and so did God. Abbot John could recall Abbot Edmund's grumpy voice across the decades.

News of the bishop's death came after a few years. By that time John Wells had grown indissolubly part of Croyland. His decision to become a novice was taken and approved, and in the course of time he took his vows and entered the order. Because he shone as a scholar they had sent him to Buckingham College, the hall of his order at the university across the fens in Cambridge, which monks from Croyland had helped to found.

After six years of study he returned to the abbey and performed such a miracle of estate management in the office of cellarer that he became the acknowledged heir apparent to Abbot Richard and succeeded to the abbacy despite the claims of the prior and others senior to him.

'Bishop Russell was a second father to me,' he acknowledged.

'But what was the purpose of his visit,' demanded Aske, 'if it was so long and unusual?'

The chancellor's smile returned – an ugly gash which laid bare his black stumps and the gaps between. Before he could say anything, the abbot spoke.

'What he bequeathed to this house remains here. We hold it in trust. It can never leave Croyland.'

'But such knowledge as he imparted to us, my lord,' begged the prior, 'God would wish us to use in His cause, would He not?'

'What have you and Brother Thomas done?' The abbot's voice was as soft as the velvet he wore, but his tone conveyed the accusation of a mortal sin.

'I acted as I thought for the good of the house,' replied the prior, groping his way nervously through the words. 'In your name, my lord. I would not presume otherwise.'

'Did you consult the cellarer?'

'It did not seem appropriate on this occasion. The cellarer's duties—'

'Have you parted with anything?'

'How could you think that we would take such a step without your express command? Our visitors were pressing and I could not know how long it would be before your return. I summoned Brother Thomas and—'

'—and he refused to part with anything?'

'He advised awaiting your coming. As precentor he has charge of the archives, of course, and I decided not to overrule him.'

The abbot blessed Brother Thomas. He could picture the scene. There was not another brother in Christendom whose meekness was as deceptive as Brother Thomas's. However abject his obedience, it rarely prevented him from doing what he himself judged best. After overcoming the prior's weak resistance the chancellor must have cursed this unforeseen obstacle.

'Has anyone but Brother Thomas examined the records?'

The prior shook his head with righteous vehemence and the abbot uttered a second silent blessing.

'We agreed that the investigation which these gentlemen requested should be commenced. Faced with the bishop's wishes, we felt it would be wrong not to accede. What was asked seemed to us to be for the Church's salvation. Already the houses of God are being levelled to the ground, as Master Aske says. We believed that no time should be lost. Surely, my lord, we were not in error?'

'You are too stern with your brethren, my lord,' Aske rebuked the abbot. 'Is it a sin for them to respect the bishop's word? Their loyalty to you is not in question, I can assure you. Your librarian, Brother Thomas, guards his manuscripts like holy relics.'

'He was informative, however,' added the chancellor maliciously. 'I have learned something during these last few days.'

'Dr Rayne has been telling us of the records at Lincoln and St Alban's,' said the prior, 'and noting how ours compare. It appears that we have the finest chronicles in the country.'

'And what did you agree to do with them?' The abbot's

saddle sores were forgotten. Though he shifted uneasily, he was trying to estimate the extent of other and much more serious damage.

'We arranged that Brother Thomas should put to one side his chronicle of recent events and turn instead to the past. This has long been his wish. You know, my lord, how much time he spends reading the books and manuscripts which we obtain from other houses.'

'Did you give him permission to study all the archives, including those I have specifically forbidden him to touch?'

The prior hung his head. 'Without those he would not proceed. He was adamant that all the evidence must be open to him. You know how insistent Brother Thomas can be. Forgive me, my lord.'

The abbot masked his alarm. How dared they disobey his commands and God's? In the twelfth century, when the nearby church of Ramsey was held as a fortress by the godless Geoffrey de Mandeville, blood was reported to have gushed from the walls as a sign of divine displeasure. He looked around him now, half expecting a similar manifestation: blood rising from the rushes, oozing through the wainscot, seeping under the door.

'Forgiveness is God's prerogative,' he said. 'Fortunately for all of us His mercy is infinite.'

'Will you withdraw your refusal?' demanded the chancellor. 'Or must I report your defiance?'

With misgiving the abbot judged it safer to proceed than draw back. 'Let us say that my refusal has been circumvented.'

'So the investigation goes on!' The chancellor was jubilant.

'You will not regret your decision, my lord abbot,' Aske told him.

The abbot ignored them both. 'Send for Brother Thomas,' he ordered the prior.

'But it is vespers time,' the prior protested. 'He will be in church.'

'Send for him,' the abbot repeated, and the prior, shocked, went and gave orders for Brother Thomas to be summoned at once.

6

'He will succeed if anyone can,' said the prior loyally while they awaited his coming. 'He is not yet thirty, but a scholar of exceptional learning and ingenuity of mind.'

'He will need both,' declared Aske, 'and more. I do not doubt that he will probe every fragment of evidence and not spare himself in the search for a ruler who will protect our Church instead of destroying it. But his experience must be narrow. His knowledge is confined to the cloisters. What he has learned of the world he has learned from books.'

'Yet he has rare powers of concentration and deduction,' said the prior proudly. 'He is a disciple of St Thomas Aquinas. He believes in divine revelation and the human intellect in partnership. Last year, for instance, we had a theft. Brother Thomas recovered some silver vessels stolen from the sacristy. He led me to one of the beds in the infirmary, although he had not been there himself beforehand. I looked underneath, and there they were.'

'How did he know?' the chancellor demanded.

'With God's help he deduced the culprit. He knelt for a day in prayer: in his cell with his eyes closed.'

The chancellor grunted in scorn. 'A lucky guess. He will need his eyes this time.'

'He will use them,' the prior assured him. 'Last month during Lent it was reported to me that someone was stealing carp from the fish-pond. It was Brother Thomas who caught the thief.'

While they talked, the abbot tried to calm his troubled mind at the window, presenting them with nothing more revealing than his broad straight back. If only his venerable brother of Hayles had been less long-winded in convocation, he might have been home in time to nip the bud of this conspiracy. At Hayles they had a phial of the Holy Blood and, with men like Thomas Bedyll at large, the old man had cause for concern. But eloquence would not save his relics, any more than martyrdom. It could be that Master Aske was right and the time for open rebellion had come.

Outside, darkness was falling like a curtain lowered tenderly from Heaven. Beyond the grey outline of the gatehouse the village was disappearing before his eyes. In the other direction he could distinguish the river's narrow curling thread and the leper huts beyond. The isle of Croyland it had been in the age of King Ethelbald, bounded by the Shepishee and the Southee to east and south, by the Nene to the west and an arm of the Welland to the north. These had been the abbey's walls against the world.

The waters were tamer now but running still, making their contribution to the service of God by irrigating the fertile silt-land. The community had long since burst their bounds. The saint himself had started the policy of enclosing and draining the surrounding swamps.

Invisible beyond them to the south lay other communities: Thorney, Ramsey, Peterborough. To the west, far out of sight, ran the king's highroad linking the southern capital at London with the northern at York. Between and on all other sides crouched the familiar fenlands. To the north and east they stretched on and on, leading nowhere, until they became the Wash and the Wash became the sea.

Not for Croyland the remote beauties of the north and west. The abbot had visited Fountains and Tintern and knew the parts of England which filled the spirit with the joy of being alive. Here it was easier to concentrate on bliss beyond the grave.

What a place in which to plot the rise and fall of kings! Far from Westminster or Windsor or any other centre of government. Out of sight of any castle or secular lord's seat of power. Without strongholds where rebels could muster. No more than three old and two young men, divided in loyalties, beliefs and motives.

Yet one place, one set of men became as good as another if the time proved ripe. The king was past forty and still had no male heir. Queen Anne had succeeded Queen Katharine and herself fallen into disfavour. She was under arrest in the Tower and not likely to be released. In London rumour whispered that Parliament would soon be summoned to declare the daughters of both marriages illegitimate. Who would be the heir then? The abbot could guess: either the doubtful issue of yet another marriage or a successor nominated by letters patent. The latter would be Henry, duke of Richmond, the king's bastard, and no one would accept him after his father's death.

Meanwhile the king's affairs could not rest. Henry was shorter of money than ever. Like all kings, except his father, he was extravagant. Worse, owing to the unimagined quantity of gold and silver being found in America, the coinage was depreciating. Prices were rising fast and the royal revenues, paid in fixed sums, amounted to less and less in value. There was no war to provide him with an excuse for imposing taxes. On Cromwell's advice he had declared himself Pope in England and diverted the tithes from Rome. Now these were no longer enough and the monasteries must be milked dry.

As a politician the abbot understood the king's dilemma. As an abbot he detested his policies. As a man he detested the king himself.

Rising prices were not the king's concern alone. Everyone suffered and discontent too was rising. There was lack of employment, for which the king must take the blame. The attack on the monasteries had not brought him popularity, since it was suspected that all the spoils would go to him and to his cronies at court. Even those who hated monks could not see how the common people would profit from it. It was a time of rumours and gossip, grumblings and threats. Omens foretold violence.

In these conditions the king's spies were everywhere, snuffling out incipient treachery. Every conceivable candidate for the throne was under observation or arrest. The abbot knew them all: pale sprigs of the white rose. Now Robert Aske and Brother Thomas were to burrow in the past and unearth another. Then he too could be disposed of, and as part of the reckoning over-mighty Croyland would be levelled to the watery ground from which it had risen. The pickings would be rich; revenge on a defiant abbot sweet.

A draught of cold air told him that the door had opened. Someone entered. The very noiselessness told him who it was. He spoke without turning.

'Welcome, Brother Thomas.'

'Welcome home, father.'

He stood in the doorway, the quintessence of humility

and diffidence, a slight figure in his long black habit. The hooded head was bowed, the face concealed in shadow.

The abbot was not deceived. He felt anger against his favourite son, so outwardly obedient, so inwardly wayward. There stood the only member of his community whose intellect rivalled his own in clarity and depth. If so minded, Brother Thomas could have frustrated the prior's unwisdom and delayed matters until his own return. Only too certainly, it was his determination to study forbidden archives which had decided him otherwise. Temptation had not been resisted.

'You may be seated.'

Brother Thomas crept across the room and sat down. Candles had been brought with the onset of evening, and in the brightness and splendour of his lordship's parlour he lowered his cowl cautiously. He seemed ill at ease, as though guilt had soured his joy at the abbot's safe return – the return for which he had so earnestly prayed – a return from the shadow of noose and knife.

7

For in the chapterhouse, not a month before, whispers of 'High treason' had run round the stalls like wind through the fens outside. Like the wind, they chilled the assembled brethren. The abbots were making a stand at last and the king had ordered their leader to be seized and charged with treason.

This was what rumour from London reported, brought to Croyland by an itinerant friar. It further reported that the abbots' leader was the abbot of Croyland.

While the prior devoutly intoned the opening prayers and began the humdrum business of the day, Brother Thomas had sat wondering whether he possessed the strength of body and purpose to share his abbot's martyrdom. Every day the brethren met before compline to deliberate on mundane and domestic affairs. He seldom paid much attention, and that day less than ever until he heard his own name spoken.

'Brother Thomas must investigate.'

It had been the cellarer who spoke, their level-headed and worldly-wise administrator. The prior was presiding, but they were all aware of the abbot's strict command, whenever he left them, that the cellarer be consulted on important questions. 'So far as his vow of obedience to me as your deputy permits,' the prior would beg, being a stickler for the rules of the order. 'As you say,' the abbot would answer with a sigh.

'But Brother Thomas is our precentor. He has musical and literary duties. Surely—' The prior had fluttered his wizened fingers in his usual state of indecision.

'Surely,' the cellarer repeated firmly, 'you recall his recovery of the silver paten and pyx.'

'Yes indeed. Thanks be to God and St Guthlac.'

'We must ask him to invoke St Guthlac's aid again. We must pray for divine intervention. With the saint's prayers and our own, God will reveal the name of the culprit to Brother Thomas. Otherwise we shall starve.'

Brother Thomas had listened dimly, his mind on the abbot's mortal peril. He wanted to discuss it with Brother Henry, who was the only other member of the community not present. Would the abbot choose to suffer the extremities of pain alone or would he welcome company in death? Brother Henry would know. He was not blessed with cleverness but his instincts were sound. Ever since their novitiate together he had been Brother Thomas's closest friend, until the dark moment in the depth of winter when he had left the cloister to become master of the leper house.

Fish, the prior had had to explain to him in the tone of an indulgent teacher to a pupil caught asleep. Fish had risen to the surface of the agenda. They were discussing the mysterious disappearance of carp from the abbey pond, and whether the community could survive Lent without starvation or – which would be nearly as bad – paying the villagers exorbitant prices for their mud-flavoured pike. Guards had been posted to no avail. Thefts were still occurring nightly.

It was a steep descent from martyrdom to fish, but Brother Thomas had accepted the assignment.

The next morning he had taken a stroll outside the monastery along a stretch of water where Brother Henry had taught him the skills of fishing. Fowlers were out with their nets wringing the necks of wild duck which they had ensnared. Abbey servants trapping eels greeted him. He walked on towards solitude, where he could squat and watch the stream uninterrupted.

After an hour he rose and took a causeway through the reeds to the Spalding road where two of Brother Henry's lepers were begging for alms outside the village boundary. He forced himself to look into their God-forsaken faces and bid them a good day in His name.

The afternoon he had spent kneeling at the saint's tomb, and before nightfall he ordered the withdrawal of the guards from the pond.

In the evening, after dark, he had led an expedition of kitchen and scullery staff equipped with spades and barrows. In two hours of hard work they surrounded the pond with a coating of fresh damp earth and smoothed away their footprints. Then he sent them to bed bound by a vow of silence and went to his cell to pray for cloud to cover the moon.

At first light he had gone to the pond to inspect the footprints. A pair of big bare feet had left their mark on the loose soil. He allowed himself a small wry smile of triumph.

The leper colony lay isolated in the water meadows on the far side of the gentle stream named Shepishee. Brother Thomas walked to the bank and shouted until someone in the huddle of huts woke and roused Brother Henry for him.

They had stood on either side of the water and Brother Thomas saw to his horror the mark of the disease on his friend's face, swollen and ulcerous with sores.

'Come over,' he invited.

Brother Henry shook his head. 'I must keep my distance.'

'Then I will move away. But we must talk.'

'We can talk as we are.'

'No. You must come across, Henry.' 'Henry' he had said, not 'brother' as he should.

Henry had come reluctantly, unmooring the skerry and poling himself across the few yards of the stream's breadth.

Brother Thomas retreated towards the pond until they stood either side of it. 'Compare your footprints with those,' he said. 'They are the spoor of a thief.'

Brother Henry had wept, explaining how his lepers were ailing for want of proper food, until Brother Thomas defied the taint of leprosy and rushed round the pond to embrace his friend.

That evening in the chapterhouse the prior had announced that the identity of the carp thief was known and the thefts would cease. He named no names and Brother Thomas was looked at in wonder. Later the cellarer announced an increase in rations for the leper house.

It was three weeks afterwards when the prior summoned the precentor to solve another mystery, and Brother Thomas gladly turned his thoughts from the abbot's martyrdom to the prospect of saving him. And saving Croyland too. And all the other great abbeys. And the realm of England itself.

Standing now in the abbot's parlour, he could hear the voice of God calling him.

Part Two

THE INQUIRY

I

'How is the brothers' singing?' inquired the abbot.

'Joyful,' Brother Thomas replied. 'They worship from the heart.'

'That I do not doubt. It is their tunefulness which concerns me. I trust the chancellor will not dispute that the chanting of our liturgies and canticles takes second place to none. Croyland's musical tradition, Master Aske, goes back beyond the Conquest. To maintain and develop it is a heavy weight on our precentor's frail shoulders.'

Brother Thomas recognised at once the drift of the abbot's mind. Music was a precentor's first duty. Librarianship came second. Investigations nowhere.

'As I remember your commands, my lord, my deputy has charge of the music while I am at work on the chronicle. Our standards are safe with the succentor, and my own frailty is fortunately of no consequence. The father prior will confirm that God is still praised in tuneful unison at Croyland.'

The abbot noted that he was being 'my-lorded' instead of 'fathered', a sign that Brother Thomas was preparing to be difficult. 'The fact that the succentor is doing your work does not absolve you from responsibility,' he said. 'There have been complaints.'

'They have not been brought to my notice. I pray that they do not come from your lordship himself.'

Brother Thomas's eyes were downcast, either from the strength of the light or from humility in the presence of his superiors. His voice was meek, his words softly uttered. Yet might there not be an implication in them that the abbot attended the daily services in church too seldom to be entitled to form a judgment of his own? Knowing Brother Thomas, the abbot felt there might indeed, and his anger grew.

'The chronicle must not occupy you to the exclusion of all else.'

'No, my lord; though I am mindful of our reputation as a seat of learning.'

'The pursuit of knowledge is a proper occupation, acceptable to God, provided it does not interrupt the ordained routine of worship. The chancellor knows how strict is our obedience to our rule. Our recent visitor, Master Bedyll, would have found the same if his concern had been with the life of the spirit. In these days there must be no relaxation of our devotions to God.'

'Men being God's creation,' declared Brother Thomas, 'in discovering the truth about them I feel myself growing nearer to Him.'

'But you have broken off your continuation of the chronicle.'

'At the father prior's command.'

'And the beckoning of your own inclination?'

'I could not find it in my heart to disobey.'

'Yet you have disobeyed me? You have opened the archives I forbade you to touch?'

'You were not here. The chancellor was insistent. The prior and I had to judge what your wishes would be. If I erred, forgive me, my lord.'

The abbot made no gesture of forgiveness.

'Tell us your conclusions,' said Aske.

'Two days is a short time to reach conclusions.'

'Then you can have two weeks. Two months if need be. But no more.'

'Patience, my friend,' the chancellor admonished. 'The brother is a scholar. He is not to be hurried. His conclusions must be soundly based and tested. But he will, I am sure, inform us of his studies as they proceed.'

'With his lordship's permission.' Brother Thomas raised his eyes for the first time. They were grey and rheumy, accustomed to close reading. At greater distances the world grew blurred, and for this he was thankful. Without mundane distractions he could concentrate on the accumulation of knowledge and the keenness of his insight. He did not need his eyes now to inform him of the abbot's mood.

'Let us pray,' said the abbot, 'and then you may speak if you must.'

They followed him into the little chapel, filing under Abbot Theodore's skull. Brother Thomas went last, as was fitting. He wore his expression of piety, but while the others contemplated and praised their Maker his mind was darting like a bat, corner by corner, into the dark recesses of history.

When they returned to the parlour, the abbot pushed back his chair from the fireside and seated himself apart as a mark of dissociation. His guests left a seat between them for Brother Thomas, and the prior faced them, confidently expecting the revelation of salvation.

'It has been necessary to go back a long way,' said Brother Thomas: 'as far as the reign of the third Edward, who fathered too many sons for the good of the realm. If his eldest son, the prince of England, had lived, it would have been different. But he died, worn out by fighting, and his son succeeded to the throne. Richard wore the crown but he was a boy and his uncles ruled in his name.'

The abbot listened behind closed lids, alert for errors in the familiar blood-for-blood story of Lancaster and York.

John of Gaunt had been the ablest of Richard's uncles. As

duke of Lancaster he possessed estates almost as large as the king's. While he lived the young king lived in his shadow. When he died Richard took his revenge. The estates of Lancaster were seized from the new duke, his son. That was the beginning of a quarrel which took a hundred years and the best blood in England to resolve.

John of Gaunt's heir had been born not far from Croyland at the Lincolnshire castle of Bolingbroke. He was not a man to accept banishment and the loss of his estates. He returned to claim them by force, and while he was at it he took the crown too.

'He put the lawful king to death,' said Brother Thomas. 'He slew the Lord's anointed. He became King Henry IV, and his son King Henry V, and his grandson King Henry VI. But no one could forget the crime that had set this dynasty of Lancastrian Henrys on the throne.'

Might is right, thought the abbot. Henry Bolingbroke and his son were warriors. They were too strong to be gainsaid. But Henry V died young, leaving an heir less than a year old. More than that, he had married the French king's daughter, and the royal house of Valois suffered the curse of hereditary madness. King Henry VI was both an infant and a simpleton. No usurping dynasty could survive that.

'Henry VI was gentle and God-fearing,' said Brother Thomas. 'He had a simple soul and a clouded mind. He rebuilt the Confessor's abbey at Westminster. He founded colleges at Eton and Cambridge. When he came to Croyland he wished to stay. He was not a good king, but many have called him a saint.'

The abbot nodded. A king was one thing, a saint another. No man in England had been both since the Confessor. Henry was too saintly for a king, but also too kingly for a saint.

What other man had been crowned in both Westminster and Paris – king of England and king of France? The burden of double sovereignty had been too much. Both his kingships were disputed, and he lost them both – first France, then England. He ruled only by right of his father's and his grandfather's conquests, and he lost them to other conquerors. When he died, glad to be rid of his royal trappings, he was laid to rest in the abbey at Chertsey, away from the world. That should have been the end, but his body was reclaimed as a king's and reburied royally at Windsor. Poor Henry! He had not sought power – he was born to it and could not escape to answer his call to the cloister. In his blend of piety and incompetence, the abbot reflected, he resembled the prior.

Brother Thomas had moved on to the rival house of York. 'When men became discontented with Henry's misrule they turned to Richard, duke of York, who was descended from two sons of Edward III, one of them senior to John of Gaunt. The duke became Protector. He did not press his claim to the throne. But when the king's supporters killed him his eldest son had no choice but to seize the crown in self-defence. He ruled as Edward IV, with Henry deposed.'

'Murdered,' amended the chancellor. 'Henry Bolingbroke was not the only man to shed the blood of the Lord's anointed. Edward did the same to Henry VI and brought the same retribution for the sin of regicide on his house. His own heir, the boy king Edward, was slain by his uncle, who usurped the throne as Richard III.'

'And Richard,' demanded Aske. 'Was he not in turn slain by our present king's father, Henry Tudor, who had no claim to the throne whatever? Retribution is due once more. Overdue, some would say.'

'Nonsense,' cried the chancellor. 'Henry Tudor was the

heir of the Lancastrian dynasty which had ruled England for three generations before the Yorkists thought fit to put forward their claim. Henry VI was descended from Edward III in an unbroken male line through John of Gaunt. The house of York's male line came through a younger son. Their descent from Lionel, duke of Clarence, the eldest son after Prince Edward's death, ran through a female line. William of Windsor died an infant and Lionel of Clarence had no son. John of Gaunt came fourth.'

'Inheritance through a female is valid,' said Aske. 'That is the law. There are precedents enough: the claim of the first Plantagenet was through his mother. But examine, if you dare, the claim of the house of Tudor. It is based on force and nothing more. And what force has done force can undo, as it has before.'

'You are speaking treason again, Master Aske,' the chancellor warned him.

'And you are assuming the lawfulness of our fat Tudor's tenure of the throne. Prove it and I will confess to treason.'

'It is not for me to prove it; it is for Brother Thomas to disprove it,' the chancellor replied. 'That is why we are here.' He rubbed his plump hands expectantly.

2

But Brother Thomas, having sparked the visitors into argument, was content to listen.

'The Tudors are no more than peasants,' declared Robert Aske. 'They tilled the land in Anglesey, the most backward part of the kingdom.'

'Do you deny that Henry Tudor was descended from Edward III?' The chancellor thumped the table under his companion's nose.

'Not at all, but through a female line – which you do not recognise as valid.'

'And you do.'

'Not when it is flawed by a double bastardy. Henry Tudor's grandfather crept into the bed of Katherine of Valois, Henry V's widow. He was a chamberlain of her household, a low-born adulterer fortunate not to be executed for defiling the memory of the hero of Agincourt. So much for the Tudors. On the female side Henry Tudor did better but not well enough. His mother was a Beaufort, descended from the bastard stock of John of Gaunt and his paramour Katherine Swinford. That is the Tudor connection with the house of Lancaster: far-fetched and illegitimate.'

'Have you forgotten that John of Gaunt married his paramour after his wife's death and that their children were legitimised by royal decree?'

'Have you forgotten that the decree expressly debarred them and their heirs from the royal succession? Make no pretence about Henry Tudor, Dr Rayne. He was a usurping regicide. With the passage of time the house of Lancaster had a fair claim. The house of York had a better. Both were Plantagenets, members of the family who ruled our country for three and a half centuries. It is time one or other of them returned to the throne to guide this poor kingdom back to God's ways.'

The chancellor snorted down his boar's snout.

'One can see that you make an able advocate, Master Aske,' he said. 'You take what is needful to your argument and leave unregarded whatever does not suit it. First, there were no other surviving members of the house of Lancaster.

All were killed except Henry Tudor. Second, you conveniently overlook his marriage to the Princess Elizabeth, eldest daughter of Edward IV and sister to the boy King Edward V. If you admit the claim of Lancaster, there is no one to support except Henry Tudor's son, our present King Henry. If you prefer the claim of York, the rightful heir is the son of the Princess Elizabeth – our own King Henry again. His claim is impregnable.'

'Our guests are divided,' said the abbot, intervening. 'Are you sure, chancellor, that you wish the investigation to proceed? If, as you believe, we already have an undoubted king, how can it profit us to pry into the past when there is so much of the present to occupy our minds?'

'The present and the past are indivisible,' Brother Thomas pronounced. 'Our judgments in the one depend on our learning from the other.'

The abbot frowned. 'Let Dr Rayne answer, my son.'

'Gladly,' said the chancellor. 'I do not pretend to treasonable pursuits, nor does my lord bishop. But he informs me that the king's health is poor. Should God choose to call him, who will govern us? The Princess Mary is the fruit of an annulled union. The Princess Elizabeth is the fruit of a union not recognised in the rest of Europe. Even if the question of legitimacy were overcome, there is no precedent for a woman becoming our sovereign lord. Even the Empress Matilda's claim was not recognised. We do not seek a replacement for our liege, but a successor.'

'Who is we?' asked the abbot softly.

'I speak in the bishop's name.'

'And the bishop? In whose name does he speak?'

'The bishop is his own master.'

'I think not. You are the bishop's vicar-general. His authority is exercised through you, and the clergy of this diocese must obey you. Above the bishop is the head of our Church. He has his vicar-general, to whom the bishops owe obedience. We should be told whether you are here on behalf of the vicar-general of all England, Master Thomas Cromwell.'

The name brought silence. No one moved except the prior, who involuntarily crossed himself to ward off evil. Aske sat tense, his eye fixed on the chancellor.

'I am grateful to the lord abbot for his intervention,' he said. 'Bishops today make strange accommodations. Is Cromwell, the anti-Christ, privy to our enterprise? That is a fair question. Answer it.'

The chancellor grunted like a cornered hog.

'Since you are blunt I will be blunt too. I am the bishop's ecclesiastical arm. In matters of politics he does not confide in me. But you may have my opinion for what it is worth. Master Cromwell is the king's minister. What he knows cannot be kept from the king. Since no man welcomes precautions against the event of his decease – kings least of all – I do not doubt that this matter has been kept from the king and therefore from his minister.'

'We note your opinion,' said the abbot, not concealing his disbelief, 'and the reason you state for wishing the investigation to proceed. Would Master Aske now wish to withdraw from this inquiry?'

'Only if the search is likely to prove unavailing,' Aske replied. 'Not from any other cause, I assure you. But if the chancellor is right about the legitimacy of our fat Tudor's claim, there can be no profit to me in proceeding. In the north we can neither wait for successors nor accept second-best claimants.'

'In that case—' the abbot began. But Brother Thomas humbly interrupted him.

'I beg your pardon, my lord, and the forgiveness of the chancellor, but I feel bound to express my conviction that he is mistaken.'

For all its meekness Brother Thomas's tone somehow suggested collaboration with One from Whom he had received information not granted to others.

'In which direction does my error lie? I await instruction from the learned brother.' The chancellor's dignity was affronted. Bandying words with an abbot was one thing. Suffering rebuke from one of his brethren quite another. He swallowed his anger only for the sake of the investigation.

'Let us first dismiss the house of Lancaster,' said Brother Thomas, 'since on this point there is no dispute. Henry VI was the last Lancastrian king. His queen, Margaret of Anjou, bore one child only, known as Edward, prince of Wales. It was said at the time that the king had not been near the queen's bed for several years before the birth of the prince. He described it as an act of God, though others held the duke of Somerset responsible. But the question of legitimacy became unimportant. Edward was killed by Yorkists at Tewkesbury and the direct line of Lancaster died with him.'

'Except for the Beauforts,' the chancellor insisted.

'Barred from the succession,' Aske reminded him.

Brother Thomas went on. 'The house of York, on the other hand, is not extinct. Their last king was Richard III. His son, like Henry's, was known as Edward, prince of Wales. He too died before his father. Richard had no other legitimate children, but he had heirs. There was his nephew, the earl of Warwick, son of George, duke of Clarence.'

'The earl is not alive,' said the chancellor. 'He was imprisoned in the Tower as a traitor to Henry VII and beheaded, leaving no heirs. In any event the line was attainted at the time of Clarence's execution, also for treason.'

'For that reason,' said Brother Thomas, 'King Richard changed his mind. When he died his heir was another nephew, a sister's son, John de la Pole, earl of Lincoln.'

'Long since dead,' declared the chancellor.

'Yes, he was killed in battle against Henry Tudor.'

'And his heirs, what of them?' demanded Aske.

'His successor was his brother Edmund, who became earl of Suffolk. Edmund fled abroad and was protected by the Archduke Philip.'

'But Henry had him killed, like the others?'

'He asked for him to be returned, but the archduke's mother was a sister of King Richard, and the archduke would not surrender his cousin. Unfortunately, on a voyage from the Low Countries to Spain, a storm blew him ashore on the coast of Dorset and Henry would not allow him to continue his journey until he had promised to hand over the earl.'

'And the archduke agreed?'

'On condition that the earl's life was spared.'

'Did Henry honour his promise?' Aske's voice expressed his disbelief.

'Yes; but his son, our present sovereign lord, did not.' Brother Thomas paused in silent rebuke. 'After seven years in the Tower the earl was executed.'

'Had he a son?'

'No. His successor was his brother, William de la Pole.'

'And he was killed too?'

'It is my belief that he is alive today.'

'Then he is our king. If he is the direct heir of King Richard his claim must take precedence.'

'If he is still alive he is in the Tower. One move in his favour and he would be dead.' Involuntarily, Brother Thomas brought his hand down on his thigh with a thud like the fall of the headsman's axe.

'Then he must escape.'

'He would be an old man, unaccustomed to liberty.'

'Age and imprisonment do not take the edge off a man of spirit.'

'William de la Pole has not been seen outside the Tower for thirty-five years.'

'Thirty-five years!' Aske exclaimed. 'For the crime of being a Plantagenet he has been imprisoned since before you or I were born!'

'For none other that I know of. He is held in secret and there is no record of his ever being publicly tried.'

'For men who feel assured of their right to rule, these Tudors behave very strangely. Under their sovereign graces Henry VII and Henry VIII it has become a capital offence to have Plantagenet blood in one's veins. Are there no Plantagenets left at all? What of Edward III's other sons?'

'The descendants of the youngest son, Thomas of Woodstock, became dukes of Buckingham. Our present king had the third duke executed fifteen years ago.'

'Not peasants,' cried Aske, 'but wholesale butchers. If anything proves the weakness of the Tudor claim, this is it. It is their own sense of guilt which makes them chop off the head of every man of royal blood on whom they can lay their usurping hands. Is there not a single one spared to lead us?'

'You have heard our brother,' said the abbot. 'I can vouch for his persistence, but every path leads to a dead end. A handful remain, but their claims are weak.'

'Except one,' corrected Brother Thomas. 'Forgive me, father, but King Richard's elder brother, Edward IV, had two sons.'

'That is well known,' said Aske. 'They were the boy King Edward V and his brother Richard, duke of York. They were murdered in the Tower by their uncle. They died when still boys, too young to leave heirs of their body.'

'It is true that they were said to have been murdered.'

'Ah!' The chancellor leaned forward and opened his thick rough lips. 'Now we are coming to the nub.'

Aske searched Brother Thomas's face in sudden hope. 'Are you telling us that the report of the murder was false?'

'It is God's will,' cried the prior. 'Let us pray that the boy king is still alive!' He fell on his knees intoning 'Edwardus Quintus, Angliae et Galliae Rex, Dominus Hiberniae. . . . Our true sovereign in the sight of God and man.'

The abbot remained seated and far from elated. He ordered the prior to pull himself together. 'Even if it were true it would be of no consequence. You cannot re-proclaim a king from three reigns ago.'

'How old would he be?' Aske demanded.

'He was last seen fifty-three years ago at the age of twelve.'

'The evidence,' demanded the chancellor. 'Where is your evidence that he is still alive?'

3

The great bell of the abbey church summoned the brethren to compline. The prior rose to excuse himself and Brother Thomas followed him from the room.

The abbot made no move to accompany them. For how many years, through day and night, had bells at Croyland marked the hours and called the faithful to prayer? According to tradition, the first church bells ever to sound in England had been rung here. If they were not to be silenced at last, there were more important matters than obeying their call.

'Brother Thomas is anxious to please,' he told his guests. 'Set him a challenge and he will meet it. It is in his disposition to oblige.'

'Then he is Heaven-sent,' said Aske. 'Let him trace this left-over king and we will set him on the throne again.'

'He would be sixty-five,' said the abbot. 'Older even than I. I do not believe he can be alive. If he is, would he have lain so long concealed if he had a mind to be king? The quest is not worth pursuing. Lead your own revolt, Master Aske, if you must have it.'

'The commons would not rise for me, but with King Edward at their head we could sweep Henry off the map of England.'

'What do you say to that, chancellor?'

'I say that if Edward lives he would not choose to lead a rebellion against his own nephew. He or, more likely, his children could succeed on the king's death.'

'But suppose the king marries again, as we believe he intends, and fathers a boy at long last?'

'The prince would have need of a Protector during his infancy. Who more fitting than a royal cousin?'

Aske laughed. 'Does the chancellor really expect us to believe that Tudors will stop killing Plantagenets and welcome them with loving arms? If I were Edward I would meet Henry at the head of an army or not at all.'

When the prior and precentor returned, food was brought – roast fowl with bread and fruit and wine, all from the abbey's estates. 'Sanctus Benedictus benedicat.' The abbot said grace and they ate without speaking until the chancellor pushed away his platter and rounded on Brother Thomas.

'So you claim to have resurrected a king for us?'

'The conclusion is yours, not mine, Dr Rayne. I did not assert that King Edward lives. I remarked that he was said to have been murdered.'

'Implying that you do not believe it.'

'Nor do I. In my inquiries I can find no evidence of his death.'

'To disbelieve what everyone else accepts as true, you require strong counter-evidence. Where is it?'

'It comes from the study of our records.'

'Then I must see them, brother.'

'There is no single document or passage in our chronicles where it is baldly stated. The issue is confused. Much examination and collation has been necessary, and a familiarity with the history of the times.'

'You are prevaricating. The evidence must be produced and brought to Lincoln. And you too for interrogation. Do you understand?'

'I forbid it,' said the abbot sharply. 'Let us not fall out again over the chronicles. Here they were written, here they will remain while I and my successors have any authority left.'

'I stand beside the chancellor for once,' Aske declared. 'Croyland is not the sole repository of learning. There are scholars at Lincoln and elsewhere who could help Brother Thomas uncover the truth. Unless we move quickly, my lord abbot, you may have no successors.'

'Let the scholars at Lincoln study their own records,' replied the abbot. 'They have plenty, though none to compare with ours. Rather than see the Croyland chronicles leave their home, I would have them destroyed. Let there be no misunderstanding about that.'

The chancellor smiled. 'Destroyed? Along with all the evidence of charters, grants and titles to your estates? All the proofs of ownership of your abbey's possessions? Is that not your famous chronicles' chief concern?'

The abbot smiled back and made no answer.

'The proofs may not bear too close inspection,' suggested the chancellor. 'After the Conquest many abbeys forged documents to show the lawfulness of their titles. Your eminent predecessor Ingulph wrote after a fire had destroyed your deeds and charters. He might have been more concerned with Croyland than the truth. Maybe you follow his example?'

'Abuse me and Brother Thomas if it pleases you, but do not defame the dead.'

'Yet that is what your Brother Thomas is doing. On evidence he will not produce, he is accusing the king's father of lying in his account of the murder of the two princes. The whole gruesome affair was fully investigated at the time and reported so particularly that the story is universally known and accepted. How can you here, so far from the hub of events, presume to gainsay it?'

'Have I leave to speak, father?'

Brother Thomas waited for the abbot's reluctant consent. When it came, he spoke with a glitter of pride. 'Our authority cannot be bettered. It is the good bishop himself: John Russell of Lincoln.'

'Chancellor of England.' Aske cracked a nut between the legs of a silver Eve.

Brother Thomas nodded. 'Yes. Under Richard III he held the highest office in the realm. Before that he had been one of Edward IV's most trusted advisers; for the last nine years of his reign Keeper of the Privy Seal. Bishop Russell was acknowledged by many to be the wisest, most virtuous, most knowledgeable man of that time.'

'And he came to Croyland,' said the prior. 'We were

talking of it earlier. I can remember him celebrating mass.'

Brother Thomas looked surprised. 'You have a good memory, father prior. The bishop was here fifty years ago today. He came in April of 1486 and left in May. After Richard III's death and Henry Tudor's accession he journeyed here in his old age to write in secret what could not then be publicly recorded. He has left us a history of occurrences in which he himself was intimately concerned. The word of such a man cannot be doubted.'

'This is as I have long suspected,' said the chancellor. 'But how can you be sure it is the truth the bishop tells? Old men forget. All men deceive themselves. Politicians seek to justify their deeds.'

'He was a good man,' said the abbot simply. 'Better by far than the cardinals we have had since – Morton and Wolsey. I knew all three. Wolsey was too ambitious. Morton was a rogue. Russell was a man of moderation and honour and genuine piety.'

'There are worse ambitions than the throne of St Peter,' said Aske. 'If Morton and Wolsey were lower than Russell in the scale of virtue, how much lower have we sunk now? What are the ambitions of the present Keeper of the Privy Seal, our friend Thomas Cromwell?' He pointed the nutcrackers accusingly across the table.

The chancellor ignored the question. 'Let us return to the princes,' he said. 'It is well known that they were suffocated on the orders of their uncle Richard so that he could wear his dead brother's crown. They were imprisoned in the Tower and buried in secret there. Does Bishop Russell deny all this?'

'No, he does not deny it.' Before the chancellor could pounce, Brother Thomas quickly added: 'Nor does he state it.'

'Then he must have been concealing his knowledge.'

'He wrote three years after the supposed murder. He wrote for posterity alone. His aim was to leave a record of the truth. Why should he wish to conceal what would have been the most terrible event of his lifetime?'

'Guilt,' suggested the chancellor. 'Tell us his words and let us judge for ourselves.'

'He writes of a rumour being spread that the sons of King Edward had died a violent death, but it was uncertain how. Not that they had died, but that a rumour was deliberately spread to that effect.'

'Does he claim that the princes were alive when he was writing? Does he state that?'

'Not explicitly,' Brother Thomas admitted. 'He does not say that they were dead, nor that they were alive.'

'Is it possible that he could have been ignorant of the truth?' asked Aske.

Brother Thomas shook his head. 'I do not believe it. If any man outside the Tower knew the truth, he would. According to the story of their death the princes were killed between July and September in 1483. By that time Bishop Russell had been appointed chancellor. The lord abbot and many others bear witness to the bishop's probity. If the princes were dead he would have known and plainly set it down. But if they were still alive prudence might have made him cautious. When he wrote, Henry Tudor was already king. By clearly declaring the fact of their survival he could have endangered the princes' lives.'

'So you have no evidence,' sneered the chancellor, pushing back his chair. 'Only speculation.'

'What is evidence?' asked Brother Thomas. 'To a lawyer it is one thing, to an historian another. My speculation, if that is the word you prefer, is firmly based. Bishop Russell's history makes curious reading. He was an adherent of Richard III, his facts speak in Richard's favour. Yet his comments belie the facts. He reveals the validity of Richard's kingship, but describes him as obtruding himself into the marble throne in the great hall at Westminster. Concerning Richard's grief at the death of his son, he comments on the vanity of the thoughts of a man who desires to establish his interests without the aid of God. The battle of Bosworth, where Richard was killed, he calls a glorious victory granted by Heaven. Henry Tudor, the victor, is said to have been acclaimed as though an angel.'

'But if these words are contrary to his belief,' said Aske, 'is it certain that Bishop Russell wrote them?'

'If he did I know his purpose, since they do not affect the substance of what he wrote. He was protecting the living.'

'But you say that he does not expressly deny the story of the princes' death?' the chancellor insisted.

'How could he?' Brother Thomas replied sweetly. 'It had not yet been invented.'

4

'Henry Tudor is the key to the mystery,' Brother Thomas continued. 'While the Yorkist kings reigned, he was an exiled adventurer living on little more than a grain of hope. After their defeat at Barnet and Tewkesbury the remaining Lancastrian supporters gathered round him in Brittany only for want of a worthier heir to their cause. Fourteen years later, against all expectation, he became King Henry VII. To disguise the weakness of his claim he blackened the name and reputation of the king he had killed.'

'Good King Richard,' said Aske. 'The city of York officially recorded its great sorrow at his death, and men in the north call him that to this day.'

'But according to Henry,' Brother Thomas went on, 'no crime was too heinous for Richard to have committed. After the battle at Tewkesbury he ran his sword in cold blood through the body of the young Lancastrian prince of Wales. As Constable of England to his brother King Edward, he had charge of the Tower and executed with his own hand the poor dim-witted Henry VI, who had been deposed and re-enthroned and deposed again. He contrived the death of his own brother, George of Clarence. He murdered his own wife so that he could thwart Henry Tudor by marrying his own niece, Elizabeth. All these accusations were levelled against Richard the instant he was dead. These and others. But of the murder of the princes there was not one word.'

'That cannot be the truth,' the chancellor protested.

'Yet it is. I have read the Act of Attainder promulgated against Richard after his death. It contains no mention of the princes, although by that time Henry had control of the Tower and the means to interrogate everyone in it. It was less than two years since the rumour reported by Bishop Russell that the princes had been murdered. How is it possible that if they were really dead Henry would not have discovered the facts and published them to add to the catalogue of crimes said to have been perpetrated by Richard?'

The chancellor grunted his disagreement. 'Of course he published the facts. How else did they become known? Richard ordered the keys of the Tower to be surrendered to him for one night. He handed them to a villain called Tyrrell who undertook to do the king's dirty work when the

Constable refused. Tyrrell hired two assassins. Even their names are known. Miles Forrest and John Dighton. They smothered the sleeping princes with their own pillows.'

'I agree that this story was made public by Henry,' said Brother Thomas. 'But when? Henry became king in 1485. The story was first published in 1502. From the very first day the princes disappeared rumours circulated, everyone wondered what had happened to them, but this tale of how Richard murdered them was first told after nineteen years. For seventeen of those years Henry Tudor, dedicated to the vilification of Richard, had been master of England. It was surely an odd delay in bringing the evidence to light.'

'If the tale is false,' said Aske, 'then the truth is clear as running water. The princes must have been alive at the time of Bosworth. They were still in the Tower. Henry found them there and killed them himself. As we have learned since, the extermination of Plantagenets is Tudor policy.'

'Master Aske,' said the chancellor, 'we are all aware that in your eyes Tudors can do no right. But I cannot allow you to accuse the late king of infanticide. The boys were the brothers of his own wife. Where is your proof? Where is a scrap of evidence? There is none.'

'The chancellor is right,' said Brother Thomas quietly. 'Let us not replace one false accusation with another.'

'Why is he right?' demanded Aske less quietly. 'Tell me that.'

'Consider the early years of Henry's reign. His claim was shaky, his throne less secure than any king's before him. Inevitably there were rival claimants, pretending to be one or other of the princes. If Henry had proclaimed their death he would have strengthened his position immeasurably. Even if he had killed them himself he could still have blamed Richard. Why did he delay doing this for seventeen perilous years? The conclusion is inescapable. He did not accuse Richard, he dared not announce the princes' death, because he did not know whether they were dead or not.'

'An ingenious theory,' Aske granted, 'but a theory nonetheless.'

'It is what the facts tell us. The negative facts. One can learn from omissions as well as deeds.'

'The omission was remedied,' the chancellor reminded him. 'Belatedly, but for good reason. Until Sir James Tyrrell confessed, the positive facts did not become known.'

'I would respect your argument more, Dr Rayne,' Brother Thomas told him, 'if Sir James had indeed confessed. But he did not.'

'You are making free with common knowledge again,' the chancellor replied. 'Master Aske and I agree on one thing. You deal in theories, brother. When they do not match the facts you throw away the facts.'

Brother Thomas denied the charge. 'I discard nothing, I assure you. To me even errors have significance. The motive behind a deception may lead us to the truth. Common knowledge is sometimes common error which someone wishes to be believed. Then we must ask why.'

'You mean that Tyrrell's confession was convenient to the king?'

'Too convenient. Henry had become desperate. In turn no fewer than four feigned boys had received support as one of the princes. The king was hated and the threat of further rebellions was growing. Two of the king's three sons had died, including the heir to the throne, and the Tudor succession looked more and more doubtful. The country was suffering from Cardinal Morton's extortions, and supporters of the defeated house of York were gaining in heart and strength. One more plausible Yorkist prince and the Tudors could be brought down.'

'Times do not change.' Aske spoke to himself, but aloud.

'In these circumstances,' Brother Thomas continued, 'Sir James Tyrrell was the obvious victim. He had been Master of the Horse to King Richard. He alone among Richard's closest supporters had survived Bosworth and Henry's executions afterewards. He survived because he was not in England when the battle was fought. He was at his post as captain of one of the fortresses guarding Calais and remained abroad after Henry's victory. The garrison was loyal to him and if he had been recalled he could have escaped across the border into France. It was seventeen years before Henry ordered him to England, and even then he was reluctant to come. In the end only the royal promise of a safe conduct persuaded him to board one of the king's ships.'

'A Tudor promise!' Aske drew a hand across his throat.

'Yes, he was seized, taken to the Tower and tortured so that he should confess that the princes were dead and he had killed them on Richard's orders. But he was a brave man and loyal to his dead master. He set his soul's honour above the agony of the flesh and refused to perjure himself.'

'As, with God's aid, all of us would hope to do.'

Aske looked at the abbot as he spoke, but it was the prior who said amen.

'Sir James was executed, but without the customary speech of confession from the scaffold and without leaving a signed statement of guilt behind him. Not until he was safely dead and could not challenge it did the supposed confession appear. I have examined in every particular the story of how he took over the Tower for one night to commit the act of infanticide. There can seldom have been a less likely tale. It is riddled with improbability, unworthy of King Henry's famous cunning and ingenuity.'

'You are a young man,' the chancellor told him. 'When you have reached my age and studied history more deeply you will realise that many events have occurred far more improbable than man's inventions.'

Brother Thomas wiped his rheumy eyes with the sleeve of his cowl while he considered his reply.

'I did not intend to suggest that my own feeble powers of historical inquiry could be relied on without corroboration. As you will recall, King Henry employed his own historian, a learned brother from Italy, who rewrote the history of England to the glorification of Henry Tudor. His purpose was to show that the greatness of King Arthur had been reborn in the Tudors. If Henry's heir had lived there would have been a second King Arthur, with the blood of both houses, York and Lancaster, in his veins, born in Winchester, the old capital, where Henry had deliberately sent his wife for her lying-in. In this court chronicle Henry can do no wrong, his enemies no right. King Richard is an aberration from the line of true kings – an inhuman monster. Yet, in spite of all this, such is the implausibility of the confession made in Sir James Tyrrell's name that Henry's own historian does not credit the truth of it. In Polydore Vergil my humble deductions find support where least expected.'

The chancellor changed his ground. 'Even if the account is false it does not follow that the fact itself is untrue. The Tyrrell tale may be invented but Richard may still have done his nephew to death. It was in his interest. They stood between him and the throne.'

'So it is popularly supposed, but there is evidence to the contrary.'

'What evidence?'

Brother Thomas looked to the abbot for permission to continue, but this time the abbot did not raise his eyes from his lap.

'Proceed, brother,' Aske urged. 'If we cannot see it, tell us of it. I for one will take your word.'

'I cannot,' replied Brother Thomas. 'Not without my lord's consent.'

The abbot hesitated and then spoke himself.

'The document to which the brother refers is one to which access is strictly forbidden him, or was until the prior ordained otherwise. Its historical importance is incalculable. Bishop Russell brought it here. He laid a solemn charge on the abbey to keep it secure and hidden from the world until Tudors should cease to reign. It has been kept more private even than his chronicle. There is no other copy. Since my precentor has mentioned it I shall not deny its existence, though I have never before seen fit to admit it. But that is all. It cannot be seen.'

'But you yourself have read it?' asked the chancellor. 'Do you support your precentor's conclusions?'

'My trust in him is absolute. What Bishop Russell has written and Brother Thomas has interpreted will be the truth.'

'Then let him tell us what it is.'

While the abbot hesitated again Brother Thomas rose and flung himself at his feet. 'Speak, father. You know the truth better than I.'

Aske and the chancellor supported him.

'Tell them what the bishop told you,' Brother Thomas begged.

'After all this time, my lord,' said the prior, 'it can surely do no harm.'

5

'Bishop Russell,' said the abbot, bowing to their importunity, 'was a servant of the house of York. Since its defeat in the late wars history has been unkind to their kings. As a boy, I was privileged to listen to the bishop in his reminiscences. If it will help restore the balance of truth I will recount to you what he described as the greatest tragedy of his time.'

'Yes, yes,' cried Brother Thomas. 'That is the start. Tell them, my lord, of the death of King Edward.'

'Edward IV was the bishop's hero. After the death of his father, the duke of York, he had won the throne in battle. He became a popular king and everyone was glad that the quarrel between York and Lancaster was settled, as it seemed, for good. He brought to heel the local lordlings, who had often been behaving no better than common robbers. Lawlessness was ended, and the king's justice re-established. As well as being a strong and just ruler, Edward was the handsomest king who ever sat on a throne: fair, six foot four inches tall, merry and open-handed. And confident in his kingliness.'

'The obverse of the Tudors,' remarked Aske. 'Unsure of themselves and others, they are tight-faced and tight-fisted. Secretive and suspicious. Untrusting and untrusted.'

'You voice your own opinion,' said the abbot mildly, 'not mine. According to Bishop Russell, Edward, although he had taken the crown from his cousin, Henry VI, believed absolutely in the justice of his claim. Taking his sovereignty for granted, he had no airs about him. If you met him out riding you would think: A man like that should be king. But if you discovered that he was indeed the king, you would be surprised. He behaved so unaffectedly, so much at ease with high and low.'

'Even in bed,' jeered the chancellor, 'as your community found out for itself when here at Croyland he broke the commandment forbidding adultery.'

The abbot ignored the interruption. He was still sitting in the shadows, withdrawn from the rest of the company, his words coming as though from a distance.

'A real king does not require the trappings of majesty, the bishop used to say. Edward would have been recognised as a king naked. He should have reigned long and gloriously. But the Lord called him in the fullness of his vigour when scarcely over forty. He died suddenly and from no known cause, and with him died the happiness of his subjects. The succession was unprepared. Old wounds, not fully healed, re-opened. As the Keeper of his Privy Seal, Bishop Russell was on duty at his deathbed, and for ever after could not recall the scene without tears.'

There were no tears on the abbot's impassive face, but he broke off to blow his nose on a fine handkerchief.

'There was weeping enough at the time. The queen wept most of all, but hers were thought to be tears of rage at the presence of Jane Shore, the king's mistress, who had supplanted her in the royal bed. The bishop was forced to ask the queen to leave because she was disturbing the king's comfort, and she would not go unless Mistress Shore left too. Kings do not die in privacy and peace. When the women had gone the room was still crowded with members of the council and the royal household, all apprehensive of what would happen if the king did not recover.'

'Tell them of the will, father,' Brother Thomas prompted him. 'It is the will that matters.'

'In the presence of all, the king added a codicil to his will stating that his brother Richard should be Lord Protector of the realm until the prince of Wales came of age. Edward had had three brothers: Edmund of Rutland, killed with his father in battle; George of Clarence, who turned traitor and had been executed; and Richard of Gloucester, who had fought at Edward's side since he became old enough to hold a sword. After Edward had lost the throne thirteen years before, he and Richard had returned from exile together and regained it side by side. The protectorship was just and welcomed.'

'But fatal to the prince of Wales,' observed the chancellor.

'King Edward did not believe it would be. These were his words as reported by the bishop: My dear brother of Gloucester is my most loyal subject and will protect my son against his enemies.'

Robert Aske's eye was darting from face to face. 'The dead embers of the past do not concern us now,' he said. 'Is Edward's appointment of his brother to rule the country relevant to our inquiry?'

'Address yourself to Brother Thomas,' the abbot replied. 'It is his inquiry. I speak at his request.'

'The appointment – and what resulted from it – is crucial to my findings,' said Brother Thomas. 'The queen had been planning the regency for herself. She was ambitious to rule. Her family, the Woodvilles, held all the power at court. There were many of them and she had seen to it that honours and titles and appointments came to them. While the king lay on his deathbed they took control of London and Westminster. The duke of Gloucester was their only rival and they hated and feared him. A few years before, when he saw that the king had fallen into their hands, he had retired out of their reach to his castle in the Yorkshire dales. He preferred the outdoor life there to the court with its mincing deceits and boudoir intrigues. As Lord of the North he kept the Scots in their place. After the king himself, he was the most famous warrior in England.'

'He should have continued to spurn the softness of the south,' said Aske, 'and stayed in Yorkshire.'

'Without the codicil he might have done so. He had no ambitions like the queen. But he was loyal. Once his brother had bequeathed to him the safety of the realm, he could not refuse. The king's infatuation with the queen had parted them but not dissolved their trust. In the end, when King Edward had to choose between his brother and his wife, he chose his brother. To Richard the queen was an evil, scheming woman, with the blood of his brother George on her hands. To her he was the one obstacle between her and the exercise of sovereign power.'

'It seems to me,' said Aske, 'that Richard had Mistress Shore to thank for the codicil. Was the king clear in his mind when he signed it?'

The abbot inclined his head. 'So the bishop swore. It was set out in the king's own words, and only when it was signed and witnessed would he make his last confession and place his soul in God's merciful keeping. Then he lay on his back with his face to the ceiling. His eyes were open but without sight, so that all the company thought him dead. Some were already praying for him in Purgatory when he moved with the last of his giant strength, heaving himself on to his side. But not to the privacy of the wall. He turned to face the company, searching, with his failing sight, for his son.'

'But he was not there!' Brother Thomas could not contain his surprise. 'You have never told me this before, father. When the king died in the palace at Westminster, the prince of Wales was in the marches at Ludlow.'

'I refer to the younger boy. Richard was at Westminster. The bishop used to say that he tried to leave with his mother but was prevented. He reached no higher than the waists of the attendants and at first no one realised whom the king sought. One of the physicians went forward, then the chancellor with the Great Seal, then Lord Hastings, the king's closest friend. All were met with a frown. When the boy was brought to the bedside at last, he spoke.'

'The king?' exclaimed Brother Thomas. 'He spoke to the prince?'

'*Richard*, he said, *we are of the royal house of York, you and I. My father was duke. Before I became king I was duke. Now you are duke. Trust your uncle. Be loyal to your brother. Be worthy of our house. Our emblem is the rising sun. See that it never sets.* Those were King Edward's last words. The bishop was standing by the head of the bed and the king signed to him to take the boy's hand and lead him away. Then he groaned and the breath escaped for the last time from his great body.'

'Great indeed,' said Aske fervently.

'Great at wenching,' added the chancellor.

'That,' said Brother Thomas sadly, 'was the cause of the trouble to come.'

6

The abbot relapsed into silence and at the guests' prompting Brother Thomas resumed the account of his investigations.

'Once Edward IV was dead, the prince of Wales became Edward V. The boy was at Ludlow castle in the care of an uncle, the queen's brother. In London the queen and her eldest son – a son by her first marriage and the new king's half-brother – seized the government. They took money from the treasury in the Tower and equipped a fleet under the command of another of the queen's brothers. They had to get the king to Westminster and crowned before Richard, the Lord Protector, could arrive from Yorkshire. Once he was crowned, the protectorship would lapse unless its continuance had first been provided for in accordance with the law, and this they intended to leave Richard no time to contrive. Government would then be conducted by the queen's family and their nominees on the king's council.

'According to Bishop Russell's chronicle the old king died on the ninth of April. The new one was to reach London by the end of the month and be crowned on the fourth day of May in unseemly haste.

'When news of his brother's death and the terms of the will reached Richard in Wensleydale, he wrote to Ludlow arranging to meet the young king and his escort at Northampton so that they could enter London together. He could not have known all the queen's plans, but he distrusted her and must have suspected that she intended to rule in her son's name, as Edward II's mother had done. Richard, too, knew that in order to rule he must secure the king's person.

'As he rode south he heard that the royal escort had been enlarged into an army. When he reached Northampton it was to discover that the rendezvous was not to be kept. The king was already at Stony Stratford, fourteen miles nearer to London. What could Richard do, heavily outnumbered?'

The abbot appeared to be dozing and the prior wrapped in prayer, but Aske and the chancellor were following closely and both opened their mouths to answer. Brother Thomas, absorbed in his own story, did not heed them.

'He rode on to Stony Stratford with a handful of men. He

took charge of the king. He dismissed the army and arrested the queen's brother. No one dared raise a finger against him, such was his boldness and power of command.

'So the queen's plot failed, and when the king and his Protector entered London together she took refuge in Westminster Abbey with her younger son and the princesses. The council appointed Richard as Regent with full powers. The coronation was postponed for three weeks to allow time for unhurried preparations. The king was installed in the royal apartments in the Tower, and the queen was persuaded to release the young duke of York from sanctuary to keep his brother company.

'During the three weeks' delay a further postponement of the coronation was announced. Eventually it took place on the sixth of July and was said to be the most splendid in all our history. Nearly every peer and prelate in the realm attended to swear fealty in person to the new sovereign. But that sovereign was not the young Edward. His brief reign had come to an end. It was Richard of Gloucester who was anointed and crowned. Edward and his brother did not attend the ceremony. They remained in the Tower and were never again known to be seen outside it.'

'Richard showed courage and resource,' said Aske approvingly. 'If what you say is true, he took lawful steps to secure his protectorship. But whatever happened to the boys he should not have stooped to snatch the crown from his nephew.'

The chancellor was quick to disagree. 'I hold no brief for Richard. He was a regicide and infanticide and you will not convince me of his innocence. But we should recognise reality and not give way to sentiment. There can be only one fate for a deposed monarch. To be deposed is to be dead: statecraft demands it. Was Henry VI allowed to live? Or

Richard II? Or Edward II? What legal title to the crown could Richard have, what authority over his subjects, while his nephews still lived?'

'The best,' Brother Thomas replied. 'He was his brother's heir.'

'How can that be if his brother had sons?'

'Not all sons are heirs.'

'You mean the boys were bastards? If that is so, why is it not known?'

'Because, because—' Brother Thomas could not suppress his excitement at the revelation '—after Richard's death Henry Tudor destroyed all record of it. Every record, that is, except one.'

'Ah,' said the chancellor. 'At last we have it. So that is the precious document Bishop Russell brought here.'

Brother Thomas nodded. 'At Croyland we have incontrovertible evidence which has lain hidden from the eye of the world for half a century.'

'And which your abbot insists on returning to its hiding place unexamined by any external authority?'

'I am content to take the brother's word,' said Aske. 'I accept that Henry Tudor would not scruple to destroy inconvenient evidence. If he was set on blackening Richard's name it would be essential to condemn him as a usurper.'

'There is more to it than that,' Brother Thomas announced. 'Do not forget that Henry Tudor married the eldest of the princes' sisters, the Princess Elizabeth of York. If they were bastards, so was she, and if she was a bastard any rightful claim to the throne in his wife's name was annulled.'

Aske's eye glinted. 'I follow you at last, brother,' he said. 'Your findings are pertinent and welcome. Our king, the son of Henry Tudor, does not even have a legitimate claim through his mother. The fat Tudor's majesty is flawed, not by two bastardies, but three. He now has nothing left but brute force. Wretched Henry! No wonder he stands so much on his dignity and cuts off every head in reach.' Ignoring the chancellor's glare, he laughed contemptuously.

'Is this sure?' the chancellor demanded of Brother Thomas. 'For you are meddling in matters of the highest importance.'

'I do so at your command.' Brother Thomas was all humility.

'Then add conviction to your assertion. How could the boys be bastards? Edward IV married Elizabeth Woodville in secret, as all the world knows. It brought retribution on his head by offending the earl of Warwick, who had set him on the throne and was negotiating with the French king for a state marriage. But when the secret was revealed, no one doubted the evidence. If this had not been produced, neither the earl nor anyone else would have recognised the union.'

'That the ceremony took place there is no doubt. Edward was amorous, as we know. He gave his heart and loins full play. When he took Elizabeth Woodville to wife he lowered himself and put his throne in hazard, and he did it for lust – because she would not let him possess her otherwise. Except as a queen she would not lie with him, and he in the heat of his lechery agreed to pay the price.'

'How could he so demean himself?' Aske's face expressed disgust.

'It had happened before.'

'You refer to Dame Elizabeth Lucy,' said the chancellor. 'That is an old tale. She was no more to him than Jane Shore became. He would never have plighted his troth to a strumpet.'

'But if his passion was for an honourable lady, member of a noble and esteemed family, he might have become betrothed to her. And that he did. When he made his promises to Elizabeth Woodville his troth was already plighted to the Lady Eleanor Butler, daughter to a hero, the soldier earl of Shrewsbury. The contract between them was binding in the eyes of God and the law. It was witnessed by John Stillington, bishop of Bath and Wells, a man of unimpeachable honesty who became chancellor of England during Edward's reign.'

'If this is true, why in God's name did Chancellor Stillington permit the Woodville union? If he was a man of honesty, as you state, why did he not protest?'

'There is evidence that he did. He became chancellor after Elizabeth Woodville was recognised as queen, but later he was dismissed for no stated reason. That, I believe, is when he raised the issue of the earlier contract, because his conscience grew troubled about the succession.'

'You are speculating again.' The chancellor shook a fat gnarled fist across the table.

'Where there is no certainty,' Brother Thomas conceded, 'one must make do with probability. For instance, if we are to judge King Edward's taste by Elizabeth Woodville he was susceptible to widows and women older than himself. The Lady Eleanor Butler was a widow, too, and older than the king. In each case, what is more, there was the daring of consorting with his enemies – both ladies came from Lancastrian families.'

'Is that all you can tell us, to bolster this tale?'

'Another clue lies in the death of George, duke of Clarence. He was the middle surviving brother, junior to Edward and senior to Richard; as disloyal to Edward as Richard was faithful. If his brother were to die without legitimate issue he would succeed, and the throne was his ambition. When, after Stillington's dismissal, he was executed for plotting against Edward, the bishop was imprisoned – again for no known cause. To me the conclusion is inescapable that the bishop had been ordered to keep the pre-contract secret but had told Clarence of it and so spurred the duke's ambition that he demanded recognition as his brother's heir. It was the queen who persuaded Edward into signing the warrant for Clarence's execution. The bishop was released afterwards but never again regained favour. Bishop Russell writes that all the Woodville faction hated him bitterly, for a reason that no man could discover while Edward lived.'

'He should have spoken out,' said Aske. 'The legal position is plain. Whether or not the ceremony has been performed, a marriage contract has the force of law. It was his duty to make the existence of a pre-contract public knowledge.'

'He would have lost his head,' said Brother Thomas, 'and to what purpose? While Edward lived it made no difference. As soon as he died the bishop did reveal the truth. That is why the coronation was postponed a second time and why, when it did take place, it was Richard, Edward's remaining brother, who was crowned. The bishop's story, showing the children to be bastards, was accepted not only by Richard but by the council, by Parliament and by the citizens of London. The evidence he produced is not stated by Bishop Russell, but it must have been strong. Richard did not seize the throne therefore. Parliament offered it to him, begged him to accept, and his title was confirmed by statute.'

'What statute?' the chancellor demanded. 'I know of none.'

'That is the document we have, the document of which all other copies were destroyed by order of Henry Tudor.'

'Do you confirm this, my lord?' The chancellor swivelled his ugly head and raised his voice at the abbot, who opened his eyes and, seeming not to like what he saw when they rested on the chancellor's features, closed them again.

'Your endorsement of your precentor's words, if you please.' The chancellor grew bullying and brusque.

'With Brother Thomas's able assistance,' said the abbot dryly, opening his eyes once more, 'you have snuffled out our secret. We have here what Bishop Russell assured us to be the only surviving copy of Titulus Regius, a statute which establishes Richard's legal claim to the throne and answers the Tudor charge that he was a usurper. It sets out the oath which King Edward swore before Almighty God, that he would marry the famous Talbot's daughter Eleanor – an oath taken before ever he met Elizabeth Woodville – and it officially declares the illegitimacy of the offspring of the Woodville union. One of these children, as the precentor has remarked, was Elizabeth of York, our reigning king's mother. Like her brothers, she was bastardised by an Act of Parliament, which may, however, have been repealed by her husband. I leave it to those learned in constitutional niceties to determine how far this affects the sovereignty of King Henry VIII, the head of our Church. Whom God preserve.'

'The good Lord has guided me to Croyland,' Aske declared. 'When this is published in the north men will no longer be in doubt of the rightness of our cause. The laws of both church and state are on our side. Henry sits on the throne and can play at being Pope because his father won a battle fifty years ago. There is no other reason.'

7

The depth of the night sat heavily on them. The heat from the still glowing ash in the hearth oppressed them. One of the candles flickered into a wisp of smoke, exhausted.

The chancellor yawned and pooh-poohed. 'Your would-be rebel force is puny and your knowledge of the law shallow, Master Aske. Certainly the Act would have been repealed, since all Richard's wicked deeds were subject to annulment after his death – as you, my lord abbot, well know. I can detect your train of thought: if the princes were bastards there is no point in the investigation, which you still seek an excuse to evade. But I do not accept this. Your Titulus Regius is irrelevant to our argument.'

'Far from it,' cried Brother Thomas. 'The statute tells us, whether we believe it or not and whatever happened after, that they were declared illegitimate. Thus the justice of Richard's elevation to the throne was universally acknowledged at the time. In those circumstances, why should he have them murdered? Rather, it was in the interests of his good name to ensure that they were kept alive.'

'But alive,' said the chancellor, 'they would always have supporters.'

Brother Thomas shook his head. 'Except for his mother and her kin none favoured Edward V. A boy king meant dissension and weakness. Firm government was required and Richard alone could provide it. A veteran of the wars, he was a hero in the north for his defeat of the Scots. He was welcomed by the London merchants, who looked for stability in the interests of trade. The nobility were sick of slaughter and showed their support by thronging to his coronation. No; Richard was secure. Edward V had become nothing more than Edward the bastard. Is it likely then that Richard would wish to be held guilty of his nephews' death – children of the brother to whom he had been devoted and who had left them so confidently in his protection? Every instinct of humanity and policy would stay his hand.'

'Then why did he not show them to be alive? Tell me that,' the chancellor demanded. 'Once they vanished from sight there were bound to be rumours that he had had them despatched. Indeed the chancellor of France was telling the Estates General such a tale within a few months. If they were never seen again after Richard's coronation what other conclusion could be drawn?'

'That someone acted over-zealously on Richard's behalf, without his knowledge or approval.'

'Who would have dared?'

'One man – the duke of Buckingham. He emerged from obscurity when King Edward died. He offered Richard timely support. He was a Plantagenet, descended from Edward III's youngest son, neither Yorkist nor Lancastrian. As a minor he had been married to a Woodville – a great catch for them but a humiliation to him. While Edward lived he sulked on his estates in the west country and took no part in affairs. He was proud and unstable and had his revenge, as Richard's lieutenant, in preventing the realm from falling into the hands of his wife's family. He met the Protector at Northampton and never left his side until he was crowned. As a reward Richard made him Constable of England.'

'And then had him put to death,' added the chancellor. 'Like Hastings, the other man who helped him outwit the Woodvilles.'

'That was during the following year, when the duke plotted with Henry Tudor and became a rebel. Like Clarence he was aiming at the throne himself. His claim was far better than Henry's.'

'Are you now suggesting that he killed the princes?'

'He was ambitious and would have been glad, no doubt, to see other Plantagenets removed from his path to the throne. He had motive and opportunity. After the coronation Richard made a royal progress to Gloucester and York. Buckingham had charge of the Tower in his absence. There would be no time for the king to countermand an order.'

'So now you lay the guilt on Buckingham.' The chancellor sniffed. 'An ingenious supposition. You have evidence, I presume, which you will refuse to divulge but assert to be incontrovertible.'

'My supposition, as you call it, is that the princes were never killed. I was suggesting that if they had been, the duke would have been a more likely suspect than the king. Buckingham was a man who could kill children in cold blood but I believe that if he had done so it would have become known. No; the boys simply disappeared and neither Richard nor Henry after him had any idea what became of them. That is the only explanation which fits all the facts.'

Brother Thomas blinked in the remaining candlelight and paused for his theory to be challenged.

'Do you mean that they escaped?' inquired the chancellor.

'Let us suppose they did. What would have happened? The Constable and his lieutenant would have kept quiet for fear of their lives. When the king learned of it, as he must have, what would he have done? If he announced it few would believe him. Murder would be presumed. His enemies could either accuse him of the crime or choose to believe that a rival claimant was at large. The pretenders who were to plague Henry would have plagued Richard too. The duke of Buckingham—'

The abbot raised his hand for silence.

'Your tongue runs on, my son. Tell our guests whether there is any passage in our chronicles or records which states that the princes escaped.'

'Not states, father, but suggests. I read between the lines. The bishop nowhere states that he knows or even believes them to be dead. It is a strange omission. I admit that he was a man of truth and he chose his words with care. But I am convinced that he was deliberately concealing his knowledge.'

'And the welcoming of Henry's victory at Bosworth as God-given, saving the realm from tyranny and confusion? Do you believe that Richard's chancellor would have expressed such a sentiment – not as a report of what men said, but as his firmly held opinion – for any reason whatever?'

'That passage might be an interpolation, an expression of loyalty by Father Philip, who continued the chronicle at Abbot Edmund's command. I will examine it.'

'So much for your concealment by Bishop Russell!' The abbot turned to the chancellor. 'The pen passes from hand to hand. Sometimes it is that of a great personage, at others that of one of our home-bred scholars like Father Philip or, as now, Brother Thomas himself. All are anonymous; all express the truth as they see it.'

'Since Bishop Russell saw it as a Yorkist,' said the chancellor suspiciously, 'it is important to separate his words from the others. Meanwhile I am prepared to accept Brother Thomas's theory as a basis for further investigation. Let us assume for this purpose that the princes, said to have been murdered in 1483, were alive three years later when Bishop Russell wrote, and were still untraced at the turn of the century when the Tyrrell tale was made public to account for them.'

'If they have died since then,' said Aske, 'there could at least be heirs.'

The prior began to speak in hope, but the abbey's great bell drowned his faltering words. It was midnight.

'Mattins,' said the abbot between peals. 'We will join the brethren.'

They followed him down the winding stairs and out of his private doorway into the church. The nave was a cavern of darkness broken by rows of huge pillars marching towards the flickering lights in the choir. A file of black-cowled figures was descending the stairs from the dorter. Their bare feet whispered on the stone flags like falling rain.

Brother Thomas had already begun his devotions – with a prayer that the abbot might find the plain-chant tuneful – when he felt his sleeve tugged. They were still in the nave and the prior had taken the lead to usher the guests to their stalls.

'Kneel,' the abbot commanded Brother Thomas.

They knelt in the crossing. Above their heads the weight of the tower was carried by the span of four great arches, dog-toothed in ancient Romanesque. Behind and on either side, the nave and transepts had become invisible, void of light, yet filled for Brother Thomas with the mysterious presence of God.

'Almighty Father,' prayed the abbot, 'in Thy infinite mercy send down, I pray Thee, the blessing of Thy grace on our beloved brother Thomas. Let him speak with wisdom and discretion. Let him not rashly reveal to strangers the secrets of our house. Let his lips dwell no more on our precious and irreplaceable treasures, *Historia Croylandensis* and the Titulus Regius. Guide his thoughts, good Lord, and guard his steps through the dangers and temptations of the world. If he leaves us, bring him safely home. Grant, O God, that this brother of ours, gifted above others, may be the salvation of this house and not the cause of its destruction. In the name of Thy only Son, our Lord and Saviour, Jesus Christ. Amen.'

Brother Thomas, overcome, could utter only a sob.

'Amen,' the abbot repeated fiercely.

'Amen,' responded Brother Thomas, choking between sobs. 'Amen, amen, amen,' The words echoed and died, smothered in the darkness like so many little princes.

8

Robert Aske rose refreshed for lauds. After a few hours' sleep in one of the abbot's comfortable guest chambers he had awoken at his most fervent and determined.

'I came to Croyland to find a Plantagenet,' he told the abbot when they assembled in the parlour after breakfast. 'Our only prospect is the boy king Edward, your Brother Thomas tells us. We believed him dead. He may not be. We believed him legitimate. He may not be. I have thought the matter over. If he is alive the realm requires him, bastard or no. If he is our sole hope he must be sought, and sought today.'

Brother Thomas had not slept at all. His eyes were dark-ringed, his soul heavy with the weight of the abbot's displeasure. God must be angry with him, he had concluded after hours of patient self-searching in his cell. Worse still was the realisation that he minded the wrath of God less than that of the abbot.

His worldly father had died too early for Brother Thomas

to remember him. He had been a miller who supplied grain to the brothers' bakehouse. When his mother died too, giving birth to a posthumous stillborn sister, Thomas, alone in the world at nine, had walked into the monastery and announced that he had come to stay.

It was the abbot who had rescued him from scullion's work in the kitchen and sent him to the almonry school, where he became the brightest pupil within the grammar master's memory. Even so he had chosen not to become a priest, unsure of his fitness and preferring the humbler vocation of a lay brother. But when the office of precentor fell vacant, the abbot had insisted on his election and inspired him with the confidence to rise to the responsibility. Abbot John had become his father on earth as well as his spiritual lord.

'My lord abbot was right. My tongue ran away with me yesterday,' he said. 'It was an ill-judged conceit that Edward might still be alive.'

'Yet you believed it then. How can you not believe it still?'

Brother Thomas hung his head and Aske took this for assent.

'Very well. Go out and beat the thickets for him.'

'I will arrange that all doors are open to you,' the chancellor promised. 'With the bishop's authorisation no one will deny you entry.'

'But if Edward and his brother were bastards,' Brother Thomas pleaded, 'any inquiry must be futile.'

'I do not accept that they were,' said the chancellor, 'since you do not see fit to produce your evidence. Even if you did, I would remain unconvinced. What reliance can we place on words attributed to the long-dead Bishop Stillington? Might not the story of the pre-contract be the result rather than the cause of his enmity with the Woodvilles? It was a timely tale for those who were plotting to set Edward's sons aside and obtrude Richard, as even your chronicle confesses. No; the inquiry will not be futile. I will arm the brother with all needful credentials and he must go to London to burrow for the truth.'

'To London!' Brother Thomas had never crossed the nearest horizon. The extent of his world was the view from the top of the church tower.

'Have no fear. Your credentials will state that your investigations take place at the bishop's command.'

'The bishop cannot command one of my brethren,' said the abbot.

'At his request then. With his blessing. You are too particular, my lord. I am assisting you by making the responsibility his. If the enterprise goes awry you will not be blamed.'

'That is considerate of you.' The abbot bowed to the chancellor. 'But will the king's council accept your assurance on the point if I am arraigned before it for treasonable activities? Brother Thomas is mine alone to command and neither the bishop nor anyone else can relieve me of the responsibility.'

'My lord abbot,' said Aske earnestly, 'we must all take risks for the Faith. Would you have us close the curtains on a shaft of light and sit in the gathering darkness awaiting the dissolution of all God's houses up and down the country? Would you have it said in days to come that Prior Houghton, Bishop Fisher and Sir Thomas More were the only three men in England in our time with the courage of their convictions?'

His fervour was infectious and the prior caught it at once.

'My lord, I hear God in my heart telling us to let Brother

Thomas go. The Church's salvation is in our hands. The brother has been chosen from Above.'

'Let us hear from the brother himself,' said the abbot.

'My heart's desire is to obey you in all things, father.'

'And nothing more?'

'To serve God and be the instrument of His truth.'

'In other words, to pursue the inquiry.'

'Not if you do not wish it. No, no,' Brother Thomas cried; although a voice inside him was crying, Yes, yes.

The chancellor smirked in satisfaction. 'It is clear that we are all in favour of taking the matter further. You have already given your permission, my lord, for the inquiry to proceed. You cannot in good faith withdraw now it is fairly launched. There is the matter of the Titulus Regius, may I remind you? What if word of it came to the king's ear? If his commissioners are taking sacred relics, they will hardly overlook the record of an Act of Parliament. Now we know precisely what it is you are hiding, you will scarcely be able to withhold it a third time.'

'If anyone comes for it,' said the abbot, 'I promise you it will not be found.'

'It would be an unusual thing to suffer martyrdom for – you and all your community with you. I have no doubt the document would be found in the end. Or else you would have to destroy it and do the king's work for him.'

The abbot fingered the silver crucifix which hung from his neck, while he meditated on martyrdom. The rule of the blessed St Benedict exhorted him to share patiently in the sufferings of Christ that he might deserve to be a partaker of His kingdom.

'If I am to sanction the continuance of the inquiry,' he said, 'there must be a pledge of silence. No one is to be told of what you have learned here, or of the true nature of the investigation, until Brother Thomas has returned safely home.'

'You have my word,' agreed the chancellor. 'Subject to one condition. That I learn from the brother's own lips the result of his mission. As soon as he comes back I must be sent for to hear his report at the same time as yourself.'

'That is fair,' said Aske. 'You have my word too and my condition is the same.'

The abbot accepted. 'But if you play me false, either of you, you will answer for it to St Guthlac and to God Himself. Expect no mercy either in this world or the next. I swear to show you none. I swear it in the name of our Father Above. Vengeance is mine, I will repay, said the Lord.'

He stood solemnly over them and they followed his glance to the sword on the wall. The prior and Brother Thomas were embarrassed by the impropriety of the oath. The chancellor shrugged off the threat with a disbelieving twitch of the shoulders. Aske stared in wonder.

'So you are a man of mettle after all.'

The abbot ignored him. 'I have stated my agreement, but let no one expect success. These happenings were many years ago. If the princes tried to escape from the Tower they may have died in the attempt. Plantagenets do not disappear except to the grave. A successful escape would have taken them to France or Scotland where the enemies of England would not have been slow to acclaim them.'

'Fear not, father; now you have blessed it the enterprise will succeed,' said Brother Thomas. 'Last night I asked God and He told me that it depended upon you, and you alone.'

'You and the prior take up too much of God's time,' complained the abbot. 'Be sure that you are listening to Him and not the promptings of your own will.'

He led the way under Abbot Theodore's skull into the

chapel. Kneeling before the altar, they all took the vow in the name of Father, Son and Holy Spirit.

Back in the parlour, the abbot dismissed them. 'You will leave tomorrow,' he told Brother Thomas. 'I shall not see you again before you go. The Lord be with you.'

'And also with you.'

Brother Thomas made the response and prostrated himself, begging for his father's blessing and forgiveness. The request was granted with a laying-on of hands. When they were lifted, he suffered the pain of loneliness. He felt himself a child without a parent once more. Outside the womb of Croyland the world awaited him, a world he had forsworn. It was a world of crime and sin, where danger and the Devil lay in wait.

Part Three

THE TRAIL

I

When the abbot of Croyland made a journey, by river or by road, he made it with a retinue of forty of fifty men. They were necessary for his dignity and business affairs, for his protection and comfort. Brother Thomas, having no dignity, needing no comfort and carrying all his business in his head, had a bodyguard of one.

The abbot had not done him proud in numbers, but he had chosen the one with loving care. Gervase was the abbot's most trusted and intimate body-servant. That he should have parted with him to a humble brother was a mark of extreme favour.

'You can trust him with your life, my son,' the prior said. 'The lord abbot has told him to see that no harm befalls you, and with Gervase the will is the deed. Your mission must be unobserved. A larger company would attract attention and arouse suspicion.'

Secretly dismayed that only one attendant, however staunch, was to stand between him and the perils of wayfaring, Brother Thomas gave thanks and wondered what other commands Gervase had received.

In the wisps of a grey dawn they rode out of the great gate and down the silent village street to the river.

Here, instead of crossing the ford, Brother Thomas urged his horse up one of the steep stone legs of the Holy Trinity bridge. This marvel of Croyland stood without parallel in all the known world. It was triangular, with three legs spanning two arms of the river – his river, the Welland, the unhurrying, untroubled stream on whose bank he had been born. It barely moved now, still wrapped in sleep, but here and there the water sparkled at him, reflecting the first light of day.

On the quayside below, the two Yorkist kings, Edward IV and his brother, Richard of Gloucester, had embarked after their visit to the abbey. With an escort of two hundred horsemen they had come by road from Walsingham, where they offered thanks for victory to Our Lady. From here a boat had taken them along the Welland and the Nene to the family castle at Fotheringhay.

He looked up and back. The monastery buildings stood in silhouette, blurred but sharpening in the growing light. A pang seized his heart at the folly of leaving. He could not conceal from himself that he had sought the parting, sinning in boastfulness that he could discover what no man had discovered before. The abbot had not willed it: consent had been wrung from him, and he, Brother Thomas, had sided against his father in God. It would serve him justly if he never saw Croyland again.

There on the hump of the bridge he climbed off his horse and knelt at the foot of the tall cross to beg God's mercy. Then he remounted and joined Gervase, who was waiting for him, stolid and patient, the barrier between his innocence of the world and the wickedness which lay ahead. It was a Wednesday and already men were stirring to prepare for the market which had been held, by royal grant to the abbots, every week during the four hundred years since King Stephen's day. Side by side they rode out of the village into the emptiness of the fens, where nothing stood above the level of the ground and all the view was sky.

At Peterborough they rested an hour at the sister house. Their reception there was polite but cold. Because of boundary disputes the abbeys were rarely on good terms. Brother Thomas recalled some of the events recorded in the chronicles. It was an abbot of Peterborough who had encouraged the men of Deeping to occupy land belonging to Croyland – rough men who seized valuable reeds, manhandled abbey servants, even invaded the village and entered the nave of the church. They had shot at the cellarer's guard-dog with arrows and killed it. Small wonder Abbot Richard had written of Peterborough as 'our too near, I wish I could say good, neighbour'.

Before setting out refreshed, Brother Thomas visited the church on an errand of piety. It was less than six months since Katharine of Aragon, the deposed but lawful queen, had died in the Faith, supplanted by the harlot Anne Boleyn. Here in obscurity the queen was buried, and at her tomb Brother Thomas prayed for her soul and the success of his mission. Earnestly he besought God not to let the harlot triumph.

From Peterborough they travelled the main highway between London and the north. To his amazement the road was alive: with pedlars, tinkers and cobblers; with troupes of wandering musicians – minstrels, singers and tumblers; with knowing quack doctors and quick-talking vendors of drugs and herbs. There were labourers on the move, and heavy carts laden with goods. Brother Thomas could not imagine why so many people should choose to endure the hardships and dangers of travel. In his curiosity he wanted to speak to them all, but Gervase discouraged him.

'No good will come of it,' he said gruffly. 'It is best to believe every man on the highway to be a rogue.'

The first night they lodged at the bishop's palace at Buckden, and the second at the bishop of Ely's in Hatfield. At each house the chancellor's letter, bearing the bishop's seal, assured them of hospitality and every ease which could be provided.

At Hatfield Brother Thomas felt himself in Lancastrian territory. John Morton, a former bishop of Ely, had done more than any other man to place Henry Tudor on the throne. A member of King Edward's and Richard's councils, he had been implicated in Lord Hastings' plot against the Lord Protector, but Richard had spared his life. He had then stirred the duke of Buckingham against Richard, and when that rebellion failed he fled to Henry in Brittany and plotted his invasion. When Henry became king he had received his reward: archbishop of Canterbury, chancellor of England and a cardinal's hat. Richard, who had spared him, he pursued beyond the grave, blackening his name with calumny, and Brother Thomas suspected that the whole cock-and-bull story attributed to Sir James Tyrrell had been invented by Cardinal Morton. Henry Tudor and John Morton were two of a kind, and Brother Thomas spent a restless night obsessed by their wiles.

When he entered the city of London on the third day he could hardly trust his eyes or ears. None of his reading had prepared him for this. The crowds were so dense that one could scarcely get through the streets; the noise was louder than he could have conceived. When he paused to feed his wonder he was jostled and cursed without regard for his habit.

He was unprepared, too, for the finery of the clothes worn by ordinary merchants, the richness of the gold and silver on display in many shops, and the dirt and squalor in the streets. Towering above everything stood the cathedral church of St Paul, with its spire surely the tallest in the kingdom, pointing the way to Heaven. Yet everyone around him was too busy to notice this miraculous monument to man's faith in God.

'Which way?' he asked anxiously.

'To the Tower,' said Gervase, rescuing him from a friar who had seized his reins to engage him in theological dispute – doubtless about the idleness of monks.

The Tower! From being a royal residence it had become a state prison. Recent kings had chosen to live elsewhere – at Windsor or Greenwich or, now, at the late cardinal's palaces at Whitehall or Hampton – and leave the fortress to their enemies. Brother Thomas had supposed he would be lodging at the abbot's town house, not at the very scene of the crime he had come to solve.

When it came into view at the end of a narrow street it appeared a city in itself. The towers were too many to count, the walls ran on and on and out of sight. The river at its side reduced the Welland to a trickle by comparison.

The officer of the guard made no pretence of respect for monks. He received them with a surly face and made them wait in the discomfort of the gateway's passage while their credentials were taken for examination.

When at last permission to enter was granted, Gervase was conducted to the stables with the horses and Brother Thomas found himself being led in the opposite direction across the Tower green. He was alone, he realised in sudden panic, alone in the clutches of the king's men.

All the way south he had been brewing his speech to the Constable. He must gain co-operation without exciting suspicion. He must be forthcoming but not too forthcoming – open in appearance, but in appearance only. The bishop wished him to look into certain matters. No doubt the Constable would wish to oblige the bishop. The investigations would be purely historical, safely in the past. He had no desire or brief to pry into the politics of the present century.

'You should have been here yesterday, brother.'

The bearded guard escorting him had stopped in the middle of the green.

'It was a great day for the Old Faith,' he whispered. 'A day to remember. Did you not hear the cannon?'

Brother Thomas tried to remember. According to his calculation, yesterday had been the nineteenth of May, and for all his nimbleness of mind he could not guess what might have made it memorable.

'She lost her head.' The man drew a hand across the back of his neck. 'Where you are standing now.'

'Who?' Even as he asked the question, the answer passed his lips: 'Queen Anne.'

The man nodded and smacked his lips in satisfaction. 'She screamed enough to wake the dead. And serve the hussy right.'

Safely in the past! Brother Thomas felt as though he had stepped through the pages in his chronicle on to the blood-stained stage of history itself. This was the dark-eyed harlot to whose sins he had drawn God's attention at Peterborough. This was the woman but for whom the monasteries might still be undisturbed. He was overcome with compassion nevertheless. She had died and her soul was in Purgatory in need of prayer. He knelt and kissed the ground. His lips touched the turf where the long neck on which she prided herself had been severed. In his mind's eye he saw the head roll from her adulterous body. Another pitiful victim of the insatiable Tudors.

2

The White Tower formed the central keep, housing beneath its pinnacles the royal apartments and the Constable's quarters, the armoury, the treasury and the chapel royal. Here Brother Thomas and his escort were turned away, directed to a less important building, where they climbed several flights of dark stairs until it seemed they must be lost for ever in a labyrinth.

The chamber at the top proved to be the chaplain's. He was another friar and Brother Thomas sensed instantly that he shared the officer's dislike of monks. Monks and friars had been at odds since St Francis's time, and some friars – the mendicants and wandering preachers like the one who had approached him in the street – were active in urging the king to dissolve the monasteries. This one was fat and unctuous, with deep-set shifty eyes.

'You are welcome, brother, welcome indeed. Praise be to God for granting you a safe journey. The Constable has ordered me to receive you and make you comfortable. If he were not occupied with business of the utmost urgency, nothing would have prevented his receiving you in person. The lord bishop of Lincoln is deeply respected here and the Constable is most particular to oblige him in all things. But sit down, I beg you, you must be tired. I shall order food and wine if you will do me the favour of sharing a repast with me. You are a man of letters, I understand. Here we suffer overmuch from bustle and worldliness, but we are at the centre of affairs and cannot complain, though a respite is agreeable. Nothing gives me greater pleasure than conversing with scholars. I envy you your knowledge and wisdom. Your presence honours us and we are grateful indeed for your coming.'

He is a friar, Therefore a liar. While the flood of words ran between them, Brother Thomas remembered the old rhyme. He distrusted this man and pondered how many poor souls had been shriven by him at the block. Had he gabbled on like this to drown the shrieks of Anne Boleyn as the headsman swung his axe? How many other beheadings had he witnessed, how much blood – Plantagenet blood perhaps – had he seen spurt from headless trunks? Brother Thomas doubly pitied the victims whose last moments on earth had been lived to the sound of that voice.

'In the name of God I thank you for the kindness of your greeting,' he said curtly.

Throughout the meal the chaplain continued to talk. He required little response and Brother Thomas, mindful of St Benedict's injunction 'not to love much talking,' thankfully stopped listening.

'Now let me know your will,' said the chaplain at the end. 'I am instructed to spare no effort in assisting you. Command and I obey.'

'The period of my study is the troubled time before his highness's father assumed the crown.'

'So you wish to examine the state archives? That, alas, is not within the Constable's competence, but he will surely obtain the necessary permission. I myself—'

Brother Thomas held up his hand. 'I thank you, but what I wish to examine are the bodies of his late highness King Edward V and his brother, Richard, duke of York.'

'The murdered boys!' The chaplain quivered with surprise.

'Boys indeed. At the time of their father's death they were aged twelve years five months and nine years seven months. They are believed to have died shortly afterwards.'

With the wordy chaplain struck dumb, Brother Thomas crossed the room and peered through one of the slits in the wall, allowing his host time to recover his speech.

The river flowed beneath him, broad and swift. Every few moments a boat appeared and disappeared from view, laden with passengers or merchandise. Heading downstream the oarsmen took their time; against the current it was hard labour. The river resembled history, he thought. How easy to row with the tide of events! But what of men who chose to work against it, to go against the current – lovers of old ways like Robert Aske and his northerners, or delvers into the past like himself? Already his very first request had reduced the most garrulous man in England to silence.

'The story is well enough known,' he said without turning round. 'On the orders of the boys' uncle, who was crowned Richard III in the young Edward's stead, Sir Robert Brakenbury, your Constable's predecessor, surrendered the keys for one night to Sir James Tyrrell. All the boys' attendants were dismissed except for one of Sir James's men and one of the gaolers. These two came upon the children at midnight while they slept. They upturned the mattresses and pillows on them and stifled them. Their innocent souls must have flown straight up to Heaven, but their bodies remained here where the deed was done. I ask leave to see them.'

'That was many years ago,' said the chaplain. 'I know nothing of it. I could never have foreseen that you would ask this. Such a request is without precedent.'

'It is said that the bodies were buried secretly, but within the walls of the Tower. There must be someone who knows or at least suspects their whereabouts. Likewise the chamber the princes had. That would be the starting point.'

'But look outside, brother. In the solitude of your cell at Croyland your request may have seemed reasonable but, as you can see now, there are many buildings in the Tower and each building has many chambers – as many probably as in the whole of your part of Lincolnshire. Very many people live and die here.'

'But not many die as children.'

'The servants have children who die. It is a daily occurrence.'

'But not that they should be buried in the same place as princes of the royal blood. In how many of your chambers would a king be quartered? One could assume that the area in which the burial took place would lie in that neighbourhood. The quest may not be so hopeless as you suppose.'

'What purpose is there in disturbing their repose? Such crimes are best forgotten. Let the dead rest in peace, brother.'

'If there were no purpose in my mission the lord bishop would not have blessed it.' Brother Thomas sharpened his tone. 'Let the bodies of the innocent indeed lie undisturbed until the Day of Judgment, but where are they? That is what I have crossed England to find out.'

'What I can do for you I will, of course. But the affair is wrapped in the darkness of time. You cannot expect to have doors to the past unlocked for you at a word from me.'

'You have said that many people live in the Tower. Some must be old. A few would have been here fifty years ago when the crime was committed. These are the doorkeepers to the past. I seek permission to question them.'

'They will be able to tell you nothing. Here we are in one small building. What do we know of affairs in the rest of the Tower? If children were being suffocated in the room below we would not be aware of it. Consider the thickness of the walls. The loudest noises cannot be heard from room to room, let alone from building to building.'

'Rumour penetrates.'

'In the Tower rumour is punished.'

'But survives, I do not doubt. Tongues cannot be silenced when great events occur. Murder will come out at last. Tales of secret tragedies are whispered from father to son, from master to apprentice. Let me talk to the oldest among the warders and to the retainers who have been in attendance here the longest.'

'There is none who was here before Tudor times. Of that you may rest assured.'

The chaplain went on to talk resolutely of other matters until darkness gathered and he showed Brother Thomas to a room next door.

'In the morning,' he promised, 'I will speak to the Constable about your strange request.'

3

Nearly a week passed before the reply came.

After breakfast on the first day the chaplain disappeared, excusing himself on grounds of duty. In his absence Brother Thomas spoke to no one except Gervase, who occupied a chamber below his own and declared himself ill at ease.

The waiting time was not wasted. He spent it in prayer in the chapel of St Peter ad Vincula, in meditation on the green and in contemplation of the weird beasts in the menagerie. Above all he spent it in growing acquainted with the Tower. Even in the chapel his mind, which should have been on the Holy Trinity, the Virgin Mother and the Blessed Saints, kept escaping through the thick walls and up and down the mysterious winding staircases, inquisitive at what the stones could have told him.

Though he dared enter only his own, he inspected the thirteen towers in turn and identified them from what the chaplain had told him. His, by the water gate, was named after St Thomas. The Middle and Byward Towers were those by which he had entered. It was in Wakefield Tower that Henry VI had been struck down while at his prayers. In Bell Tower Chancellor More had been kept prisoner before his execution for refusing to recognise the king as Supreme Head of the Church. Beauchamp Tower, Martin Tower, Salt Tower, Broad Arrow Tower and the rest had held their victims too, no doubt. Bowyer Tower had contained the butt of wine in which it was said that George, duke of Clarence had been judicially drowned. But which was the tower of the princes?

Gazing shortsightedly across the moat, down on the blur of the city clustering all round, Brother Thomas meditated on the growth of the Tower from Julius Caesar's humble fort to William of Normandy's impregnable mountain of stone which had become the most important and most cruel building in all England.

He imagined himself to be Henry Tudor, freshly victorious from Bosworth field. He had ridden south and secured his position. He was master of the Tower, therefore of London, therefore of England. Therefore, by the grace of God, King Henry VII. His predecessor, King Richard, was dead, killed in the battle – indisputably dead, his corpse displayed to public view. But what of his predecessor's predecessor, the boy King Edward, proclaimed but never crowned, recognised and then unrecognised? For the new king to be truly secure, King Edward V too, the subject of so much rumour and so little certainty, must be shown to be indisputably dead.

Brother Thomas asked himself what he would have done in Henry's shoes. First, he would have interrogated all the officers and gaolers in the Tower until he discovered where the princes were buried. Then he would have dug them up and removed them to the royal mausoleum at Windsor. Solemn ceremonies would have been performed, requiem masses sung for the boys' souls, their remains exposed before reburial so that all men should know that they were dead and done to death during their uncle Richard's reign.

If Henry had done this, how much trouble he would have saved himself – trouble which nearly unseated him and which he must have foreseen. From the very first days of his triumph pretenders sprang up to challenge him. Lambert Simnel and Perkin Warbeck were only two among many.

Warbeck proved the most troublesome. He claimed to be the younger of the two princes and was accepted as such by the boy's aunt, Margaret of York, dowager duchess of Burgundy. The kings of France and Scotland both recognised him as the rightful king of England. If Henry knew the boy was dead why did he not produce the body and put an end to the sham? Instead Warbeck threatened him for eight years until he was executed – another victim of the Tower.

No; if Henry had known the princes to be dead when he began his reign his conduct was inexplicable. Therefore it followed that he did not know them to be dead. That they were not, in fact, dead did not follow, but the presumption was strong. Henry was clever and persistent and determined to establish a dynasty. He must have made every effort within his considerable powers to establish the princes' death. He was king for twenty-four years and never to the day of his death produced the bodies.

It was while Brother Thomas was pacing the green, his lips moving apparently in prayer but actually repeating to himself the words 'no corpse, no death', that the chaplain reappeared. He was all smiles and apologies and obsequiousness. A grizzled, honest-looking man, who might have been one of the abbot's bailiffs, accompanied him.

The chaplain talked all the way to St Thomas's Tower and up to the top, puffing between phrases. He prayed forgiveness for his neglect. He offered enough excuses for a year's absence. It was the Constable's express command that no restriction whatever should be placed on Brother Thomas's inquiry. No secret was to be kept from him, provided his exploration confined itself to the past.

'If you require us to provide you with the body of Julius Caesar himself we must produce it,' he said, rubbing his hands ingratiatingly so that Brother Thomas distrusted him more than ever.

In the chaplain's room the stranger was introduced.

'This is the head warder. He is more familiar with the Tower than any of us. Constables and chaplains come and go, but a good head warder is irreplaceable.'

Brother Thomas looked at this calm stalwart with horror. Were those the hands which had bound Bishop Fisher's wrists and trussed Prior Houghton to his hurdle? He turned gladly to the past and made his inquiries about the princes.

'But do you know, of your own knowledge, that this is true?' he asked when the old tale of Tyrrell and his assassins had been recited.

'How could I, brother? I was but newly born.'

'Are you aware that Henry Tudor became king in the year of our Lord 1485 and did not announce the death of the princes until 1502?'

'That is easily explained,' said the chaplain, 'if you will permit me to interrupt. Sir James Tyrrell was governor of Guisnes all that time and the truth was not uncovered until his return to England. The fact of their death had been known, but not the circumstances.'

'But I do not accept the story attributed to Sir James and I cannot accept a death without a body,' said Brother Thomas, wishing that the chaplain would go away. 'I require proof.'

The chaplain tutted in mock rebuke. 'Come, come, brother. One does not always require proof to be assured of the truth. There are matters of faith, as you and I well know, and other matters of certainty incapable of proof. We have no proof the sun will rise tomorrow, but I am as certain that it will as I am of the existence of God.'

'So we must add the princes' death to the creed, must we, or place it beside the divine ordering of natural phenomena?'

'However they died, it would be a natural conclusion that they are dead by now. You must grant that at least, brother.'

'I am speaking of their death as boys. May I return to the bodies and my interrogation? There must have been a search. They were the bodies of princes whose sister the king was marrying. Accounts between the two houses were being closed. He would have wished to honour their bones and mark their last resting place.'

The head warder nodded. 'There was a search, or so I have heard. It was a time of great stir here. When his highness's father became king the whole garrison changed.'

'By the whole garrison do you mean the officers and soldiers?'

'I mean all the Tower servants.'

'Was that not unusual? Gaolers and kitchen staff are not adherents of one royal faction or another.'

'It was unusual. There were families who had lived in the Tower for many generations.'

'And were they expelled before or after the search had been made and the bodies found?' Brother Thomas put the question quickly but without change of tone.

'Afterwards.'

'So the search was successful! You confirm that the bodies were found?'

'I do.'

'What are you saying?' The chaplain rounded on the head warder before he could speak again. 'If you are telling the brother that the princes' bodies were discovered you are deceiving him. It cannot be so. The Constable himself told me quite otherwise only yesterday. I have spent the last few days making inquiries on the subject. There is no record to support what you are saying. None whatever. Unless you can vouch for the truth of it you must withdraw your statement.'

'I cannot vouch for its truth.' But the man stood unruffled.

'Then why did you make the assertion?'

'Because I believe it to be true. The tale is known to some of us. We keep it to ourselves, but I was ordered to speak frankly and openly to the learned brother.'

'A private tale,' scoffed the chaplain, 'and one whose truth cannot be vouched for.'

'Say what you please. I believe it to be true.'

'How can you claim to know the truth after so long?'

'You claim to know it yourself,' Brother Thomas pointed out. 'But your truth is the opposite.'

'Mine is the truth of that time. As you said yourself, if Henry Tudor could have found the bodies he would have proclaimed the fact. Since he did not, we can assume they were never found. That is what men believed before the years closed over these events. What is not known and recorded in living memory is lost forever. Time is the enemy of truth.'

'As an historian I believe the contrary. Not until those with the motive and means to suppress the truth have passed away can what really occurred stand revealed at last. Time and truth are not enemies – far from it. Truth,' said Brother Thomas, is the daughter of time.'

4

It was many minutes before the friar completed his rejoinder. His bulk was balanced precariously on a small chair and his flesh wobbled as he spoke. What he said Brother Thomas did not hear. His own thoughts were more rewarding. Suppose he were to ask the head warder about the person in the Tower who interested him most.

Somewhere behind these walls lay King Richard's heir, William de la Pole, a descendant of the great duke of York through the female line. Figure-head of the so-called party of the White Rose, he had been imprisoned here for half a lifetime. Yet the head warder would deny all knowledge of him. It would be his duty to do so. If he told the truth it would cost him his employment, his liberty, his life perhaps.

But about the death of the princes he had no cause to lie. To him it was no longer an affair of state, and he had been told to speak out. Therefore he must have told the truth as he believed it, and in extracting it from him Brother Thomas had killed his own hopes. He had been seeking to establish the absence of bodies. If indeed they had been found he had lost his true Plantagenets. Robert Aske could only proclaim the unhappy de la Pole as William III, and at that moment the prisoner's life would be forfeit.

'Where were they buried?' he asked the warder as soon as the chaplain's flow of words ceased. 'And what happened to them when they were exhumed?'

'They were reburied in the same place. I can show it to you.'

In the same place and without public knowledge! A tremor of life quickened his fallen hopes. 'Show me, I pray you. Show me at once.'

He jumped up and the head warder led the way. The chaplain followed and Gervase, who watched below, joined them on the stairs. At the foot of their tower the head warder pointed to a small doorway in the tower adjoining.

'There,' he said. 'The place is outside that door. That is the tradition.'

Brother Thomas hurried forward. The ground outside had been cut away and a flight of stone steps led up to the door.

'Which side of the steps?' he asked. 'We must have men with spades to dig.'

'Digging will serve no purpose. They lie underneath.'

'Underneath the steps? How can that be?'

'After the bodies were reburied the steps were built on top of them.'

The chaplain laughed. 'This is the unlikeliest story I ever heard. Would you have us believe in the burial place of a king of England covered with steps so that common men may walk up and down over his corpse? Is this your truth? Small wonder such tittle-tattle has not gained a wider currency.'

Brother Thomas was perplexed. 'If we are to believe this we must believe that King Henry VII took the bodies of his wife's brothers from the ground and, instead of reburying them with full honours beside their father's tomb at Windsor, secretly reinterred them here so that they should never be discovered again. He had need to prove them dead, yet he reburied the proof without revealing it.'

He knelt in prayer nevertheless, in case the boys' remains should in truth lie in the earth beneath his feet.

'I know nothing of reasons and probabilities,' said the head warder unmoved. 'I know only the story. It is said that the discovery of the bodies was the cause of a breach between the king and the boys' mother, the late King Edward's queen. Perchance the explanation lies there.'

'The quarrel is recorded,' Brother Thomas acknowledged, his interest roused, 'but not the cause of it. Yet Henry had been king a full year and a half when it occurred.'

'That would be the time. It was then the change I spoke of was made.'

'Do you say that those who manned the Tower were not changed at the beginning of the reign, but only after eighteen months?'

'The Constable's household and the garrison were changed at once; the new king's men took over the Tower to secure it immediately. But the expulsion of retainers and their families came later.'

'Can you be sure of this? You say you were not here then yourself.'

'I was not in the Tower, it is true, but my family lived in Thames Street. I was five years old at the time and I remember it well. There was an upheaval as never before or since. Many had served the Tower all their lives and enjoyed free quarters within the walls, and their fathers and grandfathers before them. Yet every one of them had to go.'

'But your own family lived outside and was not affected?'

'My father was a waterman at the pier, but I had an aunt who was turned out and ill-treated.'

'What happened to her? Is she still alive? Tell me, I pray you.'

'I cannot say.' The head warder had said enough. He

came down the steps and asked leave to depart for his duties.

'One moment more,' Brother Thomas begged. 'The queen was ill-treated too. Although she was the widow of a Yorkist king, King Henry married her daughter and she became queen mother. Yet the king suddenly turned on her and deprived her of every dignity and possession. He shut her away where she could have no communication with the world. The quarrel must have been a severe one, and now you are telling us that it was connected with her sons' bodies.'

'My aunt Agnes suffered as badly.'

'Was she also immured?'

The man moved briskly away without replying and Brother Thomas pursued him, tripping over his habit in eagerness. Out of the corner of his eye he glimpsed the chaplain waddling after him with Gervase at his side. Both had reports to make, he surmised, one to the Constable, the other to the abbot. Neither wished to miss a crucial word.

'Was your aunt immured with the queen?'

Brother Thomas threw the words like an arrow at the broad retreating back. The head warder turned to acknowledge them with the curtest of nods before disappearing into the keep.

'The old queen is long since dead,' said the chaplain when he had recovered his breath. 'This dame will be in her grave too. It is a curious story and far from likely to be true. I hardly think you would get permission to have the steps demolished on the strength of it. Let me take you to the keeper of the rolls; he will let you browse there. If I may hazard a guess, a suspicion of the plague caused this abrupt exodus. You may find confirmation of this in the record office. Probably the queen mother was detained for her own safety.'

'I thank you,' said Brother Thomas, 'but I must take my leave.'

'You have scarcely arrived. You cannot leave already. You have not looked at the records at all. What will the bishop say?' The chaplain was bewildered and suspicious.

'Will the Constable wish to detain me?'

'Not against your will. How could you suppose it? But your inquiry has barely begun. The Constable has granted you the use of every facility. If you return to Croyland so soon with your mission uncompleted he will think that I have offended you.'

'The Constable is obliging and you no less. I shall not return to Croyland yet. Indeed I expect to return here and beg further favours of you.'

'You must tell me where you are going, brother. I may be able to ease your journey.'

The chaplain was imploring, wearing his ingratiating face again. Gervase stood silent but attentive. Between the pair of them Brother Thomas felt the gaze of the world upon him. Gervase represented the eyes of the Old Faith: the Church party which the abbot led, and Robert Aske's extremists in the north. The chaplain represented the established order and its new beliefs.

Since the gates of the Tower closed behind him on his arrival Brother Thomas had come to realise his true situation – and understand that the abbot in his wisdom had known it from the beginning. The bishop whose chancellor had urged this inquiry was a king's man first and last. Every door was being opened for him by the enemies of the church, among whom the bishop must be numbered. Every move he made was to be noted, every discovery used against his cause. The abbot had been aware of this, and so had Master Aske. The young lawyer was not rash but bold, bold in the faith. All his treasonable words were policy – to manoeuvre the abbot into committing himself by sanctioning the enterprise.

'Grant, O God, that this brother of ours, gifted above others, may be the salvation of this house and not the means of its destruction.' His heart was chilled as he remembered the abbot's prayer. He felt himself fluttering like a wild duck in a snare. He, who prided himself on the depth of his understanding, had been netted by his own stupidity.

Despite his fear he took pity on the chaplain. The fat friar would be in trouble if he could not report this prying monk's destination. What was the use of withholding it, when they could follow him to find out? He pointed across the river, Downstream, beyond the wide curve of the water, the ground was flat and marshy, reminding him of home.

'I go to Bermondsey.'

5

The lady abbess at Bermondsey was formidably bearded and not pleased to receive a person as unimportant as Brother Thomas.

A grand dame of noble birth, she viewed his travel-soiled appearance and untutored manners with high disfavour. His suitably humble behaviour did not appease her. She wished it to be known that Bermondsey was a royal foundation – sprung from a palace, no less – and he was not the kind of guest it was accustomed to entertain.

'The Lady Elizabeth Woodville spent the dying years of her mortal life in this house,' she admitted at last.

To be received and reach this point had taken Brother Thomas as long as the journey itself.

He had crossed the miracle of London bridge with its street of houses huddling above the water. The whole bridge could not have been more than twenty feet in breadth, and in all there must have been at least a hundred houses. They projected perilously over the river, and the road between them was so narrow that the carts scraped wheels as they passed. The buildings squeezed and overshadowed it. Sometimes they were joined across, making tunnels for the wayfarer to pass through. He had marvelled in turn at the chapel in the middle, dedicated to St Thomas à Becket, at the drawbridge tower, the drawbridge itself and finally, near the Southwark bank, the Great Stone Gate. All the way across, the water below raced and bubbled murderously between the piers of narrow arches.

Grinning skulls on poles had crowned the gate. Among them, a spiked centrepiece, was what had once been the nether portion of a man.

'A pesky prior who robbed the poor,' one of the guards jeered, following his gaze.

'In God's name,' he had turned and asked Gervase, 'can this be the mortal remains of Prior Houghton of the Charterhouse?'

Gervase nodded gravely and Brother Thomas had disgraced himself by vomiting. Martyrdom was real. He prayed God he would have the strength to endure it. By way of comfort Gervase whispered that Bishop Fisher's head had had to be taken down and thrown into the river because it would not putrefy. It had remained for a week seeming as fresh as when it stood on his shoulders, so that men and women had gathered to worship it – and this was a man so frail that he had to be carried in a chair to the block. When they reached Bermondsey Brother Thomas had joined the pilgrims at the famous cross and said a special prayer for the martyred prior and bishop.

His mind retravelled the journey while the abbess was still worrying over his letters of introduction. She held the bishop's and abbot's missives in her hands and made searching inquiries about those dignitaries as though to satisfy herself that Brother Thomas was not an outlaw in disguise who had come by them dishonestly.

She herself had come from the sister Cluniac house of De la Pre in Northamptonshire. For her compliance in making a voluntary surrender of herself and her ten nuns to the king, she had been permitted to retire to Bermondsey and retain her state as the abbot's helpmeet in female affairs. Unmitred she might be, but that was an accident of sex. If women had been eligible to be lords spiritual, her words would have been heard in the highest counsels of the realm. Or so, despite the poverty of her former house, she prided herself.

'To have a queen here was a great honour for this house, my lady,' ventured Brother Thomas, steering her again towards the purpose of his visit.

'It was not an unaccustomed one. There were kings and queens at Bermondsey before the Normans came. The queen was honoured too and no doubt glad to pass her last years both on royal ground and in the tranquillity proper to a preparation for the life to come.'

'But men say she was far from pleased at her enforced separation from family and friends and the courtly life she was wont to lead.'

The abbess looked as though she could not recall when someone had last contradicted her. She eyed Brother Thomas fiercely, making him feel like the rude peasant from a remote bog that he undoubtedly was.

'Men will say anything,' she answered tartly. 'About this matter, as about so many others, they are ignorant. We are a strict order and there is no relaxing of the rule here; nor was there at De la Pre. Here the queen was secluded absolutely from the world, and her heart was surely filled with gladness at the contemplation of eternity after a life of earthly struggle.'

The bristles on her chin challenged him to pursue the argument. He judged it politic to concede the point and lowered his head as a signal of surrender.

'She came with servants?' he asked.

'With one only, I have heard. More would have been vanity.'

'Is this servant still with you?'

'How can I say? We have many servants here. She may have stayed, she may have gone. Most likely she is dead. You are speaking of long ago.'

In the abbess's sharp bark Brother Thomas detected a faint undertone of fluster. He plucked up spirits and courage.

'As you remarked, my lady, men will say anything. Concerning the servant, they say that her name was Agnes and that she is still here as a dependant.'

The shaft went home. He felt sure of it from the tautening of her lips. But she gave nothing else away.

'We have many of those as well. Some have pensions; most live on the charity of our alms. If your house were as close to London you would attract the same riff-raff of abbey-lubbers. A soft life is all they want. A life devoted to themselves, not God. They give the monasteries a bad name. I have made it my duty to speak to each one of the women. If the lord abbot takes my advice he will expel them for the good of their souls.'

'But this woman will have given good service while she was able. In your compassion you would not turn her out in her old age. If she is indeed alive I ask permission to speak with her.'

'Impossible.' The jaws of compassion clamped tight like manacles.

'But—'

'I command you to be silent. Suppose I permitted anyone to come here and question our servants, where would it end? Our household is as large as your abbot's, I dare assert. We have cooks and bakers and brewers, grooms and porters and dairywomen no fewer than at Croyland. On our estates we employ labourers, both men and women, so numerous that our bailiffs can scarcely count them all. How would your abbot receive a nun who came inquiring after one such?'

'With Christian charity,' he wanted to say. Instead he rose. They were in a vestibule in the tower above the porter's lodge. She had come to the gatehouse from her lodgings to confront him, not considering him worthy of her parlour.

'My abbot and the bishop will be disappointed,' he said.

She expressed no regret but, as a sign of permission to leave, granted him the favour of her heavily ringed hand to kiss. It was coarse-haired and creased with age and he put his mouth to it in penance.

At the door he turned with a sigh and a soft reproach. 'Dear God, I fear his grace the king will be displeased.'

'The king! What has he to do with this? If you are his emissary, why did you not mention the king's grace before? Show me your authority to speak in his name. I took you for one of those seditious monks set upon thwarting the royal will. The king is right to suppress houses which are disorderly and immoral and which defy him. Others, like De la Pre, are too weak to stand alone in these wicked times. But great houses like this will not be touched. The king is truly the protector of our faith. Yet I hear that your abbot opposes him in convocation. Do you come from him or the king? You cannot come from both. If you deceive me you will rue it.'

'The prime mover in my mission is the bishop. He was formerly the king's confessor, as your ladyship will not have forgotten. I make no claim to direct authority from the king, but these letters have caused the opening of the state archives for my inspection. The Constable of the Tower has issued orders that my wishes there are to be met in every respect.'

She peered into his face, exploring the windows of his soul for villainy.

'Stay then,' she granted reluctantly, 'while I cause inquiries to be made.'

'My thanks, reverend mother.'

She veiled her beard and left him. When God created Eve, he asked himself, could He have intended abbesses?

6

Brother Thomas waited patiently. The vestibule was hung with drab curtaining and contained no furniture except two chairs and a crucifix. It led to a larger room where business was conducted with stewards and tradesmen – visitors meriting a worthier reception than himself.

Yet he felt confident. Someone higher than the king was watching over his investigation. With the whole life of the faith in England at stake, he could not doubt that. The woman he sought must be alive, and the abbess would now produce her. Queen Elizabeth Woodville had been banished to Bermondsey early in 1487. A maid of eighteen or thereabouts then would be sixty-six or sixty-seven now.

She came much sooner than he had dared hope, and he recognised her at once. An old woman in a coarse gown and shawl, she shuffled into the room. Her likeness to the head warder was unmistakable.

He stood up to receive her. 'I bring you greetings from your nephew.'

She was all too plainly puzzled and disturbed at the summons, but a smile parted the wrinkles when he spoke. It exposed two rows of bare gums. He thanked God that her mind seemed unimpaired.

'He is employed in the Tower, where you used to live. Do you remember and regret those times, or are you contented here?'

She mumbled. The words were difficult to distinguish but he made out the ending: 'I have gruel enough and a bed.'

'Do you work for your gruel?'

An emphatic nod and another mumble. She nursed in the infirmary.

'What work did you do in the Tower?'

'I was a laundry maid.' His ear had become tuned to the toothlessness.

'And you came here with the Lady Elizabeth Woodville, formerly queen of England?'

This time there was no reply. She sat twisting her fingers and glancing over her shoulder. He laid a comforting hand over hers and persisted.

'You say you were a laundress, Agnes. Yet you became body-servant to a queen. How could that be?'

Instead of answering she drew away her hand and stabbed a bony finger at the hangings. He shook his head in disbelief. How could there be eavesdroppers when he had not left the room since his interview with the abbess? The two doors were tight shut. She pointed to a corner and made a spiral movement with her finger.

Had the old dame's wits failed? At first he thought so. Then he realised that they were sharper than his own. There could well be a third small door in the corner, served by a back staircase leading up the inner wall of the gatehouse. He took a step forward and then paused. The prospect of pulling back the arras and catching the abbess stooping to overhear their words was too forbidding. Assuredly it would lead to his summary dismissal.

On an impulse he hurried Agnes out of the room, down the staircase and through the abbey gates into the roadway. The porter stared in surprise but made no move to detain them.

They crossed the road into a field and the old woman sat on a stone while she gathered her breath. She was wheezing like the plague.

'They will be coming after me,' she gasped. 'I have not walked this side of the walls before. Not since they brought me here.'

'That was nearly fifty years ago. Why have they kept you a prisoner? Tell me about it, I beg you. We have a few minutes to talk.' Brother Thomas was breathless too, but more with expectation.

'My lady will be after us. As Jesus lives, she was behind the hangings. They will never allow me to speak to anyone alone, brother.'

'Why should that be?'

'Orders.' Agnes spat on the ground.

'Orders from whom? What manner of orders? Do they concern events which occurred in the Tower? Events which you yourself witnessed? Speak quickly if you can.'

She shook her head as though intent on shaking it off. 'Never! If I speak to a single soul I am to be taken back in chains and put to death.'

'Were you told this when you first came here?'

She nodded. Her eyes were fixed on the abbey gateway.

'Many years have passed since then. Your queen died long, long ago. A new king sits on the throne. There is nothing now to prevent your speaking to me and telling the truth.'

'Except for her.'

'She has allowed me to see you. You have her permission to talk to me. Now we are here in the open she will not learn what you say. I promise not to repeat your words to her.' In his eagerness Brother Thomas fell to his knees. 'I swear it by the body and blood of our Lord, in Whose name and for Whose sake I have come.'

'Will you swear to make no other person whatever privy to what I say?' His pleading was taking effect.

'That I cannot promise, for the truth must be told. But you have my word that while you are alive I shall never reveal to any man – or woman – the source of anything you may tell me. No one shall learn that it comes from you. Now speak.'

'You come from my nephew, do you say?' She was undecided still.

'It was from him that I learned of you and where you were to be found. How else would I have known? Your family remembers you still.'

'My family!' She peered into the distance as though searching for long-forgotten kin. 'I shall not live much longer. My only desire now is to stay here. May God grant that I die in the infirmary in my own bed.'

'So you shall, so far as it is within my power.'

'This is my home. Suppose they come and take me away. Suppose they shut me up and torture me.'

Despair gripped him. The old dame was mumbling self-pityingly to herself.

'While you were in the Tower, did you see the bodies of the two murdered princes?' Now he spoke accusingly, not begging for an answer but demanding.

'No.' She denied it with vehemence.

'Were their bodies discovered while you were there?'

'No.'

'Your nephew told me otherwise. He said that they were dug up and reburied. He told me of a family story to that effect and said that it came from you.'

'They were feigned bodies.' This time her mumble was a whisper too.

He could hardly believe what he heard. Despair retreated. His voice trembled as he put his next question: 'Will you tell me who feigned them?'

By moving his position he contrived that in turning towards him she faced away from the abbey. Out of the corner of his eye he could distinguish purposeful manoeuvrings at the gate. The details escaped him but the general movement could not be mistaken. The porter and two other men had their heads together and were gesticulating in his direction. Then the abbess appeared and joined them. A retinue was collecting round her.

Brother Thomas put an arm round the old woman's shoulder. Helping her to her feet, he walked her slowly away. He must not alarm her, but every second, every syllable was precious.

'The king,' she whispered huskily. 'The king himself.'

'Is your meaning that the king ordered two bodies to be

buried, and that then they were unburied and declared to be the princes?'

'God has told you. That is as it happened.' She patted his hand.

'Whose bodies were they? Where did they come from?'

'They were paupers from the graveyard of the hospital of St Bartholomew. The man who brought them told me so himself. Afterwards he was killed so that he should not tell. It was reported that he had spoken to me, but I denied all knowledge of any bodies.'

'So they did not kill you, but you were shut up here as a precaution? Now, Agnes, tell me about the queen. How did she come to hear of it?'

'There was to be an official unburying. As the boys' mother she insisted on seeing them herself the day before. She entered the Tower without the king's permission. The coffins had already been uncovered, and she ordered them to be opened.'

'Was this done without the king's consent?'

'You are too young to remember her grace. They used to say that she ruled the land when her husband was king. I served her here until she died. Whatever she desired, she would have it.'

'When she uncovered the faces she must have seen that they were impostors.'

'No; the corpses were rotten and the faces could not be recognised. They had been three years buried. It was as the king had ordered.'

'Were the children not of the right age?'

The old woman laughed. She threw off his arm and cackled herself breathless again. She was still wheezing when the posse headed by the abbess came upon them.

Brother Thomas pretended surprise at the sight of all their

grim faces. 'Mistress Agnes felt faint,' he explained, 'so I took the liberty of bringing her out to breathe the freshness of the air.'

'May our heavenly Father forgive you,' said the abbess. 'It would have been more seemly to take her to the infirmary where she belongs. She must go there at once. Her health is frail, and we must pray that you have done her no mortal injury.'

'I pray indeed that I have caused no distress, either to her or to you, my lady. Any fault is mine, and mine alone. Our converse had hardly begun, but I will trouble you and her no further. I must return to London, where I am expected. God be with your ladyship and with you, Agnes.'

'Give me your blessing, brother.' Agnes broke away from the lay sisters who were escorting her and knelt in the dust of the road for his benediction. 'Walter Skelton,' she whispered as he prepared to call down the loving kindness of the Almighty on her bowed grey head.

'What words were those?' demanded the abbess, whose hearing was as keen as her bristles.

'She wants water,' said Brother Thomas. 'The poor soul is thirsty.' He remained on his knees, praying to St Guthlac to intercede with God about the lie.

The abbess disappeared into her domain without impeding his departure or reciprocating his goodbye. As Agnes was being taken in behind her she turned on the threshold and spoke her last words to Brother Thomas.

'Rotten as they were, she saw they were never boys. The fool had not examined the remains. They were girls' bodies.'

7

Solitary by the roadside between the abbey and the cross, a leper called out for alms. Remembering Brother Henry and his sufferers, Brother Thomas signed to Gervase to hand him the money-bag. The first coin to come to hand was a silver groat, bearing the name of King Edward and the mark of the boar's head. A coin from the brief reign of the boy king, stamped with the device of the Lord Protector, his uncle Richard – it was an omen. He threw it into the poor creature's bowl and rode hurriedly on, anxious not to linger in the territory of the bearded abbess.

Not until they had crossed the bridge did he stop again.

'Where now, brother?' inquired Gervase when they reined their horses in the shadow of St Magnus Martyr. 'To the lord abbot's lodgings?'

'To the Tower.'

'I would not counsel so.' Gervase looked over his shoulder at two horsemen who had halted behind them and were busy staring up the river towards the sunset behind the abbey at Westminster.

'Is there danger then?' Brother Thomas shivered.

Gervase shrugged his shoulders. 'I would have wagered they would not let us out this morning.'

'We must return or abandon the inquiry. There is no other choice.'

'Then we will return, but with precaution.' Gervase slapped Brother Thomas's horse on the rump and startled it into motion again, to canter up Fish Street Hill.

First, for spiritual guidance, they visited St Paul's. The nave rivalled Cheapside for bustle and business, and the transepts served as a thoroughfare for those too idle to walk round the church. The vista of arches seemed infinite, running, so Gervase said, for nearly an eighth of a mile end to end. Seeking solitude beyond the rood screen, Brother Thomas passed the tombs of King Sebba and King Ethelred and in the retrochoir, under the great rose window, found the shrine of St Erkenwald. A prince who had become a bishop and borne witness to the faith before even Croyland was founded, he was as venerated as St Thomas at Canterbury and St Cuthbert at Durham. Brother Thomas prayed for his aid, here in his own city.

Rising from his devotions, he examined the richest of the monuments – to a warrior and his wife who lay under a pinnacled canopy of alabaster. Above them hung his lance and shield, and his helmet topped with a lion rampant.

'What king's tomb is this?' he asked.

'No king has one as fine as this,' Gervase told him. 'It is John of Gaunt's.'

The sweat on his body had chilled after the hard ride, but Brother Thomas felt his anger heating it again. So this was the founder of the Lancastrian dynasty. According to the chronicles he had taken Croyland's side in a dispute with the priory at Spalding, but there was little else to be said for him. All the ills and bloodshed of the past century and a half had flowed from the fierceness of his ambition.

Abandoning prayer, Brother Thomas left the building feeling his invocation of the saint annulled. He rode in apprehension to the Tower. At the gate Gervase insisted on parting, to take their horses to the abbot's house in the city for stabling in safety. The gaunt buildings frowned on Brother Thomas in the gathering darkness as though already judging him guilty of high treason.

He hurried, stumbling up the stairs to the chaplain's lodgings, where he was greeted warmly enough. The friar interrupted an ample meal to rise and embrace him and express pleasure – too much pleasure – at his return.

'The old woman. Did you meet her? Did she talk? Be so kind as to tell me all.'

'I saw her briefly. She had no tale worth the hearing.' He felt mortified at how easily the lie slipped from his tongue – the second that day.

'I expected it would be so. The head warder has confessed to the spreading of idle rumour. After your departure he was summoned by the Constable and reprimanded.'

While the chaplain described the interview and his own part in it, Brother Thomas allowed his mind to wander into the past. He did not doubt the truth of the old woman's story. Henry Tudor had attempted a characteristic act of palpable fraud. His mother-in-law had caught him out and he had not dared to carry it through. If the trick were revealed the finger of suspicion would point to himself. So Henry had retired into silence until the old queen died. Then all he had ventured was to frame a tale which would appear confirmed if the false bodies were to stay in the earth long enough. While he lived was too soon, but in another century the bones would not betray him. The infant remains of the girl paupers would have mouldered into sexlessness.

'I can guess what you are about to ask me, brother,' the chaplain was saying, 'but I must disappoint you.'

'What am I about to ask you?' Brother Thomas duly inquired.

'I surmise you have returned to request that the stairway is dug up and a search is made for bodies underneath. I raised this point with the Constable on your behalf, but after the head warder's admission he forbade it. In view of the unlikelihood of anything being found, he judged the expense not to be warranted.'

'Is his decision final? Is there no appeal?'

'None, I fear.'

The unusual abruptness of the answer suggested what Brother Thomas had hoped to establish: that reference had been made to higher authority. That was what he would have expected, and the decision too. The discovery of the bodies, followed by a demonstration that they were nothing more than another brace of pretenders – what a triumph for him that would have been!

At least he could savour it in private. His original theory was afloat again, more buoyant than ever. Not only was there still no evidence of the princes' deaths, but King Henry had felt obliged to fabricate some after King Richard's death. Last seen in public playing at archery on the Tower green in June 1483, the boys must have remained still untraced in February 1487. Up to August 1485 Richard's men had been in occupation. His successor must have been able to interrogate them. How was it they had told him nothing? Richard was a loyal man. 'Loyalty binds me' he chose as his motto, and loyalty he both gave and inspired. His personal followers would not betray him readily, but not all of them could have been as staunch as Tyrrell. There could have been few men from whom Tudor torture would not tear a secret or a confession. Yet the secret remained unbroken.

'So what can I do for you, brother, instead?'

'Tomorrow I should like to examine the records.'

Tomorrow and tomorrow. The days in the muniment room turned to weeks, and Brother Thomas's buoyancy to despair. Then late one afternoon the words sprang at him from a yellowed scroll – 'Walter Skelton, Esquire'. He slid to his knees, putting his lips to the floor in thanksgiving until the archivist came hurrying over, calling to his clerk to fetch water.

Brother Thomas scrambled to his feet, rolled up the document to hide what had excited him and left with a word of thanks and reassurance.

Outside, he crossed the green to the ramparts and looked back to the White Tower where he had been burrowing for so long. Below him he imagined the butts set up for the princes. He pictured them at play, their strength barely sufficient to draw back the bowstring, yet practised already – Edward at any rate, trained in the Welsh marches. Every day he felt nearer to them, but somehow they eluded him. If he stood still they were there, whole and rounded in the eye of his mind. If he took a step to join them, if he so much as stretched out a hand towards them, they vanished like spirits.

A man came out of the keep and walked across the princes' line of fire, so that Brother Thomas almost cried out to warn him. The light was fading and with his dim sight it took him a moment to recognise the head warder.

'Stay!' he called. 'I have not seen you since my visit to Bermondsey and I have news of your aunt.'

The man stopped awkwardly. 'I should not have mentioned her,' he said.

'You have been avoiding me. I have been the cause of trouble for you. Forgive me.'

The reply was a long stare, and Brother Thomas felt himself being surveyed as a prospective charge. The feeling should have made him cautious. Instead a fit of rashness seized him.

'Tell me about the pretenders,' he begged. 'Perkin Warbeck was here, was he not?'

'That was before my time.'

'Lambert Simnel then. He was imprisoned for many years. You must have known him. What was he like?'

'Sorrowful, like all traitors.'

'And William de la Pole? How does he fare?'

As soon as he asked the question Brother Thomas realised that he had gone too far. The man's face betrayed the enormity of the crime. He had been guilty of inquiring whether a long-standing rival for the throne was still fit to rule.

'I have no knowledge of such a person.'

'Then what of Walter Skelton?'

'Walter Skelton!' This time the head warder was puzzled. 'There is no one here of that name. The only Walter Skelton of whom I have heard was a squire to the Constable in the time of King Richard.'

'What can you tell me about him?'

'I can tell you nothing.' The man turned resolutely away.

'I beg one favour of you: not to mention his name or that I have inquired of him.'

'You beg in vain.'

The man was gone, leaving Brother Thomas in no doubt that his questions would quickly reach the Constable. He had exceeded his permitted licence and would be imprisoned. His indiscretion would incriminate the abbot and endanger Croyland.

Back in the muniment room he found the chaplain and the archivist in consultation. They drew apart at his approach. Abandoning secrecy, he told them that he wanted information about a certain Walter Skelton who might have died at Bosworth.

'Why is he important to you, brother?' the chaplain asked.

'Everyone in the Tower at the time of the princes' disappearance is relevant to my investigation. It is well known that Sir Robert Brakenbury, the Constable at that time, rode to Bosworth to die with his king. I wanted to be sure that this man, who was his squire, went with him.'

The search did not take long. Walter Skelton had not gone to Bosworth with his master. The Constable's party was fully set down and his name did not appear.

'Could he have been at the battle nevertheless?'

'Let me make certain,' the archivist replied. 'Here is the register of the dead.' He ran his finger down the names of those who had fallen in the Yorkist cause. 'Yes, he is named. You may see for yourself.'

'I do not understand. Does this mean that he was at Bosworth but not in the retinue of the Constable, although he was the Constable's squire?'

'So it would appear.' The archivist was interested in facts, not their implication. He had moved on to a great bound volume with brass catches. 'This is the record of the Constable's own household. The last mention of Walter Skelton is in October 1483. That is nearly two years before the battle. The reason for his departure is not given, which is unusual.'

'The princes were last seen in June, Walter Skelton left in October, and you infer that his departure was irregular.' Brother Thomas's well-ordered mind was recovering from its perplexity.

'That would seem to be the case.'

'But he did not desert, if it was Richard's side he took at Bosworth.'

'That is sure. He is not listed with the king's men, but among the dead traitors.'

'Traitors indeed! Who was the king on Bosworth field?'

Brother Thomas had not been able to suppress his indignation. At the time of the battle Henry did not even have the right to the title of earl of Richmond which he used; but, by antedating his reign to the day before, he had contrived to denounce as traitors all those who fought for Richard, the lawful king. The survivors were executed on this pretext and their families stripped of all their possessions under an Act of Attainder. No other monarch in all recorded history had played such a trick.

The chaplain and the archivist were staring at him as the head warder had.

'One last question,' he begged. 'From what shire did this Skelton come?'

'Here, you may see. He is inscribed as Walter Skelton, Esquire, of Fotheringhay in the county of Northampton.'

'I thank you. Now, if you will permit me, I have promised myself a visit to the cathedral.'

'You will not leave before the Constable has had the opportunity of questioning you,' said the chaplain.

'I will return after the service,' Brother Thomas promised. Would God forgive a third lie in His cause?

Gervase was cleaning his boots outside St Thomas's Tower. At a word he went to his room and collected what could be carried unnoticed. The cool of the evening provided an excuse for wearing travelling cloaks. They walked out past the guard unchallenged, Brother Thomas's mouth dry with fear.

'To the abbot's,' he directed.

'No,' said Gervase. 'That is the first place they will search for you. If you are arrested there it will make matters worse for the abbey.'

They hastened through the streets to St Paul's. There Brother Thomas huddled in the cloisters, wrapped to the eyes in his cloak, while Gervase ran to the abbot's house to fetch the horses. The alarm had not yet been raised and he returned in safety.

'Where shall we sleep?' Brother Thomas asked as he swung himself wearily into the saddle.

'Where you sit,' Gervase replied. 'We ride through the night.'

8

By the grace of God no one stopped them at the city gate. Speeding north, they rode hard and long till dawn, braving the dangers of darkness. At last Gervase permitted Brother Thomas to dismount and they fell asleep under a hedge, not waking until the sun stood high. Then they rode on again, and between Huntingdon and Peterborough turned off the highway. After a second night under the stars Gervase brought his charge weary but safe to Fotheringhay.

Here they were near to home. The village stood by the Nene, a sister stream to Croyland's Welland. Yet the countryside was another world. Instead of open fens, they were among wooded slopes on the fringe of the Rockingham forest, which covered the shire of Northampton as far as Brother Thomas's poor eyesight could stretch. This was wildness of a different kind. A hay signified an enclosure for the king's deer from the forest, and Fotheringhay lay as isolated in the woods as Croyland in its waters.

At the foot of the village they crossed an old stone bridge. A stone building towered on either side, one to threaten, the other to greet them. On their right the castle stood impregnable. The line of the river defended its front, and round the flanks and rear ran a double semi-circle of ditches. From the keep on the high mound a standard flew, and Brother Thomas, straining his eyes, had to ask Gervase what flag it was.

'It is the king's,' said Gervase briefly. 'Can you not make out the portcullis and the double rose?'

On the other side of them stood the college and collegiate church, rivalling the castle in size. The tall tower carried a further storey above it – a six-sided stone lantern which looked down even on the keep. The windows of the church and cloisters sparkled with colour in the June sunshine.

Brother Thomas sighed with pleasure. Fotheringhay had been a Yorkist stronghold, given by Edward III to his fifth son, Edmund of Langley, founder of the house. The castle, he recognised, had been planned in the shape of a Yorkist emblem, the fetterlock. The church served as the mausoleum of the royal house.

'A pennant flies from the church too, brother. It is the fetterlock.'

Brother Thomas's heart jumped. The church was defying the castle, now fallen into alien, godless hands. Here at least, the house of York was remembered and honoured still. 'Come,' he said. 'Let us pay our respects.'

He turned from the frowning castle where, the histories told him, Richard III had been born: the youngest son of the duke of York and Cicely Neville, his duchess, sister to the earl of Warwick who made and unmade kings. In this place the future king had spent his boyhood riding and hunting, nourished on reports of victories and defeats in the wars which his father and elder brothers were fighting.

'How he must have longed for the day when he would be old enough to join them!'

In his absence of mind Brother Thomas spoke aloud, but there was no one except Gervase to hear, and Gervase was growing accustomed to the oddness of his ways.

Inside the church the duchess's tomb was the first to catch his eye. She had outlived all her sons – Edmund of Rutland, Edward the king, George of Clarence, and Richard, another king. Brother Thomas spared her a special prayer out of pity for the sorrow of her old age. Then he moved on his knees to the other monuments, gold and red and marble-white, marking the pride and splendour of a fallen house finally at rest.

Edmund of Langley, brother and rival of that John of Gaunt who was still dazzling London with his pride and splendour – where was he? Brother Thomas could not find him. But his son Edward was there, the duke of York who had fallen so young and gloriously, leading the vanguard at Agincourt. Beside him lay his nephew Richard, the famous duke who had first raised the Yorkist standard. On this duke's other side lay his son Edmund, both bodies brought here, so the inscription ran, after their infamous butchery by Lancastrians at Wakefield. The Duchess Cicely, wife and mother, had seen to that.

Brother Thomas prayed beside each tomb in turn, and when he had finished praying he remained with his eyes closed, wandering in the past. Surely here among the corpses of their grandparents and other kin the secret of the missing princes would be revealed to him.

'Unworthy as I am, dear God,' he implored, 'reveal their fate to me. I ask this for Thy sake, and, please believe me, for Thy sake alone.'

An answer came in the form of a nudge at his sleeve. He opened his eyes to find Gervase pointing. The painted windows were filled with saints and scenes from their lives. Gervase had noticed St Guthlac among them, arriving in his boat at the isle of Croyland in the year of our Lord 699 and building his little cell – the cell which had grown into an abbey like an acorn becoming an oak-tree.

It was a sign. The sun behind the window lit the saint with heavenly radiance. He seemed to be smiling and beckoning, and Brother Thomas shuffled across the floor to prostrate himself in an obeisance of supplication and hope.

'Is this the man you came to find?'

Gervase pointed downwards this time. A patch of deep

red from the saint's window was reflected on the floor of a side aisle. In that inconspicuous corner was a much humbler monument, a stone slab inscribed 'Hic jacet Walter Skelton' and 'Semper Fidelis'. A single flower had been placed on the stone. A rosebud, fresh – and white.

So Walter Skelton was dead. It could hardly have been otherwise, but Brother Thomas had trusted that God would be more accommodating. Always Faithful – did that hold a clue? The squire who had disappeared from the Tower had not deserted. He had fought and died at Bosworth and been rewarded by burial with the greatest of the house of York. Perhaps the Duchess Cicely had seen to that too. But why? What outstanding service had he performed? What else could it have been but rescuing the princes?

Gervase had left the church, and when he returned Brother Thomas sprang up. 'We must talk to one of the priests and find out who left the flower.'

'I have done so. We must leave. Our presence here is dangerous to them.'

'Who knows we are here? We were not pursued.'

'At the Tower you did not conceal your interest in a man from Fotheringhay. Once it is found that you are not in London, at the abbot's house or the bishop's, will it not be suspected that you have come here? The priest told me that there are still Skeltons in Fotheringhay. It would be more discreet to inquire privately of them.'

Before they could leave, the priest came to greet him.

'A brother from Croyland is welcome indeed. You are one of us.' His eyes were alight with the same fire as Robert Aske's. 'We have heard that the abbot is in touch with the cardinal.'

'The cardinal!' Brother Thomas was taken back.

'Cardinal Pole, who must marry the Princess Mary and

become king. The old countess's son. He who is the last hope of York and the Old Faith.'

This was the first news Brother Thomas had had of the abbot's involvement with the White Rose party of the surviving Poles and de la Poles. Margaret, countess of Salisbury, was the daughter of George of Clarence, niece of King Edward and King Richard, old but still very much alive. Her father and brother had both been executed as traitors, and it was said that she would be lucky if her head and body came to be buried in one piece. She had been governess to the Princess Mary, and Queen Katharine had wanted her daughter to marry the countess's son.

When that failed and the king turned against the Pope, the son had gone to Rome and become a cardinal. In all Europe he was the king's most vocal and defiant enemy. Men believed that his mother was only kept from the block by the king's hope that he could use her to lure him back to England. If the abbot was known to be her ally his life hung by the same thread. Brother Thomas blushed as he recalled Aske's taunts of timidity.

'How can a cardinal marry and become a king?' he asked.

'When he took his vows he omitted the vow of chastity so that he might be free to marry the princess. The Pope granted him special dispensation. As for his becoming a king, God looks to you and me for that. We must not fail Him.'

They parted like conspirators.

'Cardinal Pole is a warrior of words,' said Gervase bitterly in the porch. 'If the lord abbot still had hopes of him he would not have sent us on this fool's errand.'

9

The house stood at the end of the village street, substantial and apart.

Gervase dismounted and knocked. A girl opened the door and Brother Thomas watched them from the road. After a few words Gervase beckoned to him and he dismounted too and joined them shyly. The gibe about a fool's errand rankled.

The girl curtsied out of respect for his habit and would have kissed his hand if he had not drawn it back. She was pretty and could not be more than seventeen.

'This is Mistress Skelton, brother.'

'I greet you in God's name,' he said when he found his tongue.

'In God's name,' she repeated. 'How can we help you, brother?'

'I have come to inquire about Walter Skelton.'

'There is none by that name here. I live with my father. His name is Robert.'

'Walter Skelton is dead. Would he have been your grandfather?'

She hesitated, then shook her head as though sad at disappointing him. 'My grandfather was John.'

'You cannot pretend that you are unrelated to Walter Skelton. I have been admiring the rose you placed on his grave.'

She blushed through the brownness of her cheeks. 'You had best come in and speak to my father,' she said. 'It will be an honour for our house.'

He followed her, unable to take his eyes from the fairness of her hair. The Mother of God would have been no older when her Son was born.

'I will send a groom for your man and the horses. You have come far, I can see.'

'From London.'

'London!' There was fear in her voice. She turned to search his face again at the parlour door.

'A brother from London.' She opened it and announced him.

A man writing at a desk looked up and assessed him. It was a wary appraisal. He did not rise or invite the visitor to sit.

'You may leave us, Margaret,' he said.

'I am unwelcome,' Brother Thomas stammered, uneasy under such scrutiny. The man seemed honest enough but lacking in courtesy. The girl must have inherited her sweetness from her mother.

'That depends on your business. Men of God are always welcome here, visitors from London rarely so. In Fotheringhay we prefer to be left alone. Nothing comes from London except demands for a man's money or his head.'

'You are Yorkists.'

This brought the man to his feet. 'Who is it who says so?'

'One who has travelled from London but is not a Londoner. One who is a member of the community of the blessed St Guthlac at Croyland. One who has studied and weighed the events of the past century and can tell the colour of a man's rose.'

'I know your abbot by reputation and respect him, but I trust no man on sight. How can I be sure that you are not a spy?'

'I too am a Yorkist. I swear it before God.'

Until the confession crossed his lips Brother Thomas had never admitted to himself how far he had travelled since leaving the abbey. He, the impartial surveyor of times gone by, the seeker after truth in whatever quarter it might lurk – he had become a partisan. Not even born until the wars of Lancaster and York were history, he had chosen to enlist in the ranks of the defeated.

'Sit down, brother. My name is Robert Skelton and I now bid you welcome. Tell me your name and your business.'

Brother Thomas produced his letters of authority. His host read them with a frown.

'Since you know so much, it will not be news to you that we are all unrepentant Yorkists here at Fotheringhay. This is Yorkist territory and men in these parts do not turn their coats with the climate which comes from the south. The castle may be in enemy hands but it is still haunted by the shadows of our own kings and dukes. Their remains lie in the church where we worship. They have our loyalty still. We cling to our beliefs and look forward to better times.'

'You are men after my own heart – men of faith.'

'Yes; the Old Faith and the old line of kings. There is none here who favours upstarts and heretics.'

'There are such men throughout the midlands and northern shires. You lack nothing but a leader. Help me and I will find you one.'

'How can I help? I live quietly, having some land of my own and acting as steward for others. For what goes on outside the forest I care nothing. Do you think I wish to join the outlaws who live there, wearing the wolf's head and preying on others to keep alive.'

'Where is your faith then?'

'Not in you. You are no knave, I give you credit for that. But you are a fool. If you want a leader, go to Rome for Cardinal Pole, but keep your distance from Fotheringhay. I will not ruin myself and my family in a fruitless cause.'

'A fool?' This was the second time he had been called that within an hour.

'Yes, a fool! Can you not see that someone is using you?'

'I am guided by my abbot, who is a man of wisdom well versed in politics.'

'I do not refer to your abbot. I refer to your bishop.' Robert Skelton tapped Chancellor Rayne's letter. 'You are too innocent, brother. My advice to you is to keep your mind on the next world and not meddle in this one, lest you bring mischief to those you would least wish to harm. I do not know what game your abbot is playing, but I wish to God that he had never sent you here.'

Brother Thomas felt his knees tremble. He remembered his superior's doubts. What had guided him to Fotheringhay but his own will?

'If the bishop plays false, you may be sure that the abbot has taken precautions,' he said. 'God forbid that I should bring sorrow to others.'

He was thinking of Margaret – and how he would rather suffer a hundred years in Purgatory than be the cause of harm to her – when she returned to announce that Gervase and the horses had been fed. Should she bring food for the brother?

Before leaving with her father's assent she stooped and whispered in his ear. He glared at Brother Thomas.

'Two men rode into the village on your heels,' he said accusingly.

'What have they to do with me?' Brother Thomas's voice quavered.

'They inquired about a newly-arrived monk with one attendant. They have learned that you are in this house, and have gone to the castle to report it.'

'What manner of men are they?' He could see them talking

to the abbess outside the nunnery at Bermondsey. He could see them reining their horses near St Magnus Martyr.

'Ruffians, my daughter says. Rumour in the village has it that they are Master Cromwell's men. By God, you carry a heavy burden of responsibility, brother. Master Cromwell is no friend of monks and Yorkists, I think. Why, do you suppose, does he keep you under observation?'

'I will outwit the anti-Christ Cromwell,' boasted Brother Thomas, emboldened by fear. 'If God be on our side who shall stand against us? The weakest of His servants will defeat the mightiest of His enemies if he be armed with faith.'

'Amen,' said Margaret. He had spoken for her. The look she gave him was his reward.

'You are even more of a fool than I thought,' said her father.

'I will leave at once,' said Brother Thomas. 'You are right. I have brought you into danger. I should never have come.'

'Eat with us first and I will listen to your questions. When you leave will make little difference, now that you have led Master Cromwell to our door.'

They ate trout from the river, which flowed at the end of the garden. The girl served them herself and then sat down to join them in the meal.

'Should inquiries be made,' said Brother Thomas, 'you will be able to state with truth that I did not speak about present times. My investigation concerns the lost princes, Edward the boy king and his brother Richard of York. This is already known to Master Cromwell and his henchmen. Therefore they should not trouble you.'

'I pray not. But tell me why you do not let the dead rest in peace.'

'Are they dead? They were not killed by King Richard.'

'All the world knows they were.' Master Skelton busied himself boning his fish, so that Brother Thomas could not see his face.

'On the authority of Henry Tudor and his son.'

'Of Cardinal Morton and Chancellor More too.' The face was still averted.

'Neither of them historians.'

'Do you doubt the tale?' He looked up at last.

'There is no occasion for doubt. The tale is false.' In emphasising his certainty Brother Thomas's sleeve swept a piece of bread from the table.

'It would greatly interest me to learn how you can be so sure.'

'I can give you half a dozen reasons why Richard did not kill the boys.' Brother Thomas stooped to retrieve the bread at the same time as Margaret. Their hands touched and he blushed like a boy.

10

Only when the meal was over and Brother Thomas had thanked God for it did the talk continue.

'State those reasons,' Master Skelton commanded. He wore his wary look.

'First, if the princes had been killed, Henry Tudor would have found out and published the fact as soon as he became king. Something had happened to them which neither he nor anyone else could discover.' Brother Thomas paused expectantly, but his host's face betrayed no secret.

'Proceed with your argument, brother.'

'Secondly, such a deed was not in Richard's nature.

Loyalty and honour and courage – these were his qualities. Loyalty above all: to his illustrious family and its cause. Loyalty bound him closest of all to his brother King Edward. How could he have murdered his brother's sons, the protection of whose lives was bequeathed to him?'

'You are right. Richard was born and bred in this village. We knew him for a God-fearing man – not a nephew-slayer like King John Sansterre.'

'Thirdly, he had no necessity to kill the boys. They were declared bastards and Parliament petitioned him to accept the crown.'

'Can this be the truth?' Margaret's blue eyes widened as she asked the question. She addressed, not Brother Thomas, but her father; who made no reply.

'Fourthly, consider the behaviour of the boy's mother, Queen Elizabeth Woodville. A few months after the supposed murder she became reconciled to Richard. She brought herself and her daughters out of sanctuary and placed them freely in his hands. Would she so have trusted the murderer of her sons? The king she quarrelled with after her sons' disappearance was Henry, not Richard.'

Despite temptation elsewhere, Brother Thomas studied Robert Skelton's face while he spoke.

'Fifthly, consider the position of Cardinal Archbishop Bourchier. He it was who persuaded the queen to allow the younger boy out of sanctuary. He pledged his honour that the prince would be safe. He crowned Richard.'

'If Cardinal Archbishop Morton could lie about the murder, why not Bourchier?'

'The cases are different. Cardinal Morton had no responsibility for the princes' safety. Cardinal Bourchier did. He survived Richard. If the princes were dead, would his conscience have permitted him to remain silent? Even if we suppose him an accomplice to infanticide and determined to conceal it, would not Henry Tudor have forced him into a public confession, or at least into an apologia which placed all the blame on Richard and exonerated himself?'

'If he knew of or suspected their death,' said Margaret softly, 'he surely must have spoken out.'

'Sixthly, what can we think of the Constable of the Tower at that time? We are told that Sir Robert Brakenbury was too honourable a man to obey Richard's order to have the children killed, and that therefore he was ordered to hand over the keys to another man for one night so that the dark deed could be done. Yet this honourable man returned to his post the next day. He continued to have charge of the Tower for the remainder of Richard's reign. We are asked to believe that Richard continued to trust a man who had failed him in such a matter, and that Brakenbury continued to serve a sovereign whom he knew for an infanticide. There is no need for me to tell you, of all men, Master Skelton, what happened to Sir Robert Brakenbury.'

'He died at Richard's side on Bosworth field.'

'Yes; loyalty bound him too, and the gentlemen of his household, one of whom bore the name of Skelton. Walter Skelton.'

'My father's brother had that name.' Robert Skelton spoke with reluctance, his eye on his daughter.

'I have seen his tomb in the church and the living tribute of the white rose. My six reasons I have rehearsed so that you may have the confidence in me to reveal a seventh, which concerns your uncle. It is he I came to Fotheringhay to seek.'

'He too fell at Bosworth, brother. A small band of the faithful rode with the king in his last charge, when he challenged Henry Tudor to fight him man to man. Sir Robert rode beside the king and my uncle rode beside Sir

Robert. For his pains, when it was all over, his head was severed from his body and exposed above the east gate at Leicester as a traitor's.'

To Brother Thomas's distress tears ran from the girl's eyes as though it had happened yesterday. Her father brusquely ordered her to clear the table and, while she was about it, to look outside and discover whether they had company.

She returned to announce that two strangers were grazing their horses in the orchard on the far side of the river. They were keeping a watch on the house and had strained their eyes at the sight of her and then looked away, pretending unconcern. Brother Thomas's man was in the garden watching the watchers.

'Go and keep him company. If they approach or leave, come and tell me at once.'

'Yes, father.' She curtsied to Brother Thomas and left them.

'If a hair of her head is harmed I shall hold you to blame, brother.'

Brother Thomas felt misery. He missed his beads, forbidden by Act of Parliament, but said an Our Father and a Hail Mary under his breath before he could bring himself to speak again.

'I will go soon and never return. But first you will tell me how your uncle rescued the princes and what became of them. I know you have sent your daughter from the room so that she shall not hear.'

'You are right. My fears are all for her.'

'These men are but spies. They will report, not act.'

'And when they have reported, what then? We must put our trust in God and believe that He has sent you here. You will have heard of John Skelton, my grandfather. He sat at history's high table for one brief course.'

Brother Thomas searched his memory in vain.

'In February of 1462 the house of York was defeated in battle near the abbey of St Alban. The whole family was in danger, even those too young to fight. The duke's two younger sons, George and Richard, were hurriedly taken from here to London with the Lancastrians in hot pursuit. They escaped by ship at night and reached the court of their sister's husband in the Low Countries. When this occurred, Richard, our future king, was eight years old.'

'It was your grandfather who shipped him to safety?'

'Singlehanded. A large escort would have attracted attention. The house of York had – and has today – no servants more devoted than the Skeltons. Twenty years later my uncle was chosen to undertake the self-same duty for Richard's nephews – another Richard and—'

'—Edward the boy king.'

'Yes; Edward was there at first – until the great disaster. This time there were no Lancastrians. They had been defeated long since. The earlier Richard was on the throne. He had been crowned in place of Edward and left London on a royal progress. Unfortunately his nephews stayed, and with them a man who wished them ill.'

'Henry Stafford, duke of Buckingham.'

'Just so; a villainous man but, being of the blood royal, all-powerful. As Constable of England he commanded in the king's absence.'

'Vain, unstable and treacherous,' declared Brother Thomas. 'I have studied and suspected Henry Stafford. King Richard should not have left his nephews in the care of such a man.'

'He did not. He entrusted them to Sir Robert Brakenbury, who was under strict instructions to keep them secure. As you have truly stated, he wanted no harm to befall them, nor for anyone to say that they had suffered while under his protection. There is some truth in the old tale, but it was the duke of Buckingham, not the king, who ordered Sir Robert to surrender the keys of the Tower for one night. Sir Robert refused and the duke threatened force. The law was on the duke's side, the Constable of the Tower being answerable to the Constable of England. His men surrounded the Tower while he went in to force Sir Robert's obedience. He could not be denied entry and, sword in hand, forced his way into the royal apartments which housed the princes. You may imagine his wrath when he found them empty.'

'The princes had fled with your uncle?'

'They had. The duke's men were allowing no man or boy to pass, so on Sir Robert's orders he dressed as a washerwoman and the boys were put in girls' clothing. In this disguise they passed through the gate in the company of other menials. My uncle hurried them straight to sanctuary at Westminster but the abbot warned them to leave. The duke, he feared, was not a man to respect the rights of sanctuary.'

'So your uncle took them to the king?'

'No. The roads were guarded. If they were to escape it could only be by water. After nightfall they took a skiff downstream. My uncle's intention was to hire a boat from the city wharves which would carry them to Yorkshire, where they would join the king.'

'Tell me about the boys themselves,' asked Brother Thomas. 'What did they look like? How did they behave? Were they bold or frightened?'

'Edward took after his mother, my uncle said. He was delicate and pale, with a quick temper. The younger boy was all Plantagenet: robust and fair. They were both too young to recognise the greatness of the danger and were calmed by my uncle's reassurances. None of them was as frightened as the waterman. He begged not to have to shoot the rapids under the bridge in darkness and in such a boat. The narrowing of the river's flow between the jutting starlings round the piers made the water like a mill-race. He wanted to land them on Vintry Wharf upstream of the bridge, but my uncle forbade it for fear of the duke's men.'

'He took a mortal risk,' said Brother Thomas. 'I have seen the water beneath London Bridge and heard its roar and would not wish to be on it in the stoutest craft.'

'They were nearly through when the skiff knocked against one of the piers and the younger boy was jolted into the river. The waterman leaned over to grab him, my uncle dived to save him, and between them they overturned the boat. Edward and the waterman disappeared and the boat was swept away. My uncle reached the younger boy and clung to him while he swam searching for the others. He shouted for help but no one could have heard him above the noise of the water.'

'Mary, Mother of God!' exclaimed Brother Thomas. 'Did the boy king drown?'

'He drowned. It was the will of God. When he was nearly exhausted my uncle saw the body surface and be carried away downstream like a bundle of jettisoned clothes. The other boy he managed to bring to the bank alive. They found a ship about to sail and took passage on it. The captain was a foreigner and my uncle paid him well not to ask questions. Instead of going to Yorkshire as he had first intended, they were taken to Bruges and from there went on to Tournai to avoid the English merchants. My uncle's conscience was so burdened with Edward's death that he stayed there, passing Richard off as his own son, neither seeking out the boy's aunt whose husband ruled in Flanders nor sending word to the king. He was ill for many months and could not bring himself to make the journey home.'

'But the young king – was he dead beyond all question? Can you lay your hand on your heart and answer to posterity for that?'

'My uncle could. His certainty was absolute. After that day he lived and relived the tragedy with every breath.'

Brother Thomas closed his eyes in silent valediction. 'Yes; this must be the truth I have sought. It explains the boys' disappearance. It explains the quarrel between the king and the duke of Buckingham, which ended with the duke's rebellion and execution. It explains their silence. It explains why, when rumours began to circulate, the king could not produce the princes to refute the slander of his enemies. Neither he nor the duke wished to be blamed for the boys' death. They kept silence, waiting for news. Meantime what could they do but pretend that the princes were still in the Tower? Tell me, did Richard never learn his nephews' fate?'

'My uncle had money which Sir Robert had given him. This kept him and the boy in comfort for nearly two years while he kicked his heels in Tournai and put the young Richard to school with brethren there. At last he decided to return to England, confess to the death of Edward and restore the surviving prince to the care of the king. News had reached him of the death of the prince of Wales and he believed that the boy might be legitimised and welcomed as heir to the throne.'

Brother Thomas's thoughts were racing like the water through London bridge. His quest for the boy king was over but the younger brother would serve Master Aske's purpose as well. A true Plantagenet. Robust and fair.

'Did Richard make the journey safely?' he asked in

trepidation. 'There is no record known to me of the boy's reappearance at court.'

'They returned without mishap to London, to find the king gone to Nottingham to prepare for battle with the Tudor's invading army. My uncle rode to join him. On the way he called here and told my father his story.'

'The young Richard of York was here? In this house?' Brother Thomas's eyes shone.

'In this very room. I was in my cradle at the time but many years later my father told me of it. He opened the door to a knock one night and there was his brother whom he thought dead. The prince was disguised as my uncle's page. There were only the two of them. They arrived thus, unannounced and unattended. After resting a day or two they rode on. It was the eve of Bosworth when they left. My uncle was killed the next day. The boy must have died with him.'

'What did your father do? Did he not ride with them?'

'My father was lame. He could not fight. When he heard of the battle and my uncle's death he went to the old duchess, the king's mother, and told her the story. She it was who had my uncle's head taken down from the gate at Leicester and his body honourably buried. She searched for the boy's body in vain.'

Brother Thomas calculated. 'He was born on the seventeenth of August in 1473. The battle took place on the twenty-second of August in 1485. Would a boy scarcely twelve years of age have fought and been killed?'

'On that day, and afterwards, Henry Tudor's men spared no one who took the king's side. Tudors do not show mercy, even to women and children. It is for this reason that I fear the consequences of your coming.'

11

No sooner was the tale told than Brother Thomas promised to take his leave. He would not compromise them further by lingering.

Gervase confirmed that the watchers in the orchard were the same men whom they had seen in London. 'Say the word, brother, and I will knock them down for you, though it bring a hornets' nest about our ears.'

Brother Thomas did not say the word. Before he could speak, Margaret came running to announce that the men were stirring.

'They cannot cross the river except by the bridge,' said her father. 'You must leave this instant, brother. If you were not a monk I would ask you to take the girl with you.'

They made their farewells hurriedly. Margaret knelt before Brother Thomas and this time he did not stop her from kissing his hand.

'God be with you, sister.' He felt sickness at the parting.

'And also with you. He has sent you to us.'

He mounted glumly and rode away without a backward glance. Gervase followed, covering his retreat and urging him to hasten, but Master Cromwell's men did not appear.

'Be of good cheer,' Gervase exhorted him when they had left the village a safe distance behind. 'It will not take us many hours to reach home.'

'We are not going home.'

'But you are not well, brother.'

'We are not going home.' Croyland beckoned. He was sick from despair, sick from guilt, sick from sinful desire; yes, sick for the girl. Sick above all from failure. And that had only one cure.

'Where to then?' Gervase asked with a sigh.

'To Leicester. Where else?'

He was uncertain, when they arrived at length, whether to seek hospitality from the Franciscans or the black canons.

The canons' house was Leicester abbey where, seven years ago, had died the most powerful man in all England, a Thomas like himself, a butcher's son from Ipswich who had become cardinal archbishop of York and chancellor of England, and who, if he had kept his sovereign's favour, would have been Pope. Brother Thomas, a miller's son from the fens, counted himself fortunate in his elevation to the precentorship of Croyland. Yet the higher the climb the greater the fall. Wolsey had died in failure and disgrace. He had dragged his body across England towards a traitor's death in London, and at Leicester he had given up the struggle. 'Father abbot, I am come hither to leave my bones among you.' And so another Thomas, the evil Cromwell, had come to power.

In his present condition Brother Thomas felt that he too might be leaving his bones there. But the abbey disappointed him. It was full, or claimed to be so.

'Their abbot supports the king,' growled Gervase, rejoining him outside the gate. 'I have spoken to the porter. They will not take us in, because we are from Croyland.'

At the friary they were more successful, and Brother Thomas vowed to be more charitable towards friars in the future. In his guest-cell he thankfully fell asleep at once, although it was barely evening, and when he woke the sunshine through the window vent was already strong and bright.

Instead of rising for prayer he lay stretched out on his back, aching and brooding on the investigation. Could that fair robust boy, schooled by monks at Tournai, possibly be alive fifty-one years after the battle at Bosworth? That was the question now.

Here he lay but a few miles from the battlefield, where a hopeless adventurer had in two brief hours become master of England. Henry should never have won the battle and Richard, a man seasoned in war and skilled in generalship, should never have lost it. The result ran counter to all expectation and justice. Richard was a veteran of the civil war, as bold and battle-honoured as his Plantagenet forebears, Curtmantle and Coeur-de-Lion. His monstrous crook-back had been invented after his death by his vanquisher, a man who took no part himself in the battle, nor in any other before or after.

The two decisive encounters in English history, Brother Thomas decided, had both gone awry. Bosworth was one, Hastings the other. Richard should have beaten Henry. Harold should have beaten William. Why had God decided otherwise? He closed his eyes to ponder and fell asleep again.

When he opened them he had visitors. Gervase and a friar stood at the end of the bed, and a white-haired, white-bearded man was bending over him. The room was too small to hold them all.

'I am not ill,' he cried. 'I do not need a physician. Let me up.'

The old man nodded approvingly. 'Excellent,' he said, 'but you must have food first. I have ordered soup and pudding.'

'Neither soup nor pudding.' Brother Thomas laughed and saw the others exchange glances as though fearing for his sanity. He was too weak to explain that the phrase came from Chancellor Rayne's charge against the abbot in the report on his visitation to Croyland. The abbot, he had falsely and maliciously alleged, had taken over the office of cellarer himself in order to starve the monks to his own profit. Meals in the refectory were said to be inadequate. Perhaps they were so to the gluttonous chancellor.

'His mind is wandering,' he heard one of them whisper.

'No, no; I will eat. I have work to do.'

'I have told the friar about your investigation,' said Gervase.

'What have you told him?' Brother Thomas sat up alarmed. On the journey, to make doubly sure of word reaching the abbot, he had recounted Robert Skelton's tale to Gervase.

'That you are inquiring about the battle here, and in particular about those who fought on the king's side. That is all. The friar says that the learned doctor will assist you in this matter.'

When the food came Gervase and the friar left. The physician sat and watched. For all his years he seemed alert and clear-eyed, finely dressed and free from the slovenliness of old age.

'You must look after yourself better,' he chided. 'Your body is not accustomed to so much exertion and your mind is overworking.'

'There is nothing wrong with me. We are all in God's hands.'

'Nothing except fatigue and nostalgia. You should go home and rest. Resume your inquiries later if you must. As for God, I do not believe He exists.'

In his surprise Brother Thomas spilled his soup. 'How can you speak such blasphemy? What are you doing here, an enemy of the Church in a house of God?'

'Calm yourself, brother. I am not an enemy of the Church. I live here peacefully with the friars. Their warden is an old friend. The matter is very simple: to oblige him I try to believe, but I do not succeed.' He mopped the bed-clothes with a napkin. 'My problem is that I cannot see God, nor hear Him, nor touch, smell or taste Him. How else can I know Him?'

'In your heart.'

'There is nothing you can tell me about hearts. I studied in Padua and have dissected a score or more. No; I do not believe the heart leads anywhere except to the other organs.'

As they talked, Brother Thomas forgot his sickness. He became engrossed in the argument and in anxiety for this man so near to death whose life, without God, was meaningless but who seemed so little cast down by it. His was a soul worth saving.

He was a corrodist at the friary, so he said. He had no children and when his wife died he sold his house and gave everything he possessed to the friars for the benefit of the sick in their hospital of St Ursula.

'Even if you do not believe in Him, He will reward your generosity.'

'Then we must trust Him not to look too closely into the account. The friars have promised to give me free board and lodging and clothe me till I die, and we made our bargain nearly twenty years ago. Another twenty, and the sick will be out of pocket. Meanwhile I attend their services and salve my conscience by helping the master of the hospital.'

'If you are a citizen of the town, can you recall the great battle at Bosworth?'

'Not the battle itself, but I recall the king who died there. Before the fight he put up at the Blue Boar across the street and I saw him ride out from the courtyard there. He was grave and resolute, a young man grown old. But he looked his subjects in the eye.'

'He was born to rule,' exclaimed Brother Thomas. 'Not

like the shifty Tudor. That king never looked a man in the eye, I dare swear, except to distract his attention while he picked his pocket or had another thrust a dagger in his back.'

'I also saw the king when he returned. His body had been stripped on the field. He was tied across a horse's back, with a halter round his neck like a common felon. They brought him into the town as naked as the day he was born. His head hung loose so that it banged against the parapet of the bridge. The Tudor's men laughed to see it bruised, but the women of Leicester averted their eyes in shame. I wonder which way your God was looking then.'

'His rewards are not earthly ones. King Richard's soul is in His keeping.'

'I counted the sword thrusts in his body. There were more than fifty. His enemies attacked him bravely enough once he was dead. I have seen many corpses but never one so gashed. The mayor and leading citizens were forced to view it and be witness to his death. Then it was exhibited in a public ditch with dead dogs for all to view. After three days nothing could be seen but flies feeding on his blood.'

'They dishonoured the Lord's anointed. May God forgive them!'

'They did themselves little good by it in this region. Even today it is a matter for sorrow that a king of England was done to death by mercenaries from France and false Welshmen. Good king Dickon – that is the name by which folk call him still.'

Brother Thomas wept. 'Was he given a Christian burial at last?'

'On the third evening the friars were allowed to take the body away.'

'I must see the tomb. Lead me to the church, I pray you.'

'He does not lie in the church. If he did, he would draw as

many pilgrims as St Thomas to Canterbury and the friars would have the church pulled down about their ears. No; that was not permitted. Some day there will be a memorial. Even Henry Tudor promised it.'

'Tudor promises!' Brother Thomas rose from his bed, swaying so that he was forced to support himself with a hand on the old man's arm. 'Is the ground he lies in consecrated? Show me his resting place.'

'Tomorrow, when you are stronger.'

'Today!'

The doctor smiled at his determination and led him out into a courtyard. They crossed it and went through a covered passage leading between the church and the other friary buildings into the cloisters. Undulating the surface of the garth were mounds marking the graves of departed friars.

'He lies in the south-east corner. That mound is his.'

'In God's acre.' Brother Thomas breathed with relief. 'But is there no stone, no inscription of any kind?'

'What would our present king do if there were and the faithful thronged here?'

Brother Thomas knelt on the grass at the head of the unmarked mound. The king's body, like his reputation, was being hounded long after death, but at least his soul was out of reach of the relentless Tudors, men without mercy or pity or piety, men guilty themselves of the crimes of which they accused him – regicide and usurpation.

'Now that you are kneeling, brother, look up.'

He raised his eyes to the gargoyle which protruded from the cloister roof. The stone had been carved into the likeness of a boar's head, its mouth wide open so that the rain would run through and water the grave. On the neck, invisible except from where he knelt, Brother Thomas read the small, lovingly incised lettering: 'I am Richard of England. Pray for me.'

12

After Brother Thomas had spent a week in bed, burning like a soul in Hell, the physician pronounced him fit to travel again and agreed to take him to the battlefield.

The old man rode stiffly, but gamely enough, with Gervase at his side. High summer had come. His eyesight was sharper than Brother Thomas's and, once out of the town, he invited them to admire open meadows and distant wooded ridges which he had loved since boyhood.

'I too seek to live in the past,' Brother Thomas told him, indifferent to the beauties of nature. 'You have your memories, I my mind's imaginings. I have spent the last week with King Richard. I see him more clearly than I see you. I feel his sufferings more than the air against my face.'

'Beware,' the old man replied. 'That way lies madness.'

A few miles outside the town they turned off the road and climbed a gentle slope. Here they stood on the very heart of England, as distant from the sea as anywhere in the kingdom. The doctor reined his horse and wheeled it round as though preparing to repel an invader from any quarter of the unseen shore.

'This is where your king spent the night before the battle. Five armies in all gathered here. The Tudor's was over there and those of Lord Derby and his brother, Sir William Stanley, lay between them but away to the right. The earl of Northumberland camped with his men out of sight beyond that rise behind us.'

'Traitors all three,' cried Brother Thomas vehemently. 'The Stanleys and Northumberland brought up their men in response to the king's summons but would not join with him. They made excuses and dallied at a distance, waiting to see which way the tide would turn so that they could be sure of committing themselves to the winning side. I have read of their infamy.'

'Your history is accurate,' said the doctor. 'Yet it is not the accepted version.'

'Who would dare publicly impugn the valour and honour of the Percys? Yet what are these so-called noblemen?' Brother Thomas asked the questions aloud of himself and answered them. 'Border thieves and ruffians dressed in the trappings of nobility – superior to none except such as the Stanleys, who were in treasonable communication with the enemy. They halted where they could sway the battle either way. Once victory was assured they would move to share the spoils. They were knaves without principle, covetous for the richest pickings. If King Richard had been a cruel tyrant, as Tudor chroniclers would have us believe, they would not have been alive. They plotted against him with Lord Hastings and he spared their lives.'

'Henry Tudor, as I have heard, did not make the same mistake. The Stanleys won the battle for him, but he later had Sir William executed for treason.'

'Richard was too forbearing in a bloody age,' said Brother Thomas. 'He was too honourable, too trusting. That was the cause of his downfall. The earl of Derby was married to Henry Tudor's mother. Richard had every reason to doubt his loyalty, but when the earl gave his word he trusted him to keep it.'

'Did he not take the precaution of keeping the earl's eldest son as a hostage?'

'He did. But when the earl broke his word and betrayed him the king spared the boy's life.'

Brother Thomas dismounted and threw himself on the ground. He felt oppressed, contaminated, his fever rising again. On this bare stretch of gentle countryside, the least likely scene of great events, traitors had butchered the last king of England whose word could be trusted. Tudor rule was government by deceit: any subject who placed reliance on a royal promise was likely to lose his head. Richard's tragedy lay in this – he had outlived the age of chivalry.

With Gervase's aid the doctor dismounted too.

'Do you see that stream?' he asked. 'That is where the vanguards met and the fighting began. When the king realised that the Stanleys' treachery was beyond doubt he put his trust in your God and a frontal assault. Your God let him down.'

'You are rash to speak blasphemously of the Almighty. You may yet come to witness, before you die, that God does not desert the faithful.' In his anger Brother Thomas spoke incautiously.

'Is it I who am rash? I ask no other questions, but would not wish to see you suffer in a hopeless insurrection – although, with monastery walls already tumbling, I recognise that you and God will have to hurry.'

'You shall see,' Brother Thomas promised. 'God is not mocked.'

He sat picturing the advance of the king's army. John Howard, duke of Norfolk, had led them down the slope against the rebel vanguard commanded by the renegade John de Vere, earl of Oxford. The fighting was fierce – swords against bows, spears against daggers, foot soldiers and horsemen enmeshed in hand-to-hand combat. The king's force had the better of it until Norfolk fell and his men saw it and wavered. That was the moment for reinforcements. The king issued his royal summons to the Stanleys and Northumberland, but none of them would move or let any part of their armies go to the aid of their sovereign lord, the man to whom they had made obeisance and sworn fealty before God.

'Are there any now alive who witnessed the battle?' he asked.

'You will not find any such in Leicester. Those who lost died, those who won were strangers. There were no standers-by. The first engagement proved decisive and it was all quickly over.'

Suppose in the hazard of the struggle Oxford had fallen instead of Norfolk! Then the king would have been seen to be winning and the reinforcements would have marched. Brother Thomas's ears were filled with the clank of steel, with oaths and groans, cries of encouragement and despair, the stamp and snort of horses and the gusts of panic in the throats of the king's men as their lines began to break. Through the clamour the old man's voice came faintly as though from across the valley.

'We have our tales of the battle nonetheless. They say that the king gathered his personal bodyguard around him on this hillock. Without reinforcements he was outnumbered. With his vanguard in retreat, he had two choices. He could retire to the safety of Nottingham castle and there await the arrival of loyal troops from Yorkshire, or he could hunt down the Tudor and settle with him man to man.'

'He should have withdrawn, yet it was not in his nature.'

'Yes; he was unwise, overbold. For all his experience he had lived scarcely thirty years. I know his age because we were born in the same year. Think of that, brother. If he had survived he might still be king today and your monasteries would stand secure.'

'He must have wished for death,' said Brother Thomas. 'That alone would account for his rashness.' Richard's son had died, the only heir of his body. His wife had died, whom he loved deeply. He hated London with its politics and court life, and all the deceits and intrigues surrounding kingship. He had spent his life fighting and was tired of it all. He would not choose to live cowering behind castle walls in his own domains.

'So he galloped to his death, down that slope and up the other side.' The old man pointed the way. 'With a small body of knights he charged straight at the main rebel force, and as if that folly did not suffice he had to expose his flank to the Stanleys as he went.'

He had hacked down the Tudor standard with his own hand and killed the bearer of it. If he had succeeded in killing the Tudor himself it would have been the bravest exploit in all recorded history.

Frenzied by the thought of what might have been, Brother Thomas leaped into the saddle, dug in his heels and galloped down the hill. The breeze sang to him. 'For God, Richard and England,' he heard himself shouting and a flock of sheep grazing where the Stanleys had skulked raised their heads in alarm.

In the soft ground at the bottom of the valley his horse stumbled, but recovered its footing. They splashed through the stream and sped up the slope through the deserted fields. Brother Thomas's imaginary lance was pointing at the heart of the traitorous Tudor ahead.

Although his strength and breath were soon gone he charged on, until his horse shied at the sudden appearance of two other, familiar horsemen. Taken by surprise, he flew over the horse's head and fell heavily to the ground into the arms of oblivion.

The doctor was feeling him tenderly for broken bones when he regained consciousness. Gervase had recaptured the horse. The two horsemen had vanished: ominous as ever, like jackals scouting for a beast of prey.

'I hoped to experience the king's feelings as he led the charge.' He spoke sheepishly.

The doctor slowly straightened himself and pronounced him to be suffering from nothing worse than bruises. 'The king did not lead the charge,' he said.

'According to the account at Croyland he led his men with such fury they could not keep pace with him.' Brother Thomas felt personally slighted at the suggestion that it was not so.

'According to local legend, the king's last charge was led by a boy.'

'A boy!' It was Gervase who expressed disbelief. Brother Thomas was too excited to speak.

'The boy went first,' the old man explained, 'followed by the king and his retinue. It is curious, I agree, but that is what has been reported by word of mouth from that day to this.'

Brother Thomas recovered his tongue. 'What manner of boy?' he asked hoarsely.

'He is said to have been a page whose horse ran away with him. He carried a pennant which bore the device of a rising sun.'

The emblem of the house of York!

13

In the peace and brightness of the summer's day Brother Thomas lay on his back rejoicing. He felt himself removed to the gates of Heaven, bathed in sudden bliss.

'I have often thought of that boy and his rising sun,' said the doctor, breaking the spell at last. 'They were strangely inappropriate symbols of hope. A few minutes afterwards the sun of York had set for ever.'

Brother Thomas stumbled to his feet, unmindful of the pain. 'Half a century is not for ever. Eternity lies in the lap of God. The house of York will rise again.' The words tumbled from him.

'I begin to understand the nature of your inquiries about the battle. You pursue historical truth with a purpose.'

'The past can show us the path of wisdom which leads to God,' said Brother Thomas, cautious now. 'Tell me, I beg you, what became of the boy.'

'When he had crossed the stream his horse took fright at what lay ahead. He bolted away between the Tudor army and the Stanleys.'

'Was he pursued?'

'So it is said.'

'Was he caught?'

'No.'

'How can you answer with so much certainty?'

'Let me ask you a question in turn, brother. What is your interest in a page?'

'I am interested because he may not have been a page. Now please be open with me. Is his identity known?'

'His identity I cannot tell you, but I saw him. You are

right in supposing that he may not have been what he seemed.'

'You saw him with your own eyes!' Brother Thomas looked into them as though in search of a reflection of the boy's image. 'Was he fair-headed and brown-skinned? Was he handsome and bold, with an air of authority? Was he aged twelve years and five days and tall for those years?'

The doctor's mouth fell open. 'If I believed in the Devil I would believe that he was befriending you. From what I saw of the boy, you have described him.'

'You said that you did not witness the battle. Did the boy escape therefore? Did he ride away alone?'

'I will tell you the rest of the tale as it is told in Leicester. When the king reached the top of this rise and slew the Tudor standard-bearer, the Tudor himself refused the challenge of chivalry and drew back behind his bodyguard. At that crucial instant the Stanleys' men moved at last, charging the king's knights in the flank so that few of them reached their sovereign's side and he was cut down almost alone in the enemy ranks. But before he fell, while he was still at the stream below, he had signalled to one of his bodyguard to follow the boy. Alone among the king's attendants, the boy and that knight survived.'

'His name? Tell me the name of the knight.'

After half a century there was little excuse for Brother Thomas's impatience and the old man took his time, breathing steadily to refill his lungs after so many words.

'You will have heard of the rhyme circulated by King Richard's enemies: The Cat, the Rat and Lovell our dog Rule all England under an Hog. The hog was Richard, of course: a reference to his emblem. The cat was his adviser Catesby, esquire of the body, who was captured here and hanged in Leicester. The rat, Sir William Ratcliffe, knight of the body, was killed in the battle. Lovell was the king's chamberlain and closest friend. He it was who rode after the boy.'

'How did you meet them?'

'The battle took place in the morning. Before noon fugitives began to arrive in the town. The victors rode in pursuit and did not scruple to slaughter them in the streets. Like others, I watched from the casement of my house. When darkness fell I was asked to attend a sick man. I went to a house near the west gate and was shown into a darkened room. There I found a wounded man and a boy.'

'Had the boy been wounded too?'

'No; he was exhausted but unharmed. No one told me their names and I knew that it would be dangerous to inquire. But it was common knowledge that the town was being searched for Lord Lovell and I guessed readily enough who the wounded man might be. How could I betray an injured fugitive? While I bound his wounds he told me that the boy was a page of one, Walter Skelton, who had been killed in the fighting. He begged me, if he died, to look after the boy. The lad said nothing for himself.'

'Why did you not believe him to be a page?'

'The man spoke so insistently of him as the page of an unknown squire that I could not but conclude that he was lying for the boy's protection. I noted how he behaved to him, even circumspectly in my presence. Beyond all doubt the boy was his superior, and he himself had been one of the most important men in the kingdom.'

'And you – did you save their lives?'

'You might say so. When soldiers came to the door hunting Lovell the dog and learned of a sick stranger within, I warned them that I suspected leprosy and they would enter the room at their peril. They ventured only to peer from the door, and when they saw the shape of a man and a boy in the bed they concluded that it could not be Lovell, for he would be alone. That is what they told each other and it gave them a pretext for not examining him more closely.'

'May God bless you, doctor! You are a good man and He will reward you despite your unbelief.'

'Is God a Yorkist then?'

Brother Thomas checked the rebuke that rose to his lips.

'Can you doubt it?' muttered Gervase, who listened but seldom spoke. 'Did any Yorkist declare himself Pope and set himself above the Church in order to destroy it?'

They mounted and headed towards the road. The doctor was tired. His head nodded, his beard spread out on the chest of his tunic. Not until they had passed through the town gate did he rouse himself.

'I have long wondered who that boy might have been. Now that I have told you so much, you may tell me this in return. Was he a bastard of the king?'

Riding by his side with Gervase behind them, Brother Thomas, after his sickness and his fall, felt as old as this old man. He swivelled stiffly in the saddle to look for Master Cromwell's spies, but they were not to be seen.

'He was the son of a king, but not of King Richard.'

'Do you mean that he was King Edward's son, the uncrowned king?'

Brother Thomas shook his head.

'Then his brother? The little duke of York?'

Brother Thomas inclined his head but said no more until they were back in the bare comfort of his friary cell. 'What happened to him?' he asked then. 'That is the question now.'

'That is the question I was about to ask you,' the old man

replied. 'When I went back after two days to change Lord Lovell's dressings the pair of them had disappeared. That was the end of it until today. But I am glad to know at last who the boy was. He seemed a lad worth saving.'

'You must tell no one else about him or that I have been making inquiries after him. You may be questioned.'

'Your secrets are secure with me. I shall say nothing. If they torture me I shall die without a struggle. At least the sick of Leicester would benefit. I have lived too long already. Permanent insensibility will be a blessing.' He lay down on Brother Thomas's bed as though stretched on a bier.

'I shall pray for your soul.'

The old man ignored the remark. 'I can tell that you believe the young prince to be still alive. If you find him, remind him of me. I often picture him leading that charge, bearing the standard of his house out of the pages of history. Who more fitting to act thus than the last duke?'

'Who more fitting to bear it back? But let me remind you that he was not the last duke. Our present king bore the title while his father reigned and his brother lived; it was part of the spoils of conquest. Now I will uncover the real duke so that men may decide whether he be the real king also. He will return to rout the anti-Christ. He must. I will not lose his trail after what you have told me.'

'You are confident in your prowess.'

'With God's help.' Brother Thomas remembered Him belatedly.

'Where will you go?'

'Where God bids me. The Lord whom you deny – He is my guide.'

14

The whole of that night Brother Thomas spent on his knees. He could not forget Margaret, and this punishment he prescribed for himself in penance for his lustful thoughts.

In the tranquillity of his cell he begged God's forgiveness and thanked him for the day's discovery, the return of his strength and the kindness of the friars. He sang a psalm to keep his voice in practice, and read from the Bible. The passage he read described how God arose and smote His enemies with the sword. When he found himself reading 'Lancastrians' for 'uncircumcised' it was time to close the Book.

Lovell, he remembered, had escaped to Ireland. There he had joined the supporters of the pretender Lambert Simnel, who at first claimed to be the young duke of York. In the end Simnel was proved beyond doubt to be the son of an Oxford tradesman. If Lovell had contrived to smuggle the real prince across the sea with him, why had he bothered himself with a base-born pretender?

It was a curious and unexplained fact that after proclaiming Simnel as Richard, duke of York, his followers changed his identity and announced him as Edward, earl of Warwick. The earl was the son of the duke of Clarence who had ended his days in a butt of wine. As nephew to Edward IV and Richard III, he stood, if neither king left a legitimate heir, as near the throne as any man. The flaw in his claim was an attainder. When his father was executed for treason the line had been expressly barred by law from the succession. But attainders, like bastardies, could be annulled. For Simnel's supporters, however, there proved to be a more serious flaw. The real earl was in Henry Tudor's hands, a prisoner in the Tower who could be produced and verified at any time.

None of this had stopped the archbishop of Dublin from crowning Lambert Simnel in his cathedral as King Edward VI of England. The lord deputy of Ireland himself had attended the ceremony. So too had the designated heir of Richard III – John de la Pole, earl of Lincoln, the son of Elizabeth duchess of Suffolk, who was sister to Richard and Edward IV. The earl had a better claim to the throne than his cousin, the genuine Warwick, yet he assisted in the crowning of a spurious one.

Kneeling on the bare stone, Brother Thomas sifted the puzzling facts. His mind twisted this way and that as though in a maze. Time and again he thought himself near to the solution, only to find the path blocked. Back he went and took a different turn, winding at last to a different halt. Then, when he believed himself blocked on all sides, he rounded a corner and stumbled across the answer. A shaft of moonlight through the narrow vent fell on his face, symbolising illumination from Above.

The mystery of Lambert Simnel, he saw now, was not the mystery of the man himself, but of other people's acceptance of him. Henry Tudor was so scornful of the palpable falsehood of his claim that when Simnel was captured he did not execute him but kept him in the Tower as a servant, exhibiting him to visitors, particularly Irish ones, whom he twitted for their guillbility. Poor Simnel – the only enemy the Tudors ever spared, because he was not worth killing! They kept him as an example, to serve them by casting doubt on the credibility of all pretenders.

It must have been an accident that Simnel, who had been well tutored by a clever priest, became the rallying point for all Richard's adherents after the disaster at Bosworth.

Troops came from Flanders to Ireland, the best of springboards for an invasion of England. The Irish were easy to recruit with promises of riches and adventure. Some of them may even have believed in their Edward VI. If they did, what purpose would Lord Lovell have served by dissillusioning them or confusing them with a rival claimant?

Brother Thomas imagined himself as Lovell, newly arrived in Dublin with his precious charge. They were fugitives. They may have spent some time hiding in England. It was possible that they escaped at first to Flanders and found there another Richard of York already recognised in the person of Simnel. The real prince's existence was unknown, his story no more plausible than Simnel's. Even if he could establish his identity, how did his bastardy stand?

On that score Brother Thomas felt no uncertainty. Henry Tudor, now Henry VII, had announced that he would marry the boy's sister. Her legitimacy was questioned no longer. She was recognised as heiress to the house of York and by marrying her Henry would unite the rival houses. If she was legitimate, so must her brother be. They were offspring of the same union.

Once that was granted, it must follow that Lovell had in his possession the rightful king of England and the natural leader of an expedition against Henry. The problem would lie in his acceptability. Would Lambert Simnel's backers change their allegiance – men who must have been expecting a rich reward from him in the event of the invasion succeeding? Or would John of Lincoln, the acknowledged Yorkist heir, be content to yield place to another cousin, said to have risen mysteriously from the grave?

Lovell was skilled in statecraft. He would have recognised the danger that the prince might be dismissed as another pretender – one produced by himself as a stepping-stone to his own ambitions. What could he lose by keeping the boy's identity a secret? If the Yorkist survivors and the Irish were ready to fight under Simnel, what need to show his hand? It would be time enough to advance the boy's claim when victory was won. That must have been the intention of the earl of Lincoln too. If the invasion were successful Simnel would be discarded, Lincoln would claim the throne and Lovell would counter-claim. If the invasion failed, only Simnel would be discredited and the others could make another attempt in their own names.

If that was what had occurred, Lovell had been wise. When the invasion did take place, two years after Bosworth, it failed utterly. Brother Thomas's heart grew heavy at the thought of it. How had the mighty fallen indeed! In a generation of war the best blood in the realm had already been shed. More than thirty years after their first encounter the proud Lancastrian inheritance had fallen to a Welsh adventurer and the noble house of York took the field of battle led by a tradesman's son.

The prospect for Simnel's men in this last clash had been bleak, but no bleaker than Henry's at Bosworth. This time, however, there was no treachery, no lack of ruthless purpose by the king. In the massacre Simnel had been captured, the earl of Lincoln killed and Lovell reported missing, believed to be dead. All their claims and counter-claims died with them.

Was Richard of York left in Ireland? He would have been almost old enough to fight and would surely not have agreed to stay behind. Was he slain with Lovell, if indeed Lovell was slain, or had he escaped unscathed from another disastrous battlefield?

'Dear God,' prayed Brother Thomas, Margaret quite forgotten. 'I have brought this boy back to life. He has been rescued from the Tower, saved from drowning, ridden unhurt from Bosworth field. Do not let him escape me now. I need him and You need him. What shall I say to the abbot if I return without him? How can Your great houses of worship be saved unless I find him?'

He begged for another sign, but this time the moon remained hidden behind cloud.

In the morning Gervase found the brother asleep on his knees and woke him roughly.

'Is this because the wench at Fotheringhay has tickled your manhood?' he asked angrily. 'If so, let the Devil have his way. You are flushed with fever again. Go to bed while I fetch the physician. You will have to stay there for another week.'

'I shall not,' replied Brother Thomas, rebelling. 'A doctor without faith can do nothing for me. It is my heart which is sick, and not for a wench. I am heartsick for a boy and shall be so until we find him. Have the horses saddled. I will leave a message for the physician and make my farewells to the warden.'

15

All the way, as they journeyed, the summer air was ripe with rumour. Travellers from the north told of bands assembling with whatever weapons they could make or seize. Resentment at the suppression of the monasteries was bursting into open resistance. Near the border the king's writ had ceased to run. At Hexham the canons had taken to arms and driven off the royal commissioners by force.

Nearer to home, discontent was reported to be swirling across the wolds and fens of Lincolnshire, from Lincoln to

Boston, from Louth to Grantham. The gentry was threatened with a new tax to fill the king's empty coffers. Common people were outraged at seeing God's houses destroyed. In another attack on the Old Faith, the clergy was suffering the humiliation of an official inquiry into its fitness to hold office in accordance with the rites of the new religion.

Much of this Brother Thomas learned when they reached the market place at Newark, where the local priest was renowned for preaching the sin and folly of new ways. Gervase spoke to the townsfolk and reported what they said, which was little in the king's favour. Newark stood where the road from London to York crossed the Fosse Way, which ran aslant the country from Exeter to Lincoln, so that news reached it hourly from all directions. Resting here, Brother Thomas felt himself at the hub of England.

Before long he became an object of interest, almost of veneration. Men and women knelt to ask for blessing or advice. In ignorance and fear they turned by instinct to a representative of God. Master Cromwell was cursed openly. They were looking to the Church, they said, to save their bodies and souls. If Gervase had not removed him down a side street he might have led his own uprising.

'Be patient, brother,' Gervase urged. 'The holy war will start soon enough. Tomorrow, or next week, or next month.'

'Who will lead it? What names are being whispered?'

'Some talk of the old countess of Salisbury and her sons. They expect her to do what Warwick the Kingmaker, her grandfather, did. One says that the leader is to be the marquis of Exeter, grandson to Edward IV through his mother. If none of the king's issue be lawful he is the heir. But another says that he is too closely watched. At the first move his head will be off.'

Brother Thomas meditated. 'What of the north?' he asked. 'Our best hopes lie there.'

'Lord Dacre is reported to be committed to the cause, he who is married to the daughter of the duke of Buckingham, whom the king executed. Another is mentioned whom men will follow – the name of Master Robert Aske is on all their lips.'

'What do they believe Master Aske will do if he prevails?'

'He will put the Princess Mary on the throne.'

'But she is illegitimate by Act of Parliament.'

'People in these parts care nothing for Acts of Parliament. They say that the Pope will order the Emperor to invade England, and that the Emperor, being Queen Katharine's nephew and cousin to the princess, will obey.'

'Alas, they are mistaken,' said Brother Thomas. 'The Emperor is at odds with the king of France. He will never come to England and leave his domains unprotected. If he did come and in arms, neither he nor any person he set on the throne at Westminster would be welcome or accepted.'

The last man to invade England with the Pope's blessing had been William of Normandy and he confiscated half the country for his Norman friends. To succeed this time, it had to be rebellion not invasion. The leader must be English. He must be of royal blood. He must be able to draw together the nobility and the gentry, the clergy and the commons, and weave their grievances into one. There could be only one such man.

'There is news from London too,' said Gervase, 'affecting the succession. The duke of Richmond, the king's bastard, is dead, and the king has not waited for Mistress Anne Boleyn's body to grow cold. He has married again. Suppose he should sire a son at last?'

'If there should be a male heir, our cause is lost. No time must be wasted.'

They were walking their horses towards the bridge, when Brother Thomas turned abruptly to the castle.

Gervase protested. 'It is too dangerous there. We must sleep in the town. The priest will find us lodgings.'

'We need assistance from the castle. Would you have me lie low and discover the true king after the rebellion is over, after the Tudor has secured his succession?'

'I am responsible to the lord abbot for your safety. This town is alive with unrest. The captain of the garrison will not hesitate to imprison a wandering monk. I say no.'

'Prevent me then.'

While they argued outside the gate a crowd gathered, and before they knew it soldiers had surrounded them. One seized Brother Thomas, and in an instant Gervase felled him with a blow of the fist. After a sharp scuffle they found themselves pinioned to the ground, faces in the dust.

At the approach of reinforcements from the castle the crowd fled, leaving them to be dragged by the heels across the drawbridge into the great fortress which stood sheer above the bank of the river, frowning on the town and holding the road and river crossing in its grip, so that townsfolk and travellers alike had all to pass under the watchful eye of the king's men.

Lying on his back trussed like a fowl, Brother Thomas philosophically weighed in his mind the impregnability of the vast keep. No man could be master of England unless he held the heart of the rich midlands. Newark, he knew, was one of the four strongholds. Like Nottingham, where King Richard had vainly summoned the loyal to muster against Henry Tudor, kings were careful to keep it in their own hands. Subjects could not be trusted with such citadels, as the other two bore witness. From Kenilworth Simon de Montfort had ridden out to conquer and capture his sovereign lord. From Warwick the Nevilles had made and unmade kings. What could Richard of York not do, astride England at Newark, if only Brother Thomas could uncover his tracks and persuade him to raise again the standard of the rising sun?

When the lieutenant of the guard arrived he ordered Brother Thomas to be unbound and raised on his feet. The abbot's letter he greeted with a sneer. 'We are loyal subjects of the king. We have no regard for abbots here.'

'Then at least pay heed to your bishop,' said Brother Thomas hotly, 'and have me taken to your commander.'

'On your own head be it.'

The lieutenant gave instructions for Gervase to remain in the gatehouse and for 'the little black crow' to be taken to the great hall, where the captain was dining with the officers of his household. They had eaten and drunk well, it seemed from the noise, and were in the mood for diversion.

'Be seated beside me, brother,' the captain invited him. 'I offer you the hospitality of my table out of respect for his lordship of Lincoln. Are you inspecting the world with a view to the future? For if I judge right you will soon be earning your food and lodging like an honest man.'

'May God forgive you,' Brother Thomas replied in his mildest and most provoking voice.

'Tonsured good-for-nothings,' said the captain, adding a belch to emphasise his contempt. 'Baldheaded, cloistered lubbers. While you and your like tell your beads and guzzle your fish some of us have been campaigning in Scotland and fighting the infidel in Spain so that Christian women and children – and monks too – can sleep safely in their beds.'

Brother Thomas nibbled at the capon's wing which had been set in front of him, sipped his ale and said nothing. The noise had died and everyone in the hall sat listening: without looking up he could feel every eye upon the two of them. The captain was a broad, bluff man, well groomed and richly dressed. Beside him Brother Thomas felt himself cutting a poor figure: slight, dishevelled and travel-grimed; his body bruised, his habit torn from the rough manhandling.

'What have your abbeys done for England but gobble up all the land and send our riches to Italy to fatten idle foreigners? Answer me that. Have you lost your tongue?'

'We pray for the souls of the living and the dead.'

'Other men can pray. What is special about monks' prayers?'

'We spend more time on our devotions. We praise God by day and night.'

'Much good that does.'

'Your ignorance does you no credit,' said Brother Thomas in a sweet and charitable voice. 'Even you cannot be unaware that we tend the sick and provide hospitality for travellers and alms for the poor.'

'Others can tend the sick. Inns provide for travellers. As for alms, you give what you have taken. When there are no monasteries, alms will not be needed.'

The captain's reply drew applause from his subordinates, and the hall grew rowdy again with jeers from all sides.

'We will have the roofs off your abbeys.'

'Give the stones to the poor for houses. That will be better than alms.'

'No more tithes to Rome!'

'Nor to abbots either!'

'Let the abbey-lubbers work like other men.'

'Do not look so glum, brother. You will soon be allowed a woman.'

'He has one already. See how he blushes.'

'The only English Pope was a monk's son.'

'Bring a girl and let us see him perform.'

Brother Thomas slowly finished eating, pretending not to hear their taunts. He thanked God for the reminder that the king did not stand alone. The fat Tudor, as Aske called him, could not impose his will without men to obey him, men with devilish thoughts like his own. Here in front of him sat the very minions of Satan who, at the king's command, were laying sacrilegious hands on what was God's. They were not afraid of His wrath, not afraid of bringing eternal damnation on their immortal souls. Did they really believe, like the physician at Leicester, that when they died that would be an end, or that God would allow them to escape punishment in the fires of Hell?

He banged his platter on the table for silence.

'My friends,' he said when they became quiet, 'you are in mortal error and it is fortunate indeed for you that God's mercy is boundless. I shall pray for you. I shall ask my fellows at Croyland to pray for you. I shall beg St Benedict, the founder of our order, to intercede with God on your behalf. Believe me that without prayer we are all lost. Prayer requires solitude, the solitude of the religious houses. Without our prayers your souls will be in danger. Without our chantries how will the souls of the dead escape from Purgatory? Without our shrines to visit how will you find remission of sins in pilgrimage?'

The ale had been strong. The room was filled with smoke from the open fire. He felt dizzy from bruising and faint from fatigue and the burden of hostility. But when he paused, the expected abuse did not come. They were heeding him and he gathered confidence and strength to continue.

'Even if you are so misled as to care nothing for your own souls and the souls of others, as your fathers and forefathers have done for centuries, be not unmindful of the poor, the sick and the traveller. I speak to you as all three and I tell you that, for all your captain would have you believe, they have nowhere to turn but to the monasteries. Even if you care nothing for souls and bodies, consider, I beg you, the glory of our churches built with love and labour by the faithful, reaching up in yearning to Him above. Consider too our stores of knowledge. Without intellect, without learning, without knowledge of God and our immortal souls, men become as beasts. Is that what you want? To roam like wild creatures without conception of right or wrong? Consider—'

'Enough,' cried the captain, pulling him down. 'What we consider is your idle lives, your jewelled chalices and gold patens, your flocks of sheep and fields of corn, your tax on every man's purchase in the markets. The abbeys hoard the good things of England while the rest of us go in want. The king himself has little enough gold to pay me and my men our pittance. It all lies in your shrines and vaults. You have taken our wealth from us and offer us prayers in exchange. Stomachs cannot be filled with prayer, and we do not want your dole. It is not charity we ask for. We want what is ours and has been taken from us by thieving monks. By the king's grace we shall have it and your monasteries will be wiped from the face of England.'

'The king shall be wiped from the face of England first.'

16

Even as the words were passing his lips, Brother Thomas sought to recall them. In his passion he had spoken out so boldly that all the company could hear.

'Hang the traitor.' That was the general cry.

The captain drew his sword and laid it on the table. Its tip pointed towards Brother Thomas's heart. The hubbub died and he spoke.

'What is that you said, Master Monk?'

'I was but reminding you that the king is mortal,' Brother Thomas replied. 'We all must die. There is no exemption for kings.' This was no occasion for martyrdom, his mission unaccomplished.

'That was not your meaning. The monasteries or the king – one of them must go and it must be the king. Thus you spoke and it was treason. You wish for the death of the king.'

'As God is my witness, I am loyal to the rightful king of this realm.'

'Then swear your allegiance to King Henry on that sword.'

'That cannot be. I can swear no oaths without my abbot's leave.'

At a signal from the captain two men seized Brother Thomas, dragged him to the window and pushed him out so that he hung suspended by the heels above the dark river far below.

'I have heard of your abbot,' shouted the captain after him in a fury. 'He is a traitor too. If I had him here the pair of you would hang there together. The king's enemies can expect no mercy here.'

'Hang me then,' Brother Thomas shouted back. 'Hang

me without a trial, hang me for being a monk, if that be your notion of justice. God is watching you.'

'He is drunk,' said the captain, 'or a madman. Take him away and lock him up. I will deal with him in the morning.'

The two men pulled Brother Thomas back into the room and showed him, none too gently, to his accommodation. They led him down narrow stairs winding within the castle wall and pushed him through a dungeon door.

The descent took so long that he thought he must be below the ground, but through a small grille he could see moonlight on water. He was at river level. The cell smelt dank. In times of flood a man would be in water up to his waist or even his chin.

Fighting against pain and sleep, he spent the night on his feet, partly on account of the dampness, partly as a penance, but mostly from fear of the rats. They scuffled and nipped at his legs until he found it hard to love them as St Francis had. By dawn he grew lightheaded and was haranguing God through the bars demanding to be told what He thought He was doing creating rats and Tudors.

In the morning, when he was brought before the captain, he was resolved to die in the Faith without a whimper. Gervase would carry the news of him and what he had discovered to Croyland, where all the brethren would pray for his soul until he reached Heaven and had the ear of God.

The captain was sunning himself placidly on the castle green. Instead of interrogating Brother Thomas as a prisoner he greeted him affably and bade him be seated. In the brightness of morning the walls looked less grim, and the two men sat together alone like neighbours in a garden.

'We were both of us the worse for ale last night,' said the captain, stroking his freshly barbered beard. 'Let us forget what was uttered in our cups. I ask pardon for the discomfort of your lodging last night and promise you better if you will stay with us. I fear I have disobliged the worthy bishop by ill-treating you and I seek to make amends.'

Brother Thomas was gratefully resting his reeling head and aching legs. But he felt a twinge of strange sorrow as the prospect of martyrdom receded.

In answer to the captain's questions he talked of his work at Croyland and spoke of the importance of knowledge. Through knowledge man grows towards God. Without knowledge he is no better than an animal, which feeds and fornicates and passes soulless to oblivion. Fervently he developed his defence of the monasteries. The abbeys were the storehouses of knowledge. Destroy them and bestiality triumphs.

'Others have knowledge,' the captain replied, and proudly confessed that he himself had learned to write. But he admitted that a monk had taught him.

They talked of Scotland and Spain and the captain's experiences; until gradually Brother Thomas reached the subject of his inquiry.

'I have been told of the battle,' said the captain. 'The village where it was fought lies three or four miles away. I will show you.'

They climbed the steps of the curtain wall to the rampart and he pointed. 'There! That is Stoke. The rebel earl of Lincoln and the pretender Simnel came from the north. They landed in Lancashire and marched through Mansfield and Southwell to seize the castle here. It was June and the river ran shallow so that they were able to ford it at Fiskerton instead of having to force the bridge. Even so the king was too quick for them. He marched from the castle to bar their way and confront them. His army was commanded by the earl of Oxford, the victor of Bosworth, and the rebels were soon scattered. They were naked Irish, ill-armed.'

'Yet I have read that the issue was uncertain for three hours. It is said that the Tudor victory at Bosworth was all but reversed.'

The captain frowned. 'There were German mercenaries in the rebel lines. They fought bravely, but neither Germans nor Irish are a match for Englishmen.'

'Englishmen fought on both sides,' Brother Thomas reminded him. 'Noblemen like the earl of Kildare and Lord Lovell marched with the earl of Lincoln. What became of them, I wonder.'

'The traitors were killed, four thousand of them, including all the men of quality. They got what they deserved and their bones lie there still.'

'I would like to see them,' said Brother Thomas, 'especially Lord Lovell's. Does he lie in the churchyard here or at Stoke?'

The captain could not say, but Brother Thomas was at liberty to make his own inquiries. An escort would be provided to guide and assist him. Brother Thomas would have declined the escort. He asked for Gervase, but to no avail. Gervase, the captain said, would not be familiar with the district.

So he took the Roman way to the south-west in the company of one of the captain's men and they were soon at Stoke.

None of the villagers could remember the battle, or none would admit to it. But one man walked with them across the fields to show where it had been fought. There, south of the village, the king's forces had deployed. There, on the high ground beyond, the earl's men had formed into line of battle after climbing from the swampy ground in the loop of the river. There, down that ravine, they had fled back to the ford after charging the royal army and being repulsed. So many of them were trapped and slaughtered there that the villagers still called it Red Gutter and declared that the pink-tinged earth was stained for ever with their blood.

All that remained of the struggle were pits of human bones. Brother Thomas prayed beside them – not only for the fallen, but also that the bones of his prince did not lie among them.

The church stood nearby, with the leper hospital of St Leonard. Here Brother Thomas received his first news of Lord Lovell. The priest did not know what had happened to him after the battle, but he revealed that although Lovell's home was in Oxfordshire he had been lord of the manor of Stoke.

'Did he then lead the army here deliberately?' Brother Thomas asked.

'Who can say? It certainly made a surprising march. He may have been seeking to recruit men from his own estates.'

An idea occurred to Brother Thomas and he insisted on talking to the master of the lepers, although it meant shouting across the churchyard wall. The man would not show his face, and Brother Thomas's throat choked with pity at his suffering and that of Brother Henry which it recalled.

'Fifty years ago,' he shouted, 'your lord was Francis Lovell.'

'He forfeited the estates with his life.'

'When the battle was over there would have been fugitives seeking to save their lives in hiding. Did some take refuge in the hospital?'

'They would not have been admitted.'

'Lord Lovell himself would not have been refused

admission, nor one of his personal retinue. Have you anyone within who came at that time?'

'We have records of all admissions. None came from the battle, nor is there any alive now from that date. Here we are more than half-way to the next world. The Lord calls us early, praise be.'

'Praise be,' Brother Thomas responded. He could not have borne the thought of his handsome prince stricken with leprosy.

Back in Newark he pursued his inquiries with the parish priest, who sharply sent the captain's man about his business before he would speak. He embraced Brother Thomas and confessed himself, as he did not flinch from declaring publicly in his pulpit, an adherent of the Old Faith. They sat closeted in his vestry like conspirators.

'What news?' he demanded to be told. 'When will your abbot and his peers raise the standard of Christ?'

'I pray God he will do so as soon as I return to Croyland.'

Brother Thomas told him of his mission and the priest told him of the good tidings which reached him every day from the north. But about the battle he had no information except for what was common knowledge.

The hero, it was said, had been Martin Swartz, the leader of the Germans, who fought like a lion. John, earl of Lincoln, the nephew of kings, refused to retreat and had stood his ground until he was cut down. The pretender had shown cowardice and fled at the first reverse. Francis Lovell had been wounded and had not stood his ground with Captain Swartz and the earl. He had fled and been drowned in attempting to swim the river to safety. No report of the battle mentioned a boy of fourteen in Lord Lovell's company.

17

Two weeks of investigation in the neighbourhood yielded nothing more. The castle, town and parish records were all put at Brother Thomas's disposal and he studied them in mounting desperation. He even took to wandering through the town and out towards Stoke speaking at random to any man or woman more than fifty years of age. At first for his pains, he heard only repetitions of the story that Lovell had been wounded, had fled and disappeared in the river. Then after a few days he became known as 'the mad monk' and exciting stories were told to him – tales which he discovered were invented to humour him.

One evening, in his quarters above the guardroom in the gatehouse of the castle, he admitted to himself that there was nothing more to be learned in Newark. The report of Lovell's death was not conclusive, but since he had never been heard of again it would be wise to presume it. What then of the prince?

If the boy had fought in the battle, had he been killed? If so, surely his body would have been identified? Henry Tudor took pains in all matters of consequence. He was careful to keep himself informed about his enemies. The battlefield would have been well searched for corpses of note. Could the prince in his disguise have been overlooked? Would his handsome Plantagenet face not have betrayed him? Of the two bodies Henry Tudor had most longed to be shown since he seized the throne, this was one. Assuredly his men would have had instructions to search particularly for any corpse resembling one of the missing princelings.

Very well then, Brother Thomas told himself, he must suppose that the boy had survived. That would explain why Lord Lovell, a man of proven courage, had failed to stand his ground. He had a more binding obligation: to ensure the escape of his precious charge. In crossing the river he himself had drowned. That left the boy alone, unknown to any man except as an unimportant page who had lost one master at Bosworth and another here at Stoke.

If his body were not on the field he must have succeeded in swimming to the far bank, putting the river between himself and his enemies. Back on the north side, where would he go? Hardly to Ireland again. Now that the expedition had failed, that would be as unsafe as England.

Flanders was the answer. Throughout the war the staunchest aid for the house of York had come from there. A daughter of the great duke of York, sister to King Edward and King Richard, had married the duke of Burgundy who ruled across the Channel in Flanders. First as duchess, then as dowager duchess, she had provided a refuge and rallying point for her family in times of disaster. It was she who had paid Martin Swartz and his mercenaries to come to Stoke. Her father and brothers were all dead, but Margaret of York and Burgundy fought on.

According to Robert Skelton's story, the young prince had already spent two years in Flanders, without, however, making himself known to his aunt. He might even have returned there with Lovell after Bosworth and met her in secret. Whatever the circumstances of their acquaintance, the boy must have been advised by Lovell to go to her if the battle were lost.

Suppose then that he had smuggled himself aboard a ship, from the Humber say, to the Low Countries? What next? Had he arrived safely or had he been shipwrecked? If he arrived, why was the fact not announced to the world? The dowager duchess would have trumpeted the news all over

Europe and demanded recognition for her nephew as King Richard IV of England.

Brother Thomas surrendered to despondency. Newark had told him nothing. The boy had disappeared from a darkened room in Leicester and all Brother Thomas's ingenuity could not hit on a theory which would keep him plausibly alive thereafter.

Next morning he announced his departure and asked for his servant and horses. They had kept Gervase from him since his arrival, continuing to supply one of the garrison in his place so that every inquiry could be witnessed and reported.

The captain was in council and not to be disturbed, but he sent his permission. The only formality took place at the drawbridge, which the lieutenant of the guard would not lower until he knew their destination.

'Have you finished meddling with the dead, brother, or are you going on to York to try your luck there?'

'What is it to you?' asked Brother Thomas.

'We must have a record of your destination. It is a regulation.'

'We are returning to Croyland,' said Gervase. 'Can you not see that the brother is ill? Now let us pass.'

'To Croyland.' The lieutenant nodded.

'No,' said Brother Thomas on an impulse. 'My servant is mistaken.'

Until Gervase spoke he had intended to return. His soul pined for the company of the brethren, the sound of plain-chant in his own church, the parchments and vellums in his own library, his own cell whose walls kept out the world. But the shame of failure held him back. He could not face the abbot yet.

York tempted him, the birthplace of Constantine, where

the emperor had been converted to the Faith and made Christianity the religion of his empire. To a man of God York stood second only to Canterbury, to an historian second only to London. To an adherent of the house of York it stood pre-eminent, beckoning.

Resolutely he put temptation aside. Chancellor Rayne had offered him the use of the bishop's library and muniment room at Lincoln. They lay but a few miles ahead. He would make his last effort there, digging blindly like a mole. Once in their burrow, moles could see, and perhaps God would open his eyes.

'We are going to Lincoln,' he said: 'pilgrims to the shrine of St Hugh. We shall be praying that the godless may turn from their wickedness and come again into the arms of Christ and the bosom of His Church. Put that in your records if you please.'

'I have been worried for you, brother,' said Gervase as they rode away to the music of the lieutenant's abuse. 'Did they ill-treat you that first night?'

'God protected me, as I trust He did you, my friend.'

'Matters went easily enough from the second day on.'

'I would never have forgiven myself otherwise. You warned me to keep away from the castle. The captain is a man who has hardened his soul against the Church, but God moved him in our cause.'

'After Master Cromwell's men had spoken to him.'

'Is that what saved me from hanging?' The light of revelation descended on Brother Thomas.

'I saw the villains arrive early in the morning. You should thank God that Master Cromwell does not want you hung. Not yet.'

The hooves of their horses clattered on the wooden planks of the bridge. Half-way across, Brother Thomas stopped to look back at the stone curtain of the castle rising from the river. Only by screwing up his eyes could he make out the little grille of the dungeon at the bottom. Here in mid-Trent he felt poised between the south, with all the iniquities of London, its conspiracies against the Faith and its lies about the old order, and the north where men of honour chose to live, like Richard III and Robert Aske. Down the road behind him lay knavery and usurpation and sacrilege. Ahead lay honesty, steadfastness and the true Faith.

'Come brother,' Gervase urged him. 'This is no place for dreaming. You will have us arrested for spying.'

They were being jostled by other horsemen, cursed by carters and stared at by all. The sentries at either end of the bridge and on the castle ramparts had them under observation.

After peering quickly down for a glimpse of some Lovell struggling to keep his head above the water, Brother Thomas turned back to the town and rode out of Newark by the north gate.

Along the Fosse Way he endured the dust in silence until a miracle jogged him from his thoughts. Ahead in distant outline arose the supreme manifestation of man's devotion to God. In France and Italy they had fine abbeys and cathedrals but none so fine as this, or so he had been taught.

It stood on a ridge overlooking the plains to south and west. At first it loomed grey and misty, like a vision of some vast city, a new Jerusalem hovering between Heaven and earth, its towers and walls an indistinguishable mass, the soaring spires triumphant.

As they drew nearer and Brother Thomas's poor eyes could serve him better, the colour of the stone grew lighter and the three towers became separate and distinct. Like the body-servants of a sovereign lord, pinnacles and pennants clustered round the central spire – the tallest in all the realm, dwarfing even that of St Paul in the capital – thrusting towards God and celebrating His majesty with upward striving.

Nearer still, when the details of the towers became distinguishable, he could see how the gracefulness was accomplished. Croyland's three towers stood solid and, he prayed God, eternal. Here at Lincoln the central tower had been decorated with a wealth of tracery, and the strength of its two western sentinels softened with window lights and parapets.

Such was the legacy of Hugh of Avalon, a humble monk of the Charterhouse whom the first of the Plantagenets had brought to England. Brother Thomas slipped from the saddle to beg the saint for another miracle on behalf of another Plantagenet.

18

An hour later, after eating and resting by the wayside, they entered the city through the main gate. On the bridge at the foot of the steep street leading up to the cathedral Brother Thomas dismounted again and handed the reins to Gervase.

Jostled this time by tradesmen and housewives, and by pilgrims who had come to Lincoln to seek favours for body or soul, he proceeded up the crowded way on his knees. It took him more than two hours to reach the Exchequer Gate at the top, and all the time children were jeering at him and curs permitted to sniff him out of curiosity.

If piety be out of place at Lincoln, he thought sadly as he dusted his knees and scrambled stiffly to his feet, then was the age of faith gone indeed. Absorbed in his devotions he had not heeded the jibes, but now they struck him like so many stave-blows. Could it be true that Master Cromwell and the captain at Newark embodied the spirit of the times? Did common people share the disbelief of the learned doctor at Leicester and regard Brother Thomas and all like him as the misguided purveyors of some superstitious mummery left over from another age? Was the cathedral no longer a living witness but the monument to a dead faith? Would there never again be other St Hughs to build other Lincolns?

Inside the close he became calmer and reassured. The visitors here were properly reverential, awed by the grandeur of the western face at close quarters. They stood in knots before the towering central arcade of stone, identifying the statues and the Bible stories carved in figures on the frieze.

Inside the building his wonder grew. Before he emerged from the fens those few short months ago he could not have imagined any glory more splendid than that of his own church and its fenland sisters at Thorney and Ramsey and Peterborough, at Sawtrey and Spalding. The cathedral of St Paul had opened his eyes, but Lincoln was surely unsurpassable.

The sublimeness of the vaulting, the rose windows in the transepts, the figures carved on the stalls – there was more than enough beauty before ever he reached the Angel Choir. There a throng of pilgrims and votaries were filing past the body of the saint, which was entombed in everlasting marble encrusted with precious metals and sparkling gems. In some eyes he detected greed and envy at the sight of such riches, but most were filled with pious wonder, lips moving in the reverence of heartfelt prayer.

As he moved round the ambulatory towards the blaze of candlelight surrounding the shrine, his attention was caught by an inscription and all joy left him. Here in this holy of holies lay buried the mortal remains of a loose woman. He bit his lip but could not restrain a spasm of anger.

In St Paul's John of Gaunt, founder of the royal house of Lancaster, had lain beside his wife Blanche. Here was the paramour for whom he had neglected her. Here was the mother of the bastard brood of Beauforts, who had become dukes of Somerset and the main props of their feeble cousin Henry VI. Margaret Beaufort had been Henry Tudor's mother. It was through her he claimed the crown and it was her second husband who had deserted Richard at Bosworth to put her son on the throne.

Without the woman here commemorated there would have been no war between York and Lancaster, no Henry VII, no Henry VIII, no Act of Supremacy, no dissolution of God's abbeys. Brother Thomas's head throbbed. His knees refused to bend in prayer for her soul. In attempting to picture her, nothing came to his mind except the last sight he would have wished for in such a context: the sweet face of Margaret Skelton. He became dizzy, reeled and fell.

It was dark when he recovered consciousness. He lay in a narrow space which could only be his tomb. That witch had put a spell upon him.

'Where am I?' he cried.

Something stirred on the floor beside him. An arm raised his head and a flask of water was put to his lips.

'You are feverish again, brother,' came Gervase's reassuring voice. 'Go back to sleep and rest until morning.'

'First tell me where we are. Are we prisoners of Chancellor Rayne? Is the bishop holding us at the king's command?'

'You imagine too much. The chancellor is in London, and so is the bishop. Father Paul, the librarian, was warned that you might come and he is looking after you. We are in an alcove off the library.'

Brother Thomas closed his eyes. How often at Croyland had he dreamed of visiting other libraries, above all the one at Lincoln! He could smell the leather now and welcomed the dust in his nostrils.

In the morning Father Paul came, bent with age and study. He was solicitous and eager to greet a fellow scholar and librarian. At the first sight of him Brother Thomas shrugged aside his illness and declared himself well enough, in spite of Gervase's grumbling, to get up and fondle the treasures around him.

Father Paul showed them to him one by one, allowing him to turn the pages of William the Norman's survey of England and unroll for himself a copy of Magna Carta from which hung the Great Seal of King John, who had died at the castle at Newark – poisoned, so Father Paul assured him, by lampreys brought too far from the king's native Gascony. Father Paul had a grudge against King John, who should have been buried at Lincoln, where they lacked the body of a king, even a bad one. Instead John had elected to be buried far away at Worcester because it had two saints and he needed one on either side to assist him into Paradise.

'You may browse here to your heart's content,' he said, 'till Michaelmas or Christmas if you so desire.'

The offer was balm to his spirit, and Brother Thomas showed his appreciation by browsing so deep that a week passed before he asked about the battle at Stoke.

'A skirmish, nothing more.' Father Paul's voice carried the ring of certainty across the low-roofed library, which was slowly darkening with the onset of evening.

'But many men were killed. It marked the climax of more than thirty years of war.'

Father Paul smiled. 'The bickerings between Lancaster and York hardly amounted to that. In all those years all the campaigns put together did not last for more than three months. That is not war as it is known in the rest of Europe. Tell me which towns were sacked. Give me the name of a single one which suffered even the privations of a siege.'

Brother Thomas could not, but he recalled how after the battle at Wakefield Croyland had hidden its treasures, guarded its gates, fortified its dykes and canals with stakes and blocked the surrounding causeways with tree trunks.

'Queen Margaret did damage, I grant you – there was some unpleasantness in Ludlow and pillaging in the countryside. But that was all. And how few were engaged in the struggle! It was a family feud, not a war, and Lancaster and York were as alike as cheese and chalk. What did it matter which side won those petty scuffles at St Alban's or Towton, Bosworth or Stoke? England suffered from lawlessness, not war. They should have composed their quarrels like men, not beasts. As if it mattered a solitary groat which of them wore the crown!'

'What are you saying, father? If York had won, the old order would have prevailed. Our Church would not be threatened. Men would respect God again.'

'Fiddlesticks! Our Church is threatened because the king must have money and there is nowhere else for him to get it. It would be the same with any other king.'

'Would any other king have put aside his lawful wife to wed a whore? Would any other king have elevated himself above His Holiness and declared himself next to Christ here on earth? Would any other king have committed wholesale sacrilege by robbing God?'

'I believe that the Church should not have so much wealth, that it should be shared among all men.' It was strange to hear Father Paul, so earnest and devout, echoing the words of the godless captain at Newark. 'I believe that any king today would plunder our monasteries and shrines, although who can say what methods he might employ?'

'I can think of a king whose actions would refute your beliefs utterly.'

'Of whom do you speak?'

'Of the heir to the Yorkist claim. I believe he was at Stoke.'

'If you believe in him you believe in a dead man. He served his time in the royal household as a turnspit, later promoted to a falconer. But he is dead now. The king told the Irish they would be crowning apes next.'

'I do not refer to Lambert Simnel,' said Brother Thomas angrily. 'I refer to Richard, duke of York, King Edward IV's younger son. He was not killed by his uncle, as those who wish to cloak the truth would have us believe.'

Father Paul nodded. 'I know it well.'

'You know it! Do you know then that he survived Bosworth?'

'I know that too.'

Brother Thomas was incredulous. 'You must know then that he was at the battle near Newark.'

Again Father Paul amazed him, but this time by saying quietly: 'If he was, I know that he did not die there.'

19

They argued through the night by the light of one thick candle. The low beams, the shelves, the desks, the stout chained volumes flickered in and out of the shadows. So did Father Paul's face.

It was a relief to Brother Thomas to converse with another historian on the subject of his mission, but every word spoken in that high precise voice carried the conviction of an absolute certainty with which he could not but disagree.

'The undoubted fact that Lambert Simnel was a false pretender,' said Father Paul, 'does not necessarily invalidate the claims of other pretenders, as King Henry VII chose to suggest. You will no doubt recall others.'

'Perkin Warbeck claimed to be Richard, duke of York.'

'And justly. I have made a prolonged investigation into the evidence and am satisfied that Warbeck was in truth the younger of the princes, as he claimed to be. His knowledge of his boyhood is conclusive proof, his account of his escape is convincing. His brother Edward had been proclaimed king and could not be allowed to live, but he was less important. There was no reason why he should not have been permitted to slip away on the promise of remaining in obscurity so long as his uncle and his uncle's heirs reigned. Bosworth absolved him from his vow.'

'Is this the sole cause of your belief that the young Richard of York survived Bosworth and Stoke? Is it because you have identified him with Warbeck, and for no other reason?'

'It is, and that is reason enough, I do assure you.'

'I too have studied Warbeck's story,' Brother Thomas replied. 'At Croyland we have a printed copy of his confession. He confessed himself the son of a merchant in Tournai named Osbeck.'

'If you or I had been Henry Tudor's prisoner we too would have obliged him by confessing to be the son of any merchant he cared to name. Martyrs to the truth are no more numerous than martyrs to the Faith. According to another account he was the son of his supposed aunt, the Duchess Margaret of Burgundy – the fruit of an illicit union with the bishop of Cambrai, if you please. Such tales are legion.'

'If he was truly Richard, why did he first impersonate Clarence's son, the young earl of Warwick, and then King Richard's bastard son, and only in the end, when it became known that those two were in Henry's hands, declare himself Richard of York?'

'These were the manoeuvrings of his advisers. Maybe the Yorkist party wished to establish the whereabouts of Warwick and King Richard's bastard and chose that means of forcing the king's hand. When he revealed his true identity, consider how many accepted his claim as genuine.' As he warmed to his argument, the gleam of the candlelight reflected in Father Paul's eye reminded Brother Thomas of the fire in Robert Aske's.

'The Duchess Margaret's acceptance is no evidence. She accepted Simnel too. She would recognise any Yorkist claimant if it would help unseat Henry Tudor from her family's throne.'

'What of her son-in-law the Archduke Philip? What of his father, the Emperor? They both accepted the claim.'

'At her insistence and from the same motives. They had no love for King Henry.'

'Very well. How about King Charles of France? He rarely found himself in agreement with the Emperor, yet he agreed in this. So too did the king of Denmark and the duke of Saxony.'

'All were enemies of England.'

'Like the king of Scotland? I grant you that in his case. But he not only recognised the claim, he gave the claimant his cousin to marry. Does that not argue sincere belief?'

Brother Thomas wrinkled his brow, determined not to be

convinced, and Father Paul, taking the determination for doubt, pressed on with his litany of Warbeck's supporters.

'Let us come now to England and consider who accepted him here in his own country. They declared themselves in secret, of course, but the king sent spies, pretending to be Yorkist agents, to Flanders. They discovered and reported some of the names. Have you read them, brother?'

'Some,' Brother Thomas admitted.

'The dean of St Paul's, the provincial of the Dominicans, the prior of Langley. These were not men to surrender their sworn allegiance lightly or follow behind some jumped-up jackanapes.'

'They were men of wisdom and courage and foresight. They recognised the anti-Christ in Henry Tudor sooner than others. That is all.'

'You are a hard man to persuade,' Father Paul complained. 'Here we have a handsome lad of the right age who looked like a Plantagenet and behaved like one. I cannot believe that a false claimant could have plagued the king with such a following and for so many years, first in Flanders, then in Ireland, then in Scotland – accepted in every country as a true sprig of York. When he landed in Cornwall and proclaimed himself Richard IV three thousand men joined his standard immediately.'

Brother Thomas ruminated on them. Naked men like Simnel's Irish: savages bribed to fight with offers of food and promises of reward. They had not the strength to capture Exeter. At Taunton they deserted him. That did not suggest staunchness of faith in their leader's claim.

'According to some reports,' he said, 'Warbeck was far from handsome and afflicted in one eye. Would the king have exhibited him to the citizens of London all the way along Cheapside and up Cornhill if he had resembled a Plantagenet? I fear he made a sorry spectacle.'

'Yet the king killed him and kept Simnel alive. He killed him with Warwick, an undoubted Plantagenet, at the urging of the king of Spain, who demanded the despatch of rival claimants before he would allow his daughter to marry the king's son.'

'Another pretender was hanged at the same time – poor Ralph Wulford – but no one ever believed him to be a real Plantagenet.'

The debate continued, broken from time to time by research into the volumes around them and the citing of authorities, until Father Paul rose and stretched himself and took the candle.

'Come, my tongue is tired. I see that your objection to admitting Warbeck's claim is insuperable. Warbeck is dead and you are bent on finding Richard of York alive. We will pray together in amity for God to enlighten you.'

Inside the cathedral the nave and transepts stood dark and silent in reverence, but behind the high altar the shrine of St Hugh still blazed and glittered in a forest of candlelight. The saint was worshipped continuously and even at this hour before dawn there was little enough room for Brother Thomas to prostrate himself.

'Blessed and beloved St Hugh,' he whispered, 'intercede with God for me, I beseech you. You who came to England with Henry Curtmantle, help me, I pray you from the depths of my most unworthy being, help me to discover where the one I seek lies hid, the last of Curtmantle's line whom, we both of us know full well, never went by the name of Perkin Warbeck. Let him be prised from his hiding place and set on the throne of this realm for the salvation of the one and indivisible Church of Christ our Saviour. I ask this in the name of all God's unworthy servants here below, who in this wicked age bear continuing witness to His eternal glory and daily expect the fires of martyrdom.'

He kissed the floor where a hundred pilgrims' feet had trodden that very night, and begged the saint for a sign. He begged and begged again, drumming his bare toes against the flagstones, until Father Paul left for bed and the candles dimmed in rays of sunrise which struck the rich reds of the window above him and seemed to smear the shrine with stains of blood. They coloured the tomb beside him too – where the good Bishop Russell lay at rest – but John of Gaunt's paramour slept in impenetrable shadow.

Two more weeks in the library uncovered nothing to advance his researches, and the saint, appealed to every night, remained unresponsive. Brother Thomas grew melancholy. He longed for Croyland and his own chronicles and records, but could not bring himself to leave. Yet it had to be. Lincoln was alien. Father Paul, for all his sweetness, was in error. St Hugh might fail a supplicant from distant Croyland, but – when he returned where he belonged – St Guthlac would not fail him. That was his last hope. So when at length Father Paul and Gervase conspired together and insisted on his going, he found no strength to resist them.

On the journey the mutterings of England's discontent sounded louder and more insistent in his ears. Common men were surly with their betters. The bishop was cursed in the streets of Lincoln itself, and at Grantham the parish priest roundly condemned him for a heretic.

'But he is your father in God,' Brother Thomas protested, shocked. They had climbed the church tower and stood looking out across the countryside, secure from the king's or bishop's spies. His native Holland beckoned, green and yellow beneath the August sun.

'The commons will have the bishop's head if he ventures from London. They know him for the king's confessor that he was. They know that he is helping to destroy the monasteries, which he pretends to protect.'

'And while he is away it seems that the chancellor does his work ably enough.'

'Chancellor Rayne,' said the priest, 'is the Devil incarnate. Men blame him for more than half the bishop's misdeeds. Last month I mentioned the Pope in a sermon. It was reported and he fined me five shillings for not saying the bishop of Rome.'

Brother Thomas leaned forward and looked down on the churchyard immediately below. 'Dear God,' he murmured, and the sin of self-destruction crossed his mind.

'All my prayer-books have been confiscated because, in hope of better times, I pinned paper over the Pope's name instead of erasing it. My parishioners are saying that Chancellor Rayne had better not ride here again or the Devil will claim his own.'

They descended from the tower and Brother Thomas set out on the last stage of his long journey with the priest's final words echoing in his ears. God is not mocked. Not for long. Vengeance is His, as the abbot had said. He will repay.

20

Croyland seemed smaller. The village and the towers of the abbey church had shrunk.

From the hump of the three-legged bridge Brother Thomas waved his hand like a returning warrior and broke into song, praising God for all to hear. His only desire now was to lay himself body and soul at the feet of his abbot, to confess his failure, to ask for absolution from his sins, the sin of pride above all, and to subject himself to total obedience and the utmost rigours of discipline. He had wandered and never again would he stray from the flock. His home and heart were here.

The brethren welcomed his return and he saluted them all in brotherly love. In the abbot's parlour the prior embraced him as though he had come back from the dead. But the abbot himself was absent and the void in Brother Thomas's heart remained unfilled, the ache of longing unquenched.

'Speak to no one of your mission till his lordship returns,' the prior enjoined. 'Those were his strict commands. I will send to London to tell him of your return and he will inform the chancellor and Master Aske in accordance with what was agreed. Until they come, keep yourself solitary or I shall be unable to restrain myself from questioning you. All the world is in turmoil outside, if reports be true, and our hopes rest on you.'

The news at home was that God had called his dearest friend. While Brother Thomas had been venturing into the world Brother Henry had slipped out of it altogether. A man of steadfast vocation, he had gladly obeyed God's every summons: into the order, to the leper house, and finally to God Himself.

The disease had bitten deep soon after Brother Thomas left for London. To the end, the prior was proud to state, Brother Henry had not neglected the holy offices. On becoming master of the lepers he had naturally ceased attending services with the rest of the community, but he joined their communion from outside, standing or kneeling at the leper's squint through which he could see the high altar. There he continued to attend, on the hottest of days and coldest of nights, but if any of the brethren attempted to speak to him afterwards he would melt away with a smile on his bleached face and a blessing on his disfigured lips.

On Sundays and saints' days he brought his flock with him, a sight to frighten the dead from their graves. They came to the squint, the abandoned and accursed, and knelt in the dirt to thank God for His blessings. Brother Henry could do nothing for their bodies apart from the provision of food and shelter, but their souls were firmly in his safe keeping.

The prior's words filled Brother Thomas with fresh determination. The Brother Henrys of England must be preserved. Did the king and his vicar-general ever spare a thought for them when they spread their tales of monkish immorality? In coveting the riches of shrines and reliquaries what care had they for lepers? He should have asked the drunken soldiery in the banqueting hall at Newark: When my abbey is levelled to the ground and I and my brethren dispersed, which one of you will take over the leper house from my friend, Brother Henry? That would have shown their bravery and bragging for what it really was. Campaigns in Scotland and Spain were one thing, leprosy another. Without monasteries lepers would have to take to the forest like outlaws. If he could save the monasteries he would save the lepers too and be worthy of his dead brother, a saint whom he had had the temerity to expose as a thief.

Alone in the church afterwards he thanked God for his safe return and prayed for Brother Henry's soul, but his mind kept straying into the labyrinth of his investigations. His deduction that the princes had not been murdered in the Tower had proved correct. He had resurrected the young Richard and kept the boy alive for four more years than history allowed him. That was the sum of his achievement.

Despite Father Paul's persuasiveness he felt more and more convinced that Perkin Warbeck was truly an impostor. Warbeck had come from a Flemish family who lived in Tournai. He must have met Richard during the prince's secret sojourn there and learned his identity. If Richard had confided in him he could have discovered enough to make the imposture plausible, and to the Yorkists plausibility was all that mattered in advancing their cause. If Warbeck had been genuine he could have established his authenticity beyond doubt by telling his adventures truthfully and in detail. Instead of the unlikely story that his brother's murderers allowed him to escape out of the kindness of their murderous hearts, he would have told of the flight to sanctuary, of the boat capsizing, of his return to England, the charge at Bosworth, the flight to Ireland and his return – as return he surely did – to disaster at Stoke.

While Brother Thomas was kneeling at St Guthlac's tomb, he suddenly sensed what he had besought in vain from St Hugh at Lincoln. Someone was interceding for him at the throne of Truth. It could only be the saint himself.

Throughout the night he knelt, his mind concentrated, his body wrapped in the ecstasy of the saint's benevolence. His physical being drifted away from him; he could feel it go, and with it went his identity. He stood in spirit beside the river Trent, a boy of fourteen with a sword in his hand. All around him lay the bleeding bodies of his ill-armed supporters, slaughtered by the heavily-armoured horsemen of the traitor John de Vere.

Should he flee or should he stand and be cut down like those other Yorkist Richards, his grandfather and his uncle, rashly outnumbered yet fearless in the circle of the enemy's steel?

Plantagenets did not flee, but this one must have. In his

vulturous pickings over the fields at Stoke Henry Tudor would not have missed the much-sought body. Any corpse resembling one of the lost princes would certainly have been exhibited to prove his death and the falseness of pretenders' claims.

Beside the boy stood the most loyal surviving servant of the house of York – Francis, Lord Lovell. Although not a member of the king's council, which had been headed by Bishop Russell of Lincoln, this man had been closer to the boy's uncle, King Richard, than any other adviser. He had been the king's chamberlain, performing the role of trusted friend which Lord Hastings had performed for Edward IV. He and King Richard had been brought up together as young squires in the household of the king-making Warwick. To him, riding at the king's right hand, had fallen the duty of rescuing the runaway prince at Bosworth. He had succeeded and kept his charge unharmed for two perilous years – only to bring him back to the threshold of death.

This was a man the young Richard would obey, and to Lovell the life of the prince would be far more precious than his own. From inside the boy's body Brother Thomas could feel the warmth of the protective arm round his shoulders as they retreated down Red Gutter towards the river, covered by the last of their retainers and the gallant Germans.

'Swim, boy,' he could hear Lovell saying. 'Swim while I hold them off.'

'Never!'

To his embarrassment Brother Thomas spoke the word aloud. It soared to the vaulting of the chancel and echoed diminuendo down the long tunnel of the nave.

'Never!' he repeated in a whisper, thanking God that the church was empty. 'I will stay and die at your side.'

'Go! I command you. In the name of your forebears.'

'I cannot leave you, Lovell,' Brother Thomas snivelled and wiped his nose with his sleeve.

'My lord, my sovereign liege, you must. Your uncle placed you in my charge. It is your bounden duty to obey my command. Go! Go at once! God willing, I will follow you.'

Brother Thomas felt the waters of the Trent closing over his head. He rose to the surface and an arrow hissed into the water not a yard away. The river was wide and his armour encumbered him, but at last he struggled out on the far bank. Not until then did Lovell abandon the fight, and it was too late. A sword stroke cut his leg to the bone. He fell on one knee and the enemy closed in for the kill. His own men fought back and dragged him to the water's edge. He half plunged, half collapsed into the river and the current carried him away, never to be seen again.

A tear fell on the saint's tomb. In his role as prince, seeing what had happened, Brother Thomas grew numb in a sweat of fear. He was alone in the world. Lovell's protecting arm had been swept away. Did anyone else know his identity? His cousin, John of Lincoln, might have been party to the secret, but he had been killed in the first clash of the battle. However parlous his situation, the boy had one remaining protection: his anonymity.

What should he do? Where should he go? The enemy would soon be across the river in pursuit. Reliving the drama after fifty years, Brother Thomas in panic resorted to prayer.

'Blessed St Guthlac, you were born a nobleman and fought as a soldier before God called you. In your lifetime men sought you from all over England and you gave them counsel freely. You told Ethelbald of Mercia how to be king. Since your death you have worked many miracles. Intercede with God for me and ask Him where my prince went and where he is to be found now, the prince who is rightfully king and will rule in accordance with God's laws.'

He was so tired that he could hardly keep awake, but a voice revived him.

'I bring you a message from God, brother. Have confidence in the gifts He bestowed on you. Search no more. Your quest is ended.'

Brother Thomas scrambled to his feet and looked about him. No one else was in the church and he did not recognise the voice, which was rough and scornful. It could only be the saint speaking to him, rebuking him.

'All my confidence is in God. I have none in my own poor abilities. I act only in humility and obedience to the will of my superiors.'

The saint laughed. Brother Thomas could see him now. He was floating above the high altar, dressed in armour, brandishing his sword.

'Who are you deceiving? If you are humble, be less humble. If you are obedient, be less obedient.' Thus the vision admonished him.

'What will the abbot say?'

The saint laughed again, a different laugh this time, and faded from sight. Brother Thomas hurried round the church from side to side and end to end, calling on the apparition to reappear. He pleaded. He shouted. He sobbed. He stumbled and fell. Gradually he calmed himself.

With calmness came doubt. The vision was false. The voice had spoken from within himself. The journey had made him sick and he had imagined it all, or he had communed with Satan in the guise of St Guthlac. Surely none but the Devil would suggest that he be less humble and obedient, he whose humility and obedience were suspect already. If those qualities were truly his, he would have bowed to the abbot's wishes and never undertaken his ill-fated mission.

The more he meditated on it, the more he realised that every word spoken betrayed his own besetting sin of pride. He gloried too much in his intellect. He had good reason, he acknowledged, and caught himself sinning again, basking shamelessly in adulation of his own powers of mind, excusing himself on the grounds that it would be more sinful not to recognise the truth. While he was thus rapt in self-praise, his back turned for the first time on the problem which had exercised him day and night for the past five months, the solution budded and blossomed in his mind.

In the half-light of the coming dawn his eye had fallen on a brass wall-tablet. It commemorated John Russell, lord bishop of Lincoln, a guest of the abbey in the years of our Lord 1486 and 1487. Brother Thomas's wandering gaze was arrested. The purpose of the first visit he knew well. But 1487 – the year of Stoke! How, until the saint directed him, could he have overlooked the second? Or not recognised the awaited sign from St Hugh when the sun's rays illuminated the bishop's tomb at Lincoln?

The cellarer and succentor, coming to prepare for the lauds, prime and mass of a new day, found him in a trance from which he could not be roused, although his eyes were open and staring at them.

The fresh morning air of the cloisters revived him as they carried him to his cell. 'He lives!' he cried.

'Christ lives indeed,' the succentor assured him.

'Not Him,' cried Brother Thomas. 'Not Him!'

Part Four

THE QUARRY

I

When the lord abbot returned to Croyland the prior reported that Brother Thomas had come home, whole in body but sick in mind. His attendance at divine service had grown irregular and when rebuked he had boasted that he was acting under direct instructions from St Guthlac, who (so he unblushingly averred) had appeared to him. According to the succentor he had gone so far as to cast doubt on the divinity of Christ Himself. The prior confessed himself sadly out of his depth.

'That I should live to hear a brother doubt the Son of God and question the value of prayer!'

'How does he occupy his time?' the abbot inquired.

'He locks himself in the library, studying the chronicles and records in secret. He asserts that, as time is short, research must have priority over prayer.'

'Is his conscience not troubled by his disobedience?'

'He says that St Guthlac, though dead, yet speaketh, like St Benedict; that the two saints have discussed the matter and agreed to grant him temporary dispensation from his vow of obedience to the Rule.' The prior, standing obediently before the abbot's chair in the parlour, shuddered at repeating such words.

'What discipline have you prescribed?'

'He appears so wild that I asked the father from the infirmary to examine him and he advised that he should be humoured. He believes that a fever caught when he was travelling abroad may have infected the brain. In the circumstances I thought it best to leave the matter of punishment for your decision, my lord.'

'Does he reveal what he is looking for in his searches or what he has discovered in his travels?'

'Not a word. I have learned from Gervase where he went, but that is all.'

'His journey has not gone unnoticed in London. I have been questioned about it by the bishop. Chancellor Rayne will be with us in a few days to learn what opportunity has transpired for doing mischief to the abbey. I should never have given my consent.'

'If there be a fault it is mine. I pressed your lordship. The incident of Brother Henry and the carp showed wits so sharp that I brought myself to the belief—'

The abbot held up his hand. 'Mine was the authorisation. Mine is the fault.'

'But suppose he has found us a king who will cherish the Old Faith! The people will rise tomorrow. Matters have been stirring here while you have been in London, my lord. The commons in Lincolnshire are calling for resistance to the king's will. They say that they will stand for no more monasteries being dissolved. They say that the king's government favours the rich, that goods cost more each year, that they are losing their common land by enclosure. They ask who will look after the poor and the sick and mend the dykes if there are to be abbeys no more.'

'Tell me what else they say.' The abbot's voice betrayed him. To his joy the prior detected, behind the mask of his lordship's face, a note of involvement and resolution.

'Rumours reach us every day, such rumours that we do not know how to believe them. Our guests bring travellers' tales of the whole country in ferment, of rioting and open defiance in Cumberland and other counties in the north.

Here in our own shire there are prophecies of great events at Michaelmas. The county is plagued by three sets of royal commissioners. One is committing sacrilege on the smaller houses. Another is assessing wealth and collecting taxes. A third has set to work in Bolingbroke, where all the clergy are to be examined to discover whether they are conforming to the new practices. Every day we expect to hear that the whole shire has risen in revolt. May God grant that it happens soon!'

'If men rebel they will be hanged – commons, gentry or clergy.'

'Not if we all rise together, Lincolnshire and the north as one!'

'It will make no difference. At Hexham the canons resisted and they have already been hanged.'

'God rest their souls! Master Aske would have saved them. He is right – we need arming and leading. I would lead them myself.'

'You would lead them to their death.'

'I would lead them to victory or eternal life.'

The abbot eyed the frail, belligerent figure in front of him and wondered whether Brother Thomas's insanity was infectious. 'Your enthusiasm does you credit, father prior,' he said. 'We live in times when the path of duty is hard to recognise. We must pray for guidance. Now will you go and fetch Brother Thomas and we will question him.'

But the prior returned alone, perplexed. Brother Thomas had refused the summons! He sent a message regretting that he could not interrupt his researches. When his conclusions were confirmed, his mission accomplished, then – and not before – would he present himself to his superior. Meanwhile he humbly begged to be excused. The prior, expecting an outburst of abbatical wrath and the ordering of the most severe penance, was disappointed. The abbot said nothing, dismissing him with a gesture.

A week later Brother Thomas attended mass for the first time since the abbot's return. He looked so pale and staring-eyed that the brethren kept their distance for fear of contagion.

Afterwards he obeyed the week-old summons. He entered the abbot's lodgings by the cloister door, climbed the stairs to the parlour, flung open the door and abased himself at the abbot's feet with a half-throttled cry of 'My lord!'

When the abbot raised him to his feet Brother Thomas saw that they were not alone. By the chapel door stood Chancellor Rayne and Master Aske.

'He has the plague,' said the chancellor at the sight of Brother Thomas's face. 'The epidemic in London spreads fast.'

It has not yet spread as far as Croyland, God be praised,' said the abbot.

In time it will devastate the whole kingdom,' said Aske, 'unless measures are taken to prevent it.'

His meaning was plain and the chancellor snorted. 'Speak, brother,' he urged. 'We have come a long distance to hear your findings, and I have urgent business elsewhere.'

'My words are for my lord's ear alone.'

'That was not the bargain we struck. Your mission was undertaken for all of us. There can be no secrets from Master Aske and myself.'

Aske spoke harshly too. 'You have spent long enough on your inquiries. Men have grown impatient for lack of leadership. Already they are assembling in arms, unbidden by any but each other. The commons of Lincolnshire have petitioned the king not to destroy the monasteries. That is a prologue to violence.'

'Has the king yet made his answer?' asked the abbot, while Brother Thomas held his breath in hope.

'He has, and your brother may read it if it will stir him.'

Aske handed a paper across the table and Brother Thomas read the opening sentence aloud. It was all they needed to hear. 'How presumptuous then are ye, the rude commons of one shire, and that one of the most brute and beastly in the realm, to find fault with your Prince.' Brute and beastly – the shire which held such jewels of Almighty God as Lincoln and Croyland!

'His highness does not err,' said the chancellor. 'Men hereabouts are no better than brutes. When I pass through their villages they snarl at me like curs. Even their priests are half-witted and insolent, like so many oxen.'

'They have wit enough to distinguish truth from falsehood,' said Aske. 'It is not their fault if their bishop and his servants are heretics.'

Aske's hand rested on the hilt of his sword. The chancellor clenched his mutton fists in rage. The abbot had taken his seat at the head of the table as though conducting the routine of abbey business. He might have been preparing to arbitrate between two unruly tenants at blows over fishing or pasturage rights. Their wills were strong but his prevailed. After a tense moment of hesitation they joined him peacefully at the table.

'Come now,' said the chancellor, 'I am on my way to Bolingbroke to conduct an inquiry into the loyalty of Master Aske's friends among the secular clerics. I cannot suffer delay.'

'I will not speak,' Brother Thomas declared passionately, 'save with my lord's consent.'

'Then give it, my lord abbot. You are sworn to it and have nothing, I warrant, to fear from the truth.'

'The truth is not to be feared,' Brother Thomas replied. 'What is to be feared is the disclosure of truth to the wicked.'

'We are all sinners,' said Aske. 'Am I the one the brother fears?'

'You are a good man, Robert Aske,' said the abbot, 'but it may be better for the truth to be kept from you. Your reward will be in Heaven.'

'Not on earth – is that what you mean to tell me?'

Instead of replying the abbot turned to the chancellor, who was grinding his gums and demanding whether it was he whom the brother accused of wickedness.

'Yes,' said Brother Thomas, wearing his most innocent expression of humility.

'You presume too far. If I were your abbot you would have such punishment as would make you rue that tongue of yours. What have you been up to, poking and prying about the king's dominions with treachery in your black heart? How is it that an abbey can house such a traitor? Croyland itself will be dishonoured when I have this meddling renegade returned to the Tower and despatched to Tyburn.'

'I poked and pried in compliance with your wishes. I took you for a Christian and all the time you were in league with the anti-Christ Cromwell, who set spies on my heels.' There was both reproach and sorrow in Brother Thomas's voice.

'Is this true?' Aske was on his feet, hand on sword once more.

'Sit down,' the abbot ordered. 'You know that it is true. You have known from the beginning where the chancellor stood. Let us spare him the sin of denying it.'

'I do deny it,' said the chancellor. Like Brother Thomas he was trembling, partly from anger, partly from fear. 'If there were such men the bishop ordered them for the brother's protection.'

'We could send and ask them,' said the abbot. 'Gervase has told me of them. They arrived here after the brother and are still in the village. Shall we interrogate them now? What do you say, chancellor?'

'I say that the brother should speak first. You gave your word to it.'

'If you insist I cannot but agree. My word was given, as you say.'

'I refuse,' said Brother Thomas. 'I gave no word. I will not obey.'

'You forget your vows,' the abbot told him. 'There has been sufficient disobedience already.'

Aske's single burning eye examined Brother Thomas, penetrating to his soul. 'He will not speak because he is too proud to confess his failure.'

'That is not so.'

Brother Thomas was stung into the admission before he could stop himself. Instantly Aske's hand gripped his arm. 'So you have found me a king?'

'Yes,' Brother Thomas confessed, 'I have discovered the true king of England.' And he prayed that in his moment of triumph God would strike him dead.

2

At the abbot's solemn insistence he told them of his journey to London, his visit to Bermondsey and his return to the Tower. In his account of Fotheringhay he was reticent about the name of Skelton, but the chancellor dragged it from him. He could only console himself that the spies would already have reported it.

Between Fotheringhay and Leicester they ate. An abbot's meal of meat and wine was served, with best white bread from the abbey bakery and fruit from the abbey orchards. The visitors ate with an appetite, the abbot frugally and Brother Thomas not a morsel.

Afterwards he described his expedition to Bosworth and the old physician's tale, then his visits to Newark and Stoke and Lincoln, and so home again.

'That is not all.' The chancellor's pig eyes were circles of suspicion. 'You have established that the younger of the two princes was not killed, that he was alive two years after his brother's death and is not even now known to be dead. That is not discovering a king. Have you found him or have you not? I want no monkish trickery. Answer me straight and remember that God will take note of your words.'

He spoke like an inquisitor, using the voice he would use to interrogate the backsliding clergy of Lincolnshire who were sinning by offering prayers from the pulpit for the Pope and cardinals.

'The brother has already announced his success,' said the abbot. 'He will speak when he is ready.'

'I do not claim to have found the king unaided. On my return I confessed my failure to St Guthlac, who led me to the truth. He appeared to me. He stood above the high altar wearing the armour of God.'

'Are you sure it was he?' asked the abbot. 'The saint put off his armour when he gave his life to the service of God. If he chose to make a miraculous reappearance it would be as a man of peace.'

'It was he,' said Brother Thomas stubbornly, 'and in

armour. He held the sword from the wall behind you – unsheathed.'

'I believe you,' said Aske. 'God has chosen you to receive and communicate to us a message from Above – a signal for action.'

'Rubbish,' said the chancellor. 'You believe what it suits you to believe, Master Aske. Can you not see that the hardships of his excursion have softened the wretched brother's wits? A saint would not appear to such as him.'

'Then leave us,' said Aske, 'and let me alone hear where the saint has led him.'

The chancellor did not budge. The abbot, his consent already given, had withdrawn, it seemed, to brood on Brother Thomas's vision, and did not urge him to proceed. It was Robert Aske who begged and coaxed him into speech.

'If Richard of York was at Stoke and survived the battle, where would he have gone?' said Brother Thomas. 'That was the question which occupied my mind for several weeks. At first I concluded that he must have escaped abroad – to Scotland or France or Flanders, or back to Ireland whence he had come. But then I realised that anywhere among the enemies of Henry Tudor he would have been publicly proclaimed as king of England. If they so eagerly supported impostors like Simnel and Warbeck, imagine the fervour of their welcome for a claimant who could not be doubted. Since he was not proclaimed, did this mean that he had chosen to go into exile unacknowledged, his identity a secret still? How in that case would he have lived? He was a Plantagenet, the last hope of the royal line. What purpose would he have in life except to regain the throne for his house of York.'

'If that be so,' said Aske, 'since we have heard nothing of him for half a century he cannot be alive.'

'So I concluded until the saint inspired me. Were there

any survivors of the prince's faction still alive at the time of Stoke and with the means to help him? Most of the Yorkist nobility and their followers had been killed at the time of Bosworth. Henry Tudor had had two years on the throne in which to dispose of King Richard's remaining adherents. What had happened to King Richard's and King Edward's advisers? Those who administered the government in Yorkist times had been dismissed and their posts given to the Tudor's friends, but they had not all been killed, nor even disgraced. They were administrators, not makers of Yorkist policy, and the most prominent were churchmen. The most eminent of all was still alive, still a bishop, and near at hand.'

'Bishop Russell!' the chancellor exclaimed.

'Yes; John Russell, our bishop's predecessor at Lincoln. He had been a member of King Edward's council and chancellor of England under King Richard. From the banks of the Trent, as I discovered for myself, Lincoln lies but a few miles up the road. Lovell would have known this well and advised the boy to flee there. Let us suppose that the fugitive prince arrived at his palace. What would the bishop have done? Would he regard himself as a loyal servant of the crown, whoever wore it? Or was he, above all else, a servant of the house of York which had raised him to the seat of St Hugh and the highest appointment in the realm? History tells us that he was considered the wisest and most upright man in England. He was old and preparing to meet his God. How would he have resolved such a dilemma?'

'The answer is simple,' said Aske. 'If he had chosen to hand the boy over to Henry Tudor the king would have announced the capture and we should all know of it. It is inconceivable that Henry would have held him secretly while Warbeck was causing him so much trouble pretending to be the self-same boy.'

'That is my conclusion. I cannot believe from what I have learned of him that Bishop Russell could have contemplated facing his Maker stained with the guilt of being an accomplice to infanticide. He would have known that in delivering the boy into King Henry's hands he would be sending him to certain death. On the other hand, I do not believe that he would have wished to bear the responsibility of continuing a civil war by smuggling the heir of York out of the country to his aunt in Flanders to assemble an army and fight again.'

'Tell us what other choice he had,' demanded the chancellor. The old man had a hand cupped to his ear in his anxiety not to miss a syllable.

'He could have offered the young Richard his protection on condition that he surrendered himself, not to the king, but to God. Might he not have judged that on those terms he could honourably grant the boy sanctuary?'

'Where?' asked Aske. 'Do you refer to a monastery? If so, which one?'

'Need you inquire?' asked the chancellor in turn.' Does it tax your brains beyond their powers to hit upon an abbey in this diocese which has long been a nest of traitors? The lord abbot and the brother have already told us of Bishop Russell's coming to Croyland and how he wrote his history here, not stating that the princes were murdered but disguising his knowledge that one of them was still alive. I have not forgotten his chronicle nor the so-called Titulus Regius in which, so the lord abbot assures us, His Highness's mother was declared by Parliament to be a bastard.'

'The bishop came to Croyland twice,' said Brother Thomas. 'The first time, in the spring of 1486, he brought the Titulus Regius and stayed to write his chronicle. It must have been this visit which decided him where to hide the prince, for he came again in the summer of the following year immediately after the battle at Stoke. On this second visit he made alterations to what he had written during the first. I have examined the manuscript and the ink is different. Every change is consonant with the desire to suggest, without tampering with the true version of events, that the cause of the house of York was beyond retrieval and its heirs gone for ever.'

'The boy!' said Aske, shaking with impatience. 'Have you proof positive that he brought the boy here with him?'

'I have been closeted with the abbey records since St Guthlac appeared to me. The bishop brought with him a boy whom the abbot accepted for the novitiate. When this novice came to take his vows two special dispensations were granted: one for those born outside the bonds of holy matrimony, the other for those who have themselves espoused a wife. There is no proof of this novice's identity with Richard of York, but Richard, like his brother and his sisters, had been declared a bastard, as the bishop and the abbot both knew from the Titulus Regius. He had been married, too, as an infant. To Anne Mowbray, the duke of Norfolk's heir. She died as a child, but they were bound by a marriage contract signed on the fifteenth of January 1478 when he was four and she was six.'

'That is proof enough for me,' said Aske. 'Tell us now under what name the boy was introduced into this community.'

The chancellor's chair creaked. He rose heavily to his feet and lumbered wild-eyed across the room. In the silence which followed, no one else moved. His words when they came were charged with the enmity of a lifetime and burst from him like a torrent of flood-water through the banks of a dyke.

'You are a fool, Master Aske, or you would not need to ask the name. I have suspected him for many years, but only recently of this. Leader of the opposition to the royal will – that is what he has so fittingly become. The traitor known as John Wells, now and long since lord abbot of this house of knaves.'

He pointed an accusing, condemning finger. Aske sprang to his feet, but the abbot sat like a carved effigy, as wooden as the chair he sat in. Brother Thomas rushed across the room and knelt before him.

'Forgive me, father,' he cried. 'I knew not what I did.'

He laid his cheek on the abbot's lap and wept like a child in a flood of grief. When the abbot moved at length and placed a comforting hand on this head he dared to look up in worship and obeisance.

'My lord!' he breathed like an abject lover. 'My sovereign liege. Richard IV, by the grace of God king of this realm of England.'

3

'Rise,' ordered the abbot. His voice was tender.

'I have brought ruin on us all,' moaned Brother Thomas.

'Rise,' the abbot insisted. His dignity was unruffled, his authority unwavering. 'The decision was mine. When I gave you leave to go I foresaw the outcome. I calculated that you would not fail. The responsibility lies with me; you have no cause to reproach yourself.'

No sooner had he helped Brother Thomas to stand than another suppliant was before him. Robert Aske knelt in homage.

'Give us your leadership,' he demanded, 'and the abbeys will be saved. Between us we shall topple the fat Tudor. You will be crowned and anointed at Westminster. I salute you, Richard, king of England.'

'I am abbot of Croyland. Even if Brother Thomas's speculations be accepted as fact, I am a man of God now. My vows have been taken, the world renounced. How can an abbot become a king? If you would have a churchman you would do better with Cardinal Pole. His Plantagenet blood is not flawed by illegitimacy.'

'The cardinal is a coward, as well you know, and will not cross the sea until others have dealt with the fat Tudor. Your illegitimacy was an act of state. Since Henry Tudor took the crown it has no force in law.'

The abbot waved him away and crossed to the door, but Aske followed to press his demand.

'Come with me now, this instant. Take off that habit and put on armour like your saint. We will ride north together and proclaim you king in York, the seat of your house. If Brother Thomas tells true, you led the field at Bosworth and fought by Lovell's side at Stoke. Fight again. Lincolnshire will follow you to a man. The northerners will flock to your standard, and the west country too when the news reaches them. All England will rise again under the sun of York and wear the badge of the white rose.'

'It is not possible.' The abbot locked the door and returned to the table, key in hand.

'Are we your prisoners, King Richard?' asked the chancellor with a sneer.

'I am not King Richard and you are my guests. But before you leave we must talk further and determine the will of God in this matter. Whether or not the welfare of the realm rests with us, as Master Aske supposes, it is certain that the safety of this house lies in our hands. That is a weighty enough consideration.'

'Talk then yourself,' said the chancellor. 'Confess yourself to be Richard of York or deny it plainly. We must know how the matter stands.'

'Be seated and have patience.' The abbot left them and went to commune with God in the chapel annexed to his parlour. It was nearly an hour before he returned, his decision taken.

'You shall have the truth,' he said. 'I am no longer Richard of York, but once I was. My birth and lineage I will not deny. My father was king of this realm; so too my brother and my uncle. My sister was Henry Tudor's queen. Our present king, whose sovereignty I acknowledge, is my nephew. From being duke of York, I have become in succession Richard the lord bastard, John Wells, Brother John, Father John and lord abbot of Croyland. No man is what he was, but I less than any.'

'The last time we met here,' said Aske, 'you told us of your father's death, pretending that the account came to you from Bishop Russell. On his deathbed he laid on you a sacred trust to strive so that the sun of York should never set. Where is your honour? Would you fail your own father in his dying wishes?'

'It is too late to turn back. I failed him long ago.'

'How can you, a Plantagenet, be so faint of heart? It is not too late. You are strong still. You are handsome like King Edward, your father, and have the power and presence to command. As abbot of Croyland you are known and respected. Where you lead, men will follow. If you have vowed never to be king we will crown another, but at least rid us of this usurping son of Satan.'

'Whom else would you crown, Master Aske?' demanded the chancellor.

'His lordship's cousin of Salisbury has other sons besides the cardinal. Lord Montague will make a king.'

'Why is he not with you, he and the so-called party of the White Rose? Lord Montague, Lord Exeter, Sir Edward Neville – even these wilting blooms of York realise that this rising you seek to foment will be hopeless. They care more about keeping their heads on their shoulders.'

'You must be king, my lord,' Brother Thomas implored. 'It is your birthright and your destiny. God wills it. Go with Master Aske and charge your enemies as you did on Bosworth field.'

'Has God revealed His will to you, my son? Are we to receive all our communications from the Almighty and His blessed saints through you?'

'He has made you valiant to fight His cause.'

'I showed no valour at Bosworth. It was a day of shame. I fled that field and the one at Stoke.'

'You were but a lad.'

'And now I am an old man.'

'You are sixty-three and as hale as a man of forty.'

'You cannot persuade me, my son. Neither you nor Master Aske. Your supposition that I went to Bishop Russell at Lincoln is correct. He made me swear at the shrine of St Hugh as a condition of bringing me here, that I would never again take up arms against Lancastrians or Tudors. He told me that the old feud must be buried for England's sake. I believed him and obeyed.'

'The good man erred,' said Aske.

'No.' The abbot turned to the window so that they should not see his face. 'How many times have I remembered my father's words and regretted my weakness in taking the oath. How often have I told myself that I should have refused the condition and continued the fight from across the sea. Yet when I kneel before God I know that the bishop was right. You cannot move me now.'

Aske's eye glittered. 'You are a traitor to your house.'

'Insults will be of no avail. I accept your reproach.'

'My lord abbot – since you spurn my homage and will not be called king – I ask you for the last time to come with me. Come, not as the heir of York and rightful king, if that be your choice. Come as abbot of Croyland, the saviour of our Faith. Come as God's chosen instrument in the defence of the true religion. Fight for Christ instead of York. Our struggle is first and foremost a religious war, not a clash of dynasties. Leave the rising sun where it sank if you must, but raise the standard of the Cross.'

The abbot shook his head. 'I admire your resolution and but for my oath I would be tempted to ride with you, but the abbeys will not be saved by force. The smaller houses are doomed, but the greater may yet be preserved. Subtler means are required if it is to be so.'

'What means? Is there any course open but force.'

'One,' said the abbot, looking the chancellor in the eye. 'The downfall of Master Cromwell. That is the task to which I have devoted myself. But it will not be achieved if you and your northerners rebel and fail.'

'We shall not fail. If you will not join us I shall lead them myself and we shall succeed without you. You will live to thank me for saving your abbey for you. Now let me go, and fear not for your secret. It will be safe with me.'

'He must not leave,' said the chancellor, rising in turn. 'If you are loyal to the king's grace, arrest him.' His voice shook and he banged the table with his fist.

The abbot took no heed. He held out his hand for Aske to kiss the jewelled ring on his finger. 'May God be your shield!' he said. Then he crossed the room, brushing past the chancellor's forbidding bulk, unlocked the door and let the rebel go.

'You have blessed an avowed traitor and called down God's protection on a treasonable enterprise.' The chancellor's jowl was heavy with menace. 'These are grave acts indeed. I must report them and these other matters. Let me pass.'

'To whom must you report them?' Even as he asked the question the abbot relocked the door and stood beside it, barring the way.

'To the bishop naturally.'

'And the bishop in his turn will report to Cromwell.'

'So you say. That is no concern of mine. The bishop must learn of Aske's treachery and your true identity. Your brother here must come with me and repeat his story. He must bring with him the chronicles and all other relevant documents. The bishop will decide what is to be done.'

'The bishop is your superior, but he is not mine, as I have ventured to point out to you before. I have renounced the rest of England, but this is my kingdom. The decision is mine and I have decided that the bishop shall not learn what you have heard.'

The chancellor paused, pursing his lips and puckering his brow while he pondered the implication of the abbot's words.

'You are as great a coward as Cardinal Pole,' he taunted. 'You fear a traitor's end.'

'My life is of no importance. What I fear for is the safety of this house. No harm shall come to it through me – that I swear before God. I did not reject Master Aske's bidding because I intended to abandon the abbey to its fate. My intention is to protect it in my own way.'

'Submission is your only hope. If you refuse to surrender

Brother Thomas and the documents, I must go and tell the bishop of your refusal. When these tidings come to the king's ear both of you will pay the price.'

'But you shall not tell the bishop. You will not be permitted to leave until you have sworn by the blood of our Saviour not to breathe a word of what has been disclosed.'

'I cannot swear that.'

'Then you cannot leave.'

They confronted each other. The abbot was taller and younger, but the chancellor was burly and choleric. Brother Thomas stood ready to lend his lord what feeble support he could.

'What reason will you give for keeping me here?'

'Your own good. There are armed bands round Lincoln. You are not popular. Men have come to know you for what you are, Chancellor Rayne.'

'You cannot force me to stay. I shall be missed at the inquiry at Bolingbroke. My servants—'

'There is no question of force. What I am saying is this: if you do not wish to die, either swear to what I ask or remain here.'

'That is a threat to my life. You will regret those words, you and your abbey. The king's vengeance will fall on both of you. It will not be long before your head is spiked above London bridge and the fowls of the air are nesting in the ruins of your choir. Imprison me here if you dare.'

He charged towards the door like a cornered boar, but the abbot stood firm and pushed him bodily aside.

'Stay!'

'Never!' bellowed the chancellor, returning to the charge.

'So be it.' This time, with a shrug, the abbot turned and unlocked the door, and with a granite countenance let him go.

'He will betray you,' Brother Thomas protested.

'Fetch the prior,' the abbot ordered him. 'Immediately.'

He was transformed before Brother Thomas's eyes. The mouth grew taut, the blue eyes restless, the body alert and more erect. The aloofness of withdrawal had gone. The whole of the abbot was back in the world.

For the first time since he was a boy Brother Thomas ran – down the stairs and round the cloisters to summon the prior from his cell. When he returned to the parlour with the old man, both of them breathless, the abbot was in his riding boots and wrapped in his travelling cloak.

'Father prior,' he said, 'I have to make an unexpected journey. The abbey is in your custody until my return. Brother Thomas will tell you of his findings, but I beg that in my absence neither of you will repeat them to a living person. Our safety depends on secrecy.'

The prior dithered in astonishment. 'Where are you going in such haste, my lord? Have the proper preparations been made? How shall I announce your departure to the brethren?'

'Brother Thomas will devise something for you to tell them. As God is my witness, the errand I undertake is not for myself but for Croyland's sake.'

He left with such suddenness that their God-be-with-you's went unheard. A glint at the tail of his cloak as it swirled at the door caused Brother Thomas to look about him in dismay.

The sword of St Guthlac was gone from the wall.

4

Brother Thomas ran down the stairs and across the outer court to the stables. The abbot was already mounted and waving the groom aside.

'Stay!' he shouted. 'Help guide the prior. Safeguard the chronicles.'

'No!' Brother Thomas shouted back, and bade the groom saddle him a horse.

'I order you to stay.'

'God orders me to disobey.'

In his haste Brother Thomas slipped and fell in a mound of dung, but was on his feet again in a trice. The groom stood undecided, so he seized a saddle for himself, fumbled with the straps until they held and scrambled up astride. He wore no cloak over his habit, and his feet were bare in the stirrups. The abbot had left him and galloped to the great gateway, where Gervase rushed out to inquire how many servants he required.

'None. Stand aside and let them open the gate.'

The porter obeyed, gaping at the sight of him, and the abbot rode out as no abbot of Croyland had ever ridden out before: without escort, without dignity, as though driven by the Devil himself.

'My lord is possessed,' the porter cried to Gervase. 'Will you ride after him?'

'Did you not hear what he said. Let none follow.' It was Brother Thomas who replied, knocking them apart on the canter. 'Which way did the chancellor go?'

'The Spalding road.'

'How many men did he take with him?'

'His servants are still here. He left in haste without a word.'

'Keep them here. Do not let them go.'

He dug in his heels and the horse reared and whinnied. Brother Thomas was no horseman, and he grazed his shoulder on the gate-post. During his excursion he had ambled without mishap; now, unfittingly clad, he must gallop. Seeing his plight, the porter rapped a stick across the horse's rump and startled it into action.

He was conscious of the villagers staring. Then, where it left the village, the road towards Spalding curved sharply. Round the bend a cur sprang out snapping. The horse shied. Brother Thomas parted company with it and fell heavily into a ditch.

God, he thought while he lay feeling his bones for fractures, God has brought me low. Even as the thought passed through his mind two horsemen sped by. Through the dust they raised he recognised them and felt a tremble of fear. They were Master Cromwell's men, the men who had trailed him across England and been lurking in the village since his return. He had not seen them since that day on the battlefield at Bosworth but, if Gervase was to be believed, they had saved his life at Newark.

He jumped to his feet and ran to secure his steed. It was munching sedge tamely by the wayside and allowed him to remount, but it took him quarter of a mile or more before he could persuade it to break from a canter into a gallop again.

The two men were not far ahead. They must have been watching the abbey and received a signal from the chancellor to deal with any pursuers. Certainly they rode as if bent on doing mischief, like hounds after a coursing hare. Unarmed and unversed in violence, Brother Thomas followed them with despair in his heart. Across the bare flat fen even he could see them plainly and the abbot beyond, a large black figure like one of the riders in the Apocalypse. In the distance he could distinguish a blur that must be the chancellor, squat and going strong. There would be no cover for any of them until they reached Spalding.

'My lord! My lord!'

His call of warning echoed across the water meadows, startling a pair of swans into flight. The chancellor was out of earshot but the others heard. The abbot looked back and saw his pursuers. He wheeled his horse abruptly to confront them. The two drew their swords and charged on towards him.

A flash of steel told Brother Thomas, thumping his horse in the ribs with his bare heels, that the sword of St Guthlac was in the abbot's hand. By the mercy of God one of his assailants rode faster than the other. The age of the prince bishops was long past in England – even four and a half centuries ago at Hastings Odo, bishop of Bayeux, had wielded a mace because men of God did not carry swords. The appearance of the abbot's weapon, Brother Thomas could tell from the sudden jerk of the charging rider's head, was beyond belief. The man realised it too late.

His charge bore him forward at full force, the point of his own sword aimed at the chest of the abbot's horse. He had no hope of reining in time. The abbot's weapon pointed to his belly and his own impetus carried him on to it. Gervase's polishing and honing of the great blade had kept it in fighting trim. The tip drove through the man's leather jerkin, clean into his body and out the other side.

Men and horses, they fell together. The man in his death agony, skewered like a carcase on a spit. The abbot's horse, floundering mortally wounded. The abbot and his attacker's horse, tumbling on top of them in the slush of the road.

Unhorsed and disarmed, the abbot rose to receive the attack of the second man with nothing save his bare hands.

For two or three seconds the man held back, confused by what had happened. In that instant Brother Thomas fell upon him.

He did not carry so much as a riding whip. Never before had he committed an act of assault. He had no desire to hurt the man, only to save the abbot's life. He flung himself out of the saddle, trying to grapple with the enemy and pinion his arms to his side.

In his anxiety he jumped too early and fell short, but grasped the man's leg in falling and tugged him off his horse. They struggled in the mud, and all at once Brother Thomas lay winded and spread-eagled on his back while the enemy, stronger and more agile, was on his feet, sword in hand.

Brother Thomas closed his eyes and committed his soul to God's merciful keeping. The blow would be but the faintest taste of the agony his Redeemer had suffered for him. He made an attempt at the sign of the cross, not to ward off the sword thrust, but to bestow on his killer his blessing and forgiveness.

When the blow did not come, he opened his eyes. A fearful sight greeted them. The stern but tender abbot whom he loved was transformed into a raging Plantagenet with the warrior blood of Henry Curtmantle and Richard Coeur de Lion singing in his veins. He had secured the dead man's sword and was attacking the new enemy with all the savagery of his ancestors.

The duel was brisk and bloody. Out of practice in sword play, the abbot thrust too boldly and left himself exposed. The other's blade was at his throat but the abbot moved quickly and it glanced by, causing a wound from which the blood spurted. In a frenzy of wrath he closed on his man, hugging him tight and imprisoning the other's sword arm under his left elbow while with his own right arm he brought the long blade down like a dagger and buried it in his assailant's back. They broke apart and the abbot hurled him to the ground.

The man groaned like a stuck boar, blood bubbling from his mouth. Brother Thomas's bowels melted in pity and he crawled over to comfort and console him.

'Stand back,' the abbot cried. He was wrenching the man's sword, his last defence, from his weakening grasp.

'In God's name, no!' Brother Thomas begged him like a suppliant. But the blade of the great sword shimmered past his eyes and plunged into the man's heart, splintering its path through his ribs and pinning him to the earth. Dust to dust.

Clouds, the harbingers of evening, were darkening the sky and wisps of autumn mist rising from the dampness of the fens. Brother Thomas vomited until his stomach was empty.

The abbot had work to do and paid him no heed. First he made sure that both men were dead. Then one by one he dragged their bodies off the highway and threw them into a dyke, and their swords after them. His own he had withdrawn and sheathed. Now he unsheathed it again to kill his horse, which was struggling and kicking in a pool of black blood. That left three horses for the two of them, and one he unsaddled and set free, dropping its harness beside the bodies in the water. Only then did he turn his attention to Brother Thomas.

'Can you rise, my son, or are you injured?'

Brother Thomas stood up, his face averted. He could not bring himself to look at the abbot or trust himself to speak.

'I commanded you not to follow me.'

Brother Thomas nodded.

'You disobeyed me, and not for the first time. Repeated disobedience is a sin meriting the most severe punishment.'

Brother Thomas nodded again.

'God has punished you already. You have lost faith in me. I thank you for saving my life, if indeed it was worth saving, and ask you always to remember that, although I broke the Lord's commandment, I killed for Croyland.'

5

They chased the chancellor till nightfall.

In Spalding he was reported to have ridden through. There Brother Thomas implored the abbot to rest a night at the priory, but the scent of blood was in his nostrils. The hunted had turned hunter.

'We shall be recognised here,' the abbot said. 'Questions will be asked and our quarry will escape.'

'You would not kill the chancellor?'

'What choice is there? And murder and mortal sin I have committed already.'

'You killed in self-defence. They would have slain you. It was no murder.' Already Brother Thomas's respect for the abbot had returned. In his love and loyalty he would defend him even against himself.

'You are charitable. They wished to apprehend me – that was all. So that the chancellor might make good his escape.'

They rode out of Spalding dusty and blood-stained. Darkness had come and, save for the woman who told them of the chancellor, they went unnoticed; which was as well. The appearance of Croyland's abbot without retinue and in such a state could not have been explained. If Master Cromwell ever learned who it was who had done his minions to death Croyland would be made an example to all abbeys who resisted the king's policies. In his mind Brother Thomas could see the site as desolate again as when Tatwin the boatman had first brought Lieutenant Guthlac ashore on the island, as the window at Fotheringhay had depicted.

The halted a mile outside the village and fell asleep under the shelter of a hedge. Towards midnight they woke and, huddling together, celebrated mattins to the accompaniment of a moaning wind. Tired but wakeful, Brother Thomas bathed and bound the abbot's wound as best he could. His own feet were raw. His body ached. He smelt of dung and vomit. Yet, alone with his hero, he was sublimely at ease. His body glowed with the sin of pride. All his study, all his inquiries had been rewarded. The king he had searched for through fifty years of history was crouching beside him, body to body, his father in God, his lord spiritual and temporal, the friend whose life – the most precious in England – he had saved.

The abbot talked. He spoke of the chancellor and the bishop and the betrayal of the Church from within. He spoke of them with compassion, not as evil men but as victims on the treadmill of worldliness. He himself had been corrupted by the necessity of playing politics. 'You were blessed in your seclusion, my son. I should never have allowed you outside our walls, after experiencing the contamination in my own soul.'

'But England has need of you, father,' Brother Thomas protested. 'How shall she prosper in goodness if all good men refuse to serve her? You have had one foot in London. Would that you had had both there, firmly planted on the footstool beneath the throne!'

'I would have done no better than the others, and I will tell you the reason. Ruthlessness is the stamp of a successful ruler. My uncle King Richard was a good man. He intended well but committed the error of showing mercy to his enemies. He spared the lives of those who conspired against him and left them their liberty to bring him down. The quality of mercy cost him his throne and his life. Henry Tudor showed no such weakness. For all his bastard blood he was a real king.'

Brother Thomas peered into the night, trying to determine from the outline of the abbot's face whether he was serious. He was too shocked to speak.

'What does the realm require of its kings?' the abbot continued. 'By executing every rival, regardless of justice, Henry Tudor secured peace after thirty years of war. By meanness and extortion he made the exchequer rich enough to pay adequately for the administration of government. His taxes were cruel, but the poor had stable prices. If the safety and welfare of the state demanded it he never hesitated to break an oath or betray a friend. That is the stuff of sovereignty. Every one of his private vices was a public virtue. Now can you understand why I have never regretted the surrender of my rightful title? Consider poor Henry VI. Where did his saintliness lead the realm? To the loss of France, to civil war and anarchy. If you believe that I have some goodness in me, how could you wish England on me or me on England?'

Once more Brother Thomas could not think how to reply. Instead he asked about the abbot's boyhood and the adventures on which he had speculated so arduously.

Listening with the ear of a chronicler, he learned that Richard, duke of York, had scarcely known his brother until they met in the Tower. Richard was brought up in Westminster while Edward, as prince of Wales, had been sent to the wild marches, which he hated. He complained of slights and ailments. He was frightened and moody and his brother confessed to feeling little sorrow at his death.

As the story unfolded, Brother Thomas asked question after question to satisfy himself on every particular. Later he would write it all, so that posterity should learn of the loyalty which bound the men of York indissolubly. Brakenbury, Skelton, Lovell, Tyrrell. These were not men to be terrorised into fealty. True loyalty was engendered by the liege lord's recognition of the obligations as well as the privileges of overlordship. The Plantagenet house of York recognised these obligations. Why else, asked the abbot, did men in these times of suspicion and spies and arbitrary arrest still speak openly of Good King Edward and Good King Richard – words which could cost them their lives under Tudor law?

In the greyness before dawn Brother Thomas put the question to which, above all others, he wanted the answer. What had happened at Bosworth?

'I believe the king my uncle wished to die. The queen his wife and the prince, his only legitimate child, were dead. He found no joy in kingship and had no fear of death. It was his duty to defend the realm and secure the succession. When Walter Skelton brought me to him on the eve of the battle he welcomed me with rapture, as though sent back to him from the grave by the Almighty. I believe that he took it as a sign from Heaven for him to depart this life. He sent at once for John Howard, the man to whom my dukedom of Norfolk had been given, and ordered him in the presence of all his bodyguard to proclaim me king if he fell in the battle. Then all, save the king himself, knelt outside his tent and did me homage.'

The sun was rising pale and watery from the distant sea and the abbot's face was visible now. The authority of the forehead, the strength of the jaw, the mouth and eyes deliberately drained of life to mask the mind – Brother Thomas noted it all and admired the mastery of emotion, knowing as he did the twin depths of anger and gentleness which lay beneath the crust.

'Except for Lovell, every man who knelt before me was killed, John Howard the first to fall. I was ordered out of the battle array but crept back. How could I wear a crown which had been won for me while I skulked in a tent? When the battle went against us and the Stanleys' treachery became apparent I could see what the king meant to do. If Henry Tudor were killed the result of the battle would not matter; his men had no one else to crown. If King Richard, whom they hated, were dead, they too would accept me. So he charged and I charged with him. He killed the Tudor standard-bearer and all but slew the Tudor himself, while I allowed my horse to run away with me.'

Something that in another might have been a tear glistened in the abbot's eye, lightening the blueness for which his father, the handsomest of kings, had been famous. Affection for the man and his cause surged through Brother Thomas, spreading out from his heart and overwhelming his entire being. Tighter than the bond between monk and abbot he felt the magic which the house of York inspired.

'Come,' said the abbot, grimly rising and shaking the stiffness from his bones, 'or the chancellor will reach Lincoln with his tale.'

They mounted and jolted their aching limbs into motion. At Boston, where they stopped for a humble meal of salt bacon and cheese and coarse bread, the town was thronged with countrymen carrying crude weapons. Brother Thomas feared violence but at the sight of monks the men cheered and pressed forward to kiss the abbot's ring and ask his blessing.

Brother Thomas's spirits rose. 'Master Aske is right,' he said as they finished eating. 'Will you not ride to York after all? If there be as many of the Old Faith there as here, the king will not be able to withstand us. The abbeys in the north are rich. They will open their treasure chests in Christ's cause. Nothing is lacking except a leader. Will you not lead the charge a second time, in His name?'

'Drink up,' the abbot replied, 'and spare your breath. I have killed two wretches. Would you have the death of thousands more on my conscience?'

The chancellor was well known and well hated in Boston. He had slept in the town, they were told, and been lucky to leave before the mob arrived. He had said that he was taking the road to Bolingbroke, where the commission of inquiry awaited him.

They followed, asking news of him at every village, until they discovered that he had left the Bolingbroke road and taken a fork which led direct to Lincoln.

'He would deceive us,' grunted the abbot. 'Pray God we catch him. For an old man he rides fast.'

The fens of Holland were behind them now. Ahead lay the rich highlands of the wolds, grazing ground for the sheep whose fleeces were the gold of England. Up they climbed, over the heights, and steeply down again into the market town of Horncastle.

Like Boston, it was occupied by contingents of a peasant army. Here the numbers were larger, the assembly more purposeful. They gathered threateningly round the abbot's horse and demanded to know his business. They were rough men, without respect. There was no kissing of rings here.

The abbot, undaunted, demanded to know their business first and they were not loath to tell it. They had come together from all over the county to march on Lincoln.

There they would demand redress for their grievances, an end to taxation and to the destruction of monasteries. If they found him, they intended to hang the heretic bishop from one of the towers of his own cathedral.

'To Lincoln,' they shouted.

'Go to your homes,' the abbot shouted back. 'Disperse or you will all be killed.'

They eyed him with suspicion, noting his dress and its condition, the dignity of his bearing and the silver crucifix on his chest.

'Let him take the oath,' they cried.

A priest was pushed to the front of the mob. The oath, he said, was one of loyalty to the commons. At Louth the day before, after the vicar had preached against the commissioners at Bolingbroke, sixty priests had taken it, some willingly, others under duress. They had then been ordered to return home and ring the church bells to summon their parishioners to arms. The bishop's registrar who was conducting the commission had been seized and the inquiry broken up. Proclamations had been made in the name of the people. The whole county was in open rebellion.

'We seek one who is more important than the bishop's registrar,' said the abbot. 'Dr Rayne, chancellor and vicar-general of this diocese.'

'Then God has guided you here.' It was the leader of the mob who spoke.

The throng parted, leaving a path for their horses across the market square. The abbot rode forward, and Brother Thomas followed. Chancellor Rayne lay sprawled against the steps of the market cross. He stared at them, but not in recognition. His bull head was swollen, his naked body black with bruises and deep red with the mark of weals.

'He defied them,' said the priest. 'He would not take the

oath. They beat him to death with their staves and divided his clothes among them. I could not save him, as I cannot save you if you are bishop's men.'

'The fat hog deserved to die,' said the leader. 'He threatened us in the name of our own Church.'

6

Brother Thomas jumped from his horse and drew down the eyelids, shutting from the old man's gaze the sinful world he had left. The wooden Christ, wearing His crown of thorns, looked down while His dishevelled servant made the corpse decent. Brother Thomas had no garment to spare, so the abbot handed down his ermine-lined cloak for a shroud. Then from his horse, while Brother Thomas knelt, he spoke the last offices.

Awed by the abbot's authority, no one interrupted the service or seized the cloak. Before the end the bells of the parish began pealing, but not for the dead man. It was a signal for the mob to march.

The leader mounted the steps to address them. He was a man of the people like themselves and they hailed him as Captain Cobbler. He told them they must be in Market Rasen before sundown. The march on Lincoln must not be delayed. Word of the chancellor's death would run ahead of them, preparing the bishop for their coming. Lastly, he announced that they had an abbot – or a prior at least – come among them to bless their enterprise in the name of God and the Old Faith.

But the abbot refused his blessing. 'Disband,' he called to

them, 'and I will gladly give you my blessing. But rebellion will not save the abbeys. It will make their destruction sure.'

The crowd jeered and drifted away to form columns for the march. The leader was anxious to be gone with them to take his place at their head, but first he faced the abbot.

'Those who are not for the commons are against them,' he said. 'We are blunt men and recognise no niceties. There is Christ, for Whose sake we march, and there is anti-Christ. Take the oath and bless our holy cause, join our ranks and march at their head with me, or die like that hog of a chancellor.'

The abbot answered by drawing his sword. Two of the captain's men retaliated by seizing Brother Thomas. The point of the abbot's sword was instantly at the captain's throat.

'Release him if you value your leader's life.'

They released him reluctantly and he remounted.

'Now go in peace,' the abbot ordered them, 'and I will let your leader follow.'

When they reached the far side of the market place he lowered his sword.

'I cannot bless your enterprise, Captain Cobbler,' he said, 'but I bless you. May God forgive you your sins and watch over you. You will have need of Him.'

The captain was not to be softened by words. He stood by his principles. After rejoining the waiting mob he ordered men back to kill the man who had blessed him. As the abbot and Brother Thomas left the square a troop of horsemen entered it, and it was only the grace of God which enabled them to escape through the narrow streets. Once Brother Thomas nearly fell, but the abbot drew quickly abreast to grip his arm and steady him in the saddle. Out of the town, they headed at speed away from Lincoln and their pursuers abandoned the chase.

Exhausted as they were, it took them till evening on the following day to accomplish the return to Croyland. Now that his desperate mission was over, the burden of his mortal sin seemed to overwhelm the abbot. The second night under the sky was spent in silent communion, and during the whole journey he scarcely spoke. The wound in his neck grew angrier but he would not allow it to be bathed. If Brother Thomas had not begged for food and drink from cottages by the way it seemed that the abbot would have been content to starve.

He showed no sign of cheer even when they reached his own boundary stone with its welcome greeting: 'This stone, I say, marks Guthlac's furthest limit.' At the place of his encounter with Master Cromwell's minions, where Brother Thomas scrambled down to commend the poor wretches' souls to God and leave a benediction with their sodden corpses, the abbot journeyed on unheeding. When the great tower of the church loomed above them he did not raise his eyes.

At the abbey he rode into the outer courtyard erect and aloof as always, but dirty, ill-clad and bloodstained, like a scourged king on a pilgrimage of penance. All the pensioners and servants came clustering round and the villagers with their wives and children burst through the gate to wonder at the sight of him. Someone ran to ring the great bell of Abbot Lytlyngton. Like the boundary stone, it spoke. 'Jesu mercy, Lady help', it was inscribed, invoking the aid of the Saviour and His Mother in time of trouble. It spoke so seldom that at its sound the brethren themselves hurried out of church, abandoning vespers in their haste.

Their father had returned, he who had unaccountably

vanished from their midst – the prior's faltering attempt at explanation had rung too false for any man's belief. Soon the entire court was full of kneeling figures. The abbot held up his hand in blessing and made the sign of the cross. He allowed Gervase to help him dismount, then without a word he disappeared into his lodgings, with Brother Thomas doggedly at his heels.

The prior hurried breathless up the stairs behind them. In the parlour, when he could speak, the words flooded from him in joy and relief. 'Thanks be to God for your homecoming, my lord. We were lost and like children without you. We knew not where you had gone or for what purpose. We feared we might never behold you again. Will you say a few words of comfort to your flock?'

'I have no comfort to offer and nothing to say,' the abbot replied. 'Before I left I recollect ordering Brother Thomas to tell you of his discovery. He did not do as I bade and I here and now countermand the order. What he discovered is buried once more. He has forgotten it. I have forgotten it. It will never be told again. The affair is closed for ever. Now tell me this. Which of the brothers has taken Brother Henry's place among the lepers?'

'It is not yet decided. There is some reluctance. We need your decision, and I thought it best—'

'You have my decision. I shall take his place myself.'

'But, my lord—' The prior was so overcome that he sat down unbidden.

'Never!' Brother Thomas spoke with all the vehemence he could command. 'I will go. Brother Henry was my dearest companion. It is the least I can do to honour his blessed memory.'

'Calm yourself, my son. The offer does you credit, but it is useless. My mind is made up.'

'But your duties,' protested the prior. 'How could you rule us from the lazar-house?'

'I am no longer worthy of my office. I shall resign. A new abbot will be appointed.'

'That is impossible,' cried Brother Thomas. 'You know that better than any man. The appointment will rest with the king. He will instal a nominee who will destroy us from within. Croyland will suffer like West Dereham. Master Cromwell's agents have already taken charge of the election there.'

'Brother Thomas is right,' said the prior. 'You cannot desert us in times like these. No one else can protect us as you can; no one else has your wisdom and experience. You are familiar with the ways of the world. You and you alone have the respect and confidence of the brethren.'

'You are in error,' said the abbot. 'They respect you more.'

'But they have no confidence in me. Your judgments are acceptable, mine are disputed. You they will willingly obey in all things. You, and you alone.'

'Then they must obey me in this and you must not seek to dissuade me.'

'How can I prevent myself when the future of our house depends upon it? Let me go to the lepers. Let Brother Thomas go. It matters not who goes provided you will stay.'

'Since you press me I must tell you that I have committed mortal sin. This is the atonement I have prescribed for myself.'

'Whatever you have done, the brethren will not accept your resignation. There is no precedent. An abbot of Croyland is abbot until God calls him. It is the irrevocable custom of our house, as well you know.'

Sensing the abbot waver, Brother Thomas seconded the

prior by flinging himself on the floor at the abbot's boots and grasping him by the ankles.

'Abasement signifies obedience,' said the abbot sharply, 'and I would remind you that Abbot Wulketul was superseded during his lifetime, when King William imprisoned him for resisting the Normans and Abbot Ingulph was elected in his stead. But since both of you are so importunate I will not resign if the brethren truly believe that this would put the abbey in jeopardy. I shall be leaving this world for the lazar-house nevertheless. I shall remain abbot in name only and the abbey will be in your charge, father prior.'

'But I am old and sick. How can I begin at my age to pick a safe path through the thickets of statecraft and litigation? I am weak and the responsibilities are too heavy.'

'They are too heavy for any man. If you do not wish me to resign you must reconcile yourself to the consequence. God will help you. So too will the cellarer and Brother Thomas. If you wish for my advice you may send me a message across the stream.'

'If you go,' said Brother Thomas from the floor, 'I shall go with you. You cannot live alone among lepers. You are accustomed to comforts and attendance.'

'You shall not come with me. Your duty is in the cloister and the choir. You must take care to secure our records whatever may befall this house. These tasks are more important than attending to my worldly wants.'

'But you will become diseased like Brother Henry and die among the lepers.'

'That is as God chooses.'

'I cannot let you suffer alone. I am guilty too. I must share your penance.'

'No,' said the abbot. 'It would be a consolation I do not deserve.'

'Then I swear here and now in the sight of God and on the martyred skull of Abbot Theodore that no word shall pass my lips until you return to us. If you do not return I shall never speak again this side of the grave.'

Brother Thomas leapt to his feet, ran across the room and stretched his hand up to the revered skull pierced by the blade of a heathen king so long ago. Then he returned, sank in tears at the abbot's feet again and kissed the dirt-stained boots.

'No, no,' said the abbot drawing him upright and holding him in his arms. 'You are distressed by the hardships of our journey. You are not yourself. The penance is mine alone. You had no share in my sin and I absolve you from all responsibility for what has occurred. Promise me you will not keep this foolish oath. I still command your obedience, remember. The vows you made to me are more binding than this.'

Brother Thomas would not promise. He shook his head to indicate that there was nothing more to be said. Nothing more to be said by him ever.

'To think that I have brought my favourite son to this!' It was the abbot's turn to weep – a sight which neither the prior nor Brother Thomas had ever seen before. It was like the miracle of tears from a statue.

'If it means so much to you,' he continued when he could speak again, 'I will not forbid the oath, but I beg you to accede to a request which I ask of you as a friend. Do not let silence fall on you until I have crossed the stream. There is one last service I wish you to assist the prior in performing for me.'

7

At four o'clock the next morning in the abbey church – black in the night like a vast mausoleum – Brother Thomas, obedient to the abbot's request, attended his burial service. The abbot had declared himself a leper and this was the ceremony the Church prescribed.

Since Brother Thomas was not a priest in holy orders, it was the prior who conducted the service. At the church door he sprinkled the abbot with holy water. Then Brother Thomas preceded them up the nave, bearing the cross of Christ. The three of them were alone in the silence of death.

At the high altar the prior said mass by candlelight, the abbot kneeling under a black cloth hung over trestles as though draped on a coffin. When the service was over Brother Thomas led them from the church into the burial garth where he and the prior threw earth at the feet of their father in God and read to him in unison from the holy scriptures.

'Be dead to the world and again living to God. May your name be written in the Book of Life.'

Together they covered the recumbent abbot with the black cloth and recited the prohibition: 'I forbid you to enter at any time into churches or market places, into mills or bakehouses. I command you not to eat or drink in any company except that of other lepers. I forbid you to wash in springs or running water. I forbid you to go abroad without your leper habit and clapper. I forbid you to touch anything outside the leper-house except with your rod. You must not speak to anyone abroad except in a whisper and up wind. You must not walk along any narrow path lest you meet another and infect him.'

The abbot's body was now corrupted, though this side of

the grave. He wore leper dress and carried a rod and bell. Rich apparel and cushioned chairs, down beds and woven hangings and silver tableware were his no longer. They walked in single file down the narrow slype, past the infirmary and its chapel, through the masons' sheds and out into the grey openness bordering the stream. There the prior stopped and knelt in the dew. Overcome, he could bring himself to go no farther.

At the fishpond the abbot paused and summoned a wan smile. 'I will try not to emulate Brother Henry in all things.'

By the bank a boat was waiting and Brother Thomas could no longer restrain himself.

'My lord, my liege, my father, my – my dearest friend – if I may call you so, my lord – you are a king. You cannot be a leper.'

'How so?' asked the abbot gently. 'King Uzziah was a leper. Henry Bolingbroke, who killed the second Richard and took his crown, became a leper. God punished him for murder, as I pray that He will punish me – here below rather than in all eternity.'

'But you are deserting us, your children, your subjects.'

'You will be better without me. These are my subjects now.' He pointed across the stream and boarded the boat. 'Perform the last duty, my son.'

'Remember,' Brother Thomas sobbed, reading from the service-book by the light of his candle, 'remember that every faithful Christian is bound to say each day the Our Father, the Hail Mary, the I believe in God and I believe in the Spirit, and to fortify himself with the sign of the cross. Worship God and give Him thanks. Have patience and the Lord will be with you.'

'And with you also.'

The abbot made the response from across the water.

Brother Thomas could see him no longer. The words came like a final chord. His heart groaned with the burden of emptiness. His lips were closed for ever. He hurried back through the abbey building to his cell, stumbling without a word past the still-kneeling prior. He knew what he had to do. The abbot had said that his discovery must be buried and never told again. But he would not obey, for posterity must hear of it. As an historian he could not suppress what he had learned. Drawing his stool to his desk, he picked up a pen and began to write.

'In the month of July in the year of our Lord 1483, after the coronation of the Lord Protector as Richard III, rumours began to circulate concerning the fate of the boy king Edward V and his brother Richard, duke of York. These rumours were spread by King Richard's enemies to such purpose that, half a century later, their truth was universally believed. The real truth, however, was thus . . .'

Part Five

THE AFTERMATH

I

He wrote and rewrote, day and night, month after month. He held the pen of the chronicler of Croyland. He was the successor to Abbot Ingulph, Peter of Blois and John Russell of Lincoln. He strove to be worthy of them. Truth must prevail. Almighty God would wish it whatever the abbot might have said.

His disobedience in chronicling what the abbot had forbidden he confessed in writing to the prior, who punished him with six months' bread and water and a hair-shirt, but did not interfere. The punishment was welcome. The fasting meant that he did not have to spend time in the refectory, and the hair-shirt prevented him from losing too many hours in sleep. His only interruptions were the services, which he attended diligently, worshipping with fervour.

News of the outside world arrived once a week when the cellarer visited him to tell of his advice to the prior on matters of policy and administration.

On his first visit all Lincolnshire was in arms – forty thousand men, according to report. They had captured Lincoln and sacked the bishop's palace. The bishop himself was prudently in London and the mob could not decide where to direct its violence next. They parleyed and argued amongst themselves instead of fighting. A gentleman from Yorkshire had joined them, the cellarer reported, the man called Aske who had lately been visiting the abbot. He tried to persuade them to march south but they would not accept his leadership or any other. Without leaders they were lost and by the following week the uprising which had swollen to such proportions had suddenly collapsed like a pricked bladder. In three weeks from start to finish it was all over, and nothing achieved.

Brother Thomas listened in despair. The leader they should have had was living in an outcast's hovel. With God's help he, Brother Thomas, had recovered for England the Plantagenet she needed, only to have him turn his back on destiny a second time.

Then came more news. Of Aske triumphant. He had slipped away from Lincoln and raised not only Yorkshire but all the six northern counties. In default of a Plantagenet he did indeed lead the rising himself. He was elected by acclaim Captain of the North. The men he commanded called themselves pilgrims, not rebels, and their movement they called the Pilgrimage of Grace. Since the sun of York refused to rise again, they marched under the banner of the Five Wounds of Christ – the pierced hands and feet, and in the middle the heart that bled for all mankind.

As week succeeded week the army of Christ marched on invincibly. York was theirs. Hull was theirs. Durham and Lancaster became theirs. They captured Pontefract castle, bastion of the north. With each instalment Brother Thomas calculated anew how he could retrieve the abbot he had buried and set him on the throne. Each day he yearned for the thunder of an army at the gate. Aske, alone of living men, shared the secret. When he brought his pilgrims down to London, would he call at Croyland on the way and demand King Richard IV in the name of Christ and His Five Wounds?

But Aske never came, nor did the march to the south. The weeks passed and it became evident from the cellarer's accounts that triumph was turning into stalemate. The pilgrims wanted guarantees that their churches and religious houses would not be despoiled or the clergy molested. The king lured them into negotiation with promises which the abbot would have recognised at once for what they were and even Brother Thomas could have told them that he never meant to keep. What chance did honest men stand against Tudor falsehood?

In the south the White Rose party made no move. Abroad the Pope, so it was said, ordered the Emperor to invade England but the Emperor was too busy quarrelling with the king of France. Cardinal Pole came north from Rome but would not cross the Channel. In all Christendom not one finger was lifted outside the six counties to help Robert Aske defy the heretic king. Brother Thomas prayed for him, and was haunted by him nightly, that rash, angular, fiery-eyed fanatic who would surely soon suffer a martyr's death and join the company of God's elect.

In spite of all that their leader could do, the pilgrims, it seemed, grew as indecisive as the men of Lincolnshire, and more divided. There were gentry and clergy among them and nobles like Lord Dacre, as well as the mass of common people. Some cared most about the suppression of God's houses, others about taxation. Some were concerned at the rising cost of food and clothing, others about enclosures of common land; others still at the Act of Succession which excluded the Princess Mary, who had braved her father's displeasure by remaining faithful to the old religion. Some wanted Henry dethroned, others believed there to be no necessity provided the princess could succeed him. Most believed that, whatever the outcome of the negotiations, the Old Faith would inevitably triumph in the end. While the cellarer in his precise voice and orderly manner spelled out the multiplicity of aims, Brother Thomas looked at the bare wall and wondered at God's desertion of His cause.

The weeks turned to months and, while the king gathered confidence and strength, stalemate turned inexorably to disaster, as Brother Thomas had foreseen. A royal army marched north and the pilgrims disbanded with promises of pardon.

At once the butchery began. Men were hanged in chains by the hundred. Their leaders, enticed to London with assurances of safe conduct, were arrested and executed. The clergy were not spared. Abbots of the great houses of Jervaux and Fountains were martyred for complicity in the pilgrimage. So were the abbot of Whalley and the prior of Bridlington. Among the seculars the cellarer reported the name of the vicar of Newark.

Brother Thomas became sick with fear. Every day he expected the thunder of a different army on the gate – one demanding in the name of the king the persons of the abbot and himself. One day he steeled himself to the prospect of martyrdom; on the next he knew that the weakness of his flesh could never bear the torture.

What tidings of Aske, he kept asking – writing the words down and thrusting them at the cellarer. When he heard, he wished he had not asked. Aske's rashness had brought him down: he had trusted a Tudor's word. The king invited him to London as spokesman of his cause and distinguished him with a special promise of safe conduct. He was seized, interrogated and condemned as a traitor. Instead of dying in the Tower like the other leaders, he was returned to the north in chains for public exhibition and hanged high above the Clifford Tower so that all in York should see for themselves the fate of overmighty subjects. There he exchanged the agony of a martyr for the ecstasy of everlasting bliss, and Brother Thomas was no longer in doubt: he and the abbot should have died by his side, however hopeless the enterprise.

The blaze in that single eye had lit a fire which would signal his devotion down the ages.

A few days later a man called at the abbey in the middle of the night. He insisted on speaking to Brother Thomas. He would give no name, state no business, nor talk with any other. Brother Thomas was awakened and went to the porter's lodge expecting arrest.

'I have a message for you and your abbot,' said the man. 'It comes from my master, Robert Aske. Before he died for the Faith he bade me bring you word that what you told him he has carried with him to the next world. Although cruelly tortured, he kept his honour and the solemn pledge of secrecy. He asks nothing in return but your prayers for his soul.'

Brother Thomas said nothing: his vow forbade him. Before he could even make a sign of gratitude or benediction the messenger was gone.

2

The months grew old and became years, and still the abbot abased himself among the lepers and Brother Thomas refused to speak.

All the news which came from the world told of the triumph of evil. The Protestant Queen Jane gave birth to a son. The leaders of the White Rose party were executed: the marquis of Exeter, Lord Montague, Sir Edward Neville – none of whom had raised a finger to help Aske's pilgrims. In the churches all images of Our Lady were destroyed. At Canterbury the bones of St Thomas, who had defied a king, were taken from his shrine and burned to ashes. The destruction of the smaller monasteries was completed, and an Act to suppress the great houses was passed. Without the abbot of Croyland the church party drifted unguided towards disaster.

The poor prior felt he could live no longer in such a world and decided to surrender himself to God. The combined affliction of his responsibilities and the wickedness around him, culminating in the threat to the very existence of Croyland, enfeebled his mind. He took to the abbot's bed and believed himself to be St Guthlac, back in happier days.

When Brother Thomas called to pay his respects he was greeted as Beccelm, the saint's servant. The prior wanted to be reassured that what he could see from the window was a sow with a litter of white piglets sheltering under a willow tree, for that was the spot where God had ordered him to build his cell.

Brother Thomas nodded to humour him, and the prior roused himself to instruct the Devil to bring stone for God's edifice. This was what the saint had done, but the prior appeared to be having trouble with the Devil. He spoke to him angrily, sometimes calling him Satan and sometimes King Henry.

At the approach of death he demanded that Tatwin, the faithful boatman who had brought him to Croyland, should be summoned to receive his blessing, and the reluctant Gervase was forced to play the part. When the old man had received the Eucharist and made peace with his Maker, his last concern was that he should be buried in the shroud given to the saint by the abbess of Repton. An old sheet was shown him and he was satisfied. With a message of farewell to Headda, the bishop of Winchester who had ordained the hermit Guthlac and been dead eight hundred years, he closed his eyes and went to sleep, not to wake again until the Day of Judgment.

In the chapter house that evening the brethren were of one mind: the death of the prior and his vision of himself as the saint foreshadowed the end of the abbey. If that was the will of God nothing could alter it, but they could not endure it without the abbot. A new master for the leper-house was appointed in case their lord could be induced to return to the world. Brother Thomas listened dumbly to what they asked of him.

When night fell he took up his post outside the church near the leper's squint. The hours passed. Then in the stillness between midnight and dawn the abbot came, nearing now his three score years and ten, but still erect, striding up from the stream like a young man, authority in every step.

Brother Thomas allowed him to finish his devotions. Then he touched him on the sleeve and peered into his face. The moon was shining and he was fearful of what ravages might greet him. Sparse hair, wrinkled and darkened skin – these might be expected from an old man. But vanished eyebrows, dilated nostrils, pouting lips, blotches and sores, ulcers and tumours – these would tell the awful truth.

When he took courage to look, there was none of them. Contagion had not marked the royal countenance, and he could not restrain a cry of joy at God's mercy.

'Keep your distance,' said the abbot sternly. His voice was strong, carrying no hint of the hoarseness of leprosy.

Instead Brother Thomas drew closer. Daringly he seized and kissed a hand.

The abbot pulled it away. 'What do you want of me?'

Brother Thomas touched his lips to remind him of his vow.

'Speak or go away.'

For the first time in three years Brother Thomas spoke.

His tongue felt cumbersome, but it delivered the words framed as his mind and heart demanded. 'The prior has died. The abbey is condemned. We are leaderless. Father Gerard is even now preparing to go to the lepers. Come back to us, father. We need your guidance.'

Since he became an outcast the abbot had softened, it seemed. Meekly he consented to consider the plea that his sin had been expiated and his duty lay now with his flock. He would consult with God.

In the morning, when a petition signed by the whole chapter reached him, he was persuaded to return to his own lodgings. There he remained, wrapped in prayer and isolated in quarantine, until the abbey's physicians pronounced him free of disease and contamination. On the following Sunday, at a triumphant thanksgiving service, wearing the Ibi et Ubi – the rich red cope reserved for high occasions, he was ceremonially received back from the grave in front of the largest congregation within living memory.

The triumph was short-lived. The monasteries could not be saved – neither his nor any other. The end came the same year, on the fourth day of December, the feast day of St Barbara and St Osmund of Salisbury, in the thirty-first year of the reign of King Henry VIII and the twenty-eighth of the abbacy of John Wells. At other abbeys – Glastonbury, Reading, Woburn and Colchester – the abbots could not bring themselves to surrender their ancient houses and were martyred after futile resistance. At Croyland the abbot met the king's commissioner at the gate and formally surrendered the keys. He performed this last duty unsmiling but with a final display of the manners which had made 'Croyland courtesy' proverbial since the day of Abbot Turketul six centuries before.

All the inhabitants of the abbey were dispersed. Those

who had lived their lives within its walls were sent 'home'. Stewards and under-stewards, surveyors and servants and labourers, grooms and porters, cooks, bakers, brewers, barbers, nurses and patients in the infirmary — away they went to kin and kith in near or distant villages, or moved into homesteads in Croyland in the hope of work or charity from new masters.

The abbot arranged everything, spoke to everyone. Every day and all day, as they left, he stood at the great gate giving them money and advice and his blessing. The money came from his private purse, for the abbey's property had been sequestered: its manors, its buildings, its sacred treasures down to the silver crucifix which used to hang from his neck. The advice came from his long experience. The blessings came from his heart.

Brother Thomas stood by his side, smiling his God-be-with-you's as bravely as he could. The brethren left last of all, carrying nothing with them but the black habits of their condemned Order and the pension of ten pounds a year which the abbot had won for them by his compliance. While they made their sad farewells at the main gate Father Gerard led the lepers away across the water meadows on a long march to Lincoln, where the abbot had arranged for them to be admitted into the hospital of the Holy Innocents.

When the two of them alone of the whole community remained, the abbot told Brother Thomas that it was time for him to go and Brother Thomas replied that he was going where the abbot went, that he had no intention of leaving his side either that day or ever again.

Together they camped in the abbot's lodgings. All the furniture and hangings of value had been removed. Outside, the other buildings were being demolished and the thud of falling masonry jarred them to the soul. The chancel of the church was first to go, then the transepts, then the cloisters with the chapter house and library, the refectory and dormitory. One by one God's buildings bowed to the royal commissioner's men, recruited from Peterborough because no Croyland man would undertake the work.

When he had levelled also the guest houses, the infirmary and even the lepers' huts, the commissioner congratulated himself on the success of his assignment and the abbot on his co-operation. He regretted that he could not spare him his lodgings, but his orders were strict. Nevertheless, where there had been no resistance it was the government's policy to treat the head of the house generously. A life pension of £133 6s 8d per annum would be paid to him out of the abbey's former revenues, which should enable him to house himself elsewhere in comfort.

The next day brought a messenger from Peterborough with a better offer. There the abbey church had been spared to become a cathedral. The former abbot of Peterborough was to be made bishop. Would the former abbot of Croyland accept the appointment of dean? The commissioner urged it. God's work was still to be done and the stipend would be higher than the pension (which, it did not escape the abbot's notice, the government would not then be required to pay).

The abbot discussed the offer with Brother Thomas, who in preparation for a new life had taken holy orders and was now Father Thomas and the abbot's self-appointed chaplain and confessor. The choice of the rival and lesser house of Peterborough for the new see was a humiliation. So would be the acceptance of such a post by the former spokesman of the old church party. But these considerations, they agreed, should not be decisive. The destruction all about them was a running wound of sorrow. Would it not be best to leave? They asked themselves and they asked God, and the answer was clear: they could not persuade themselves to desert Croyland. It was the will of God that they should stay.

One day God would call King Henry and Thomas Cromwell to account to Him for what they had done. Then might not Croyland Abbey rise again?

3

The nave of the abbey church still stood – a symbol of hope. From its earliest days the villagers had worshipped in the north aisle, and this had saved it. This part of the building was not monastic, but the parish church.

With money from his pension the abbot bought a house in the village. It faced the ruins of the great gate and the miraculously preserved western front of the church. From their garden he and Brother Thomas could still wonder at the scenes from the life of the saint carved in quatrefoil over the doorway and adore the huge figure of Christ which leaned out in eagerness to bless mankind.

Now that no monks remained to conduct the services, a rector was required. Brother Thomas exercised all his powers of persuasion on the commissioner, pleading for the abbot's appointment; but in vain. Subject to the bishop's approval the parishioners could choose their own rector, said the commissioner, but it would be contrary to government policy for them to nominate the abbot.

The abbot, however, unknown to Brother Thomas, took an interest in the appointment too, and the villagers, since they could not have the abbot himself, willingly accepted his nominee, who was Brother Thomas. So the brother who had recently become father now became first rector of the parish under the style of the Reverend Thomas Croyland; although no one in the village called him anything but Brother Thomas to his dying day. The cure brought him, in addition to his pension of ten pounds a year, free lodging in a gallery in the church formerly used as the Master of Works' office (which he now used for housing the needy) and fishing rights worth five shillings per annum (which he distributed as alms on St Guthlac's feast day).

With Brother Thomas engaged on his new duties Gervase returned from his father's house at Spalding to look after the abbot. Then one day a fourth member joined the household. Margaret Skelton arrived, on foot, exhausted and destitute. Her father had been taken to the castle at Fotheringhay for interrogation and died under torture, refusing to the end to answer questions put to him. His property was declared forfeit to the Crown, the servants had fled, and she had been evicted. She came to Croyland a fugitive from the world, seeking what sanctuary it could offer in such times.

'Whatever protection we can afford you, my daughter, you may have,' the abbot told her: 'willingly and in God's name.'

'Amen,' said Brother Thomas, quelling his excitement and alarm at the prospect of her living in the same house. His guilt at her father's suffering was a scar on his soul.

Gervase was never told the abbot's true identity but he had guessed near enough the truth. When he confided this to Margaret, she was more content than ever to serve both rector and abbot – the last of the Skeltons with the last of the house of York. In the garden she planted a bed of white roses.

On the site of the abbey, carts came and went, busily bearing away the precious stones for buildings elsewhere.

Quarried at Barnack long ago, they were good for many more centuries. The cathedrals at Lincoln and Ely and the great parish church and bell tower at Boston were built of the same freestone. They at least would endure in God's service.

Reconciled to His will, the abbot watched and bore the noise without complaint. When the new owners of the abbey's farms and the new lords of the abbey's manors sent their stewards to him for information and counsel he received them with his unfailing Croyland courtesy. The rigorous training of self-discipline enabled him to advise without rancour these greedy sacrilegious men who showed such ignorance of the needs and problems of his fen-rich former kingdom. Good-hearted arable land, lush pasturage for cattle, well-planted spinneys, hay for their fodder, thatch for their houses, wood for their fires, birds and fishes in abundance for their table – all this these men with ready cash and the king's favour had inherited. Without the abbot's guidance they would soon have allowed the sea walls and banks of the dykes to crumble, and the whole district of Holland would have reverted to the desert swamp from which the abbey had raised it in the labour of God's love.

Brother Thomas, being younger, was less reconciled. He lived for the day when the abbey, like the Lord Himself, would rise again.

'You will have need of patience,' the abbot told him. 'This resurrection will take more than three days.'

Their secret triumph was the preservation of the abbey's records, which – with St Guthlac's sword and Abbot Theodore's skull – they hid beneath floorboards in the abbot's new house. Chancellor Rayne was dead and Master Bedyll fully occupied dissolving abbeys by the hundred. The books in Brother Thomas's beloved library had been pillaged and sold to colleges in Cambridge; copies of deeds proving ownership had been seized; but the ancient charters themselves were not convertible into cash and no one came inquiring for them once the commissioner had done his work and moved on.

When it seemed certain that the despoilers would not return, the treasure was unburied and more fittingly stored in a muniment chest. As well as the chronicles and Titulus Regius for which he had fought so hard, the abbot could console himself with the charter of King Ethelbald founding the abbey, and with charters, statutes and confirmations from a royal array of succeeding kings: Offa and Witlaf (who made the subsequently revoked grant of sanctuary within the five waters of Croyland); Bertulph, Beorred, Eadred, Canute and Edward – benefactors all; and then the Normans in their turn: William, Henry and Stephen.

The abbot pored over these documents as he had never had time to do before and brooded on his predecessors: Kenulph, who came from Evesham to be the first abbot; Siward, head of the community for more than sixty years, and Godric, for more than seventy; Abbot Turketul, the friend of St Dunstan, who had possessed St Bartholomew's thumb; Wulketul, imprisoned by the Conqueror; Abbot Ingulph, who had started the chronicles and endured the famine from which God rescued the brethren by a miraculous appearance in the church of sacks of wheat and flour; and an earlier Abbot John, so hardy that it had taken a fall from a horse in his eighty-fifth year to kill him. They were good men: lords of mankind, but servants of God.

Lovingly he fingered the ancient seals depicting the abbey's coat of arms: three whips to ward off the Evil One, and three knives to symbolise the flaying alive of St Bartholomew, on whose day the abbey had been founded. For centuries, in his honour, the brethren had ceremonially given knives to all who came to worship on that day.

He made it his devout duty to complete the chronicles, telling in his own words the story of the abbey's last days. Brother Thomas's contribution he edited and annotated, particularly the part written during the brother's long silence in defiance of his command. He had no wish to suppress it; he wished only that meticulous accuracy should place the facts beyond the reach of refutation. The record of the house of York, like that of the abbey, could stand without concealment.

One other duty he performed. He assisted Brother Thomas at celebrations of the mass. Men and women walked for miles across the fens to receive the body and blood of Christ from the hands of the last of the lord abbots who had ruled them and their forefathers since the land was first populated.

After the service he would stand unobtrusively at the church door, a step or two behind the rector, and allow all who wanted it to kiss his hand. They remembered him in the days of glory in his jewelled cope and – more apt than they could guess – the abbatical vestment embroidered with the royal arms of England and France. Now he dressed in sombre black like any humble curate, but still they kissed his hand and were comforted, placing their lips on the bare finger where the gold ring of the abbots had glittered in the time of the Old Faith.

Only seven months after the dissolution the political event occurred for which the abbot had earlier striven in vain. Thomas Cromwell fell from favour and was beheaded on Tower Hill under his own iniquitous law of treason. But the king lived on and in the following year, tired of using her as a bait to lure her son the cardinal from Rome, he had the old countess of Salisbury put to death.

Since his return from the lepers, the abbot had never spoken of his Yorkist birth and blood, but the horror of his cousin the countess's death affected him profoundly. The headsman bungled his work, and at the age of nearly seventy Clarence's indomitable daughter had to be chased round the block with her head half hanging from her shoulders. If she had been a man Robert Aske would have needed to look no further for his Plantagenet.

From that day the abbot sank towards death, until one night he went to sleep and in the morning Gervase could do nothing to waken him. God rarely granted Plantagenets the privilege of dying in their beds, but He granted it to this one, who had forsaken princedom to serve Him.

His passing was the occasion of a supernatural happening long remembered in the fens. During that night and for the whole of the following day and night rain fell without pause in such torrents that the countryside was flooded for weeks and at first appeared to be reclaimed for ever by the sea. Nothing like it had been known since the great inundation of 1467, which old folk compared to Noah's flood.

If God was showing sadness, Brother Thomas went further. He was inconsolable and his grief seemed likely to carry him off too. Had any man before been required to bury an adored companion a second time?

In honour of his sovereign lord he conducted a high requiem mass, not in what had become the church, where the villagers worshipped, but in the cold bare nave where the rain blew in at the broken windows and the birds, nesting high in the mouldering clerestory, left their droppings on the stone-flagged floor. In front of the largest gathering of the faithful since the dissolution he knelt in a blaze of dancing candlelight before the spot where the altar had stood.

In his sermon he begged the congregation for their prayers

to ease the passage of the abbot's soul through Purgatory, although Purgatory had long since been abolished by royal decree. His text he took from the chronicles – words referring to the death of another abbot, who became afflicted with blindness in old age.

'Whom God loveth He chasteneth, and scourgeth every son whom He receiveth. But at last God transferred him from the wicked world and vale of tears to a region of everlasting light and peace.'

4

It was generally accepted in Croyland and the surrounding villages that the abbot's death unhinged Brother Thomas's mind. Though as conscientious as ever in the cure of souls, his smile became vacant, his attention hard to retain, his eyes focussed indefinitely on what others could not see.

The monument he erected was as extravagant as his sorrow. The site of St Guthlac's original cell lay at the foot of the abbey church's southern tower. The abbot must therefore be buried at the foot of the northern, regardless of any inconvenience caused to worshippers by the fact that this was the entrance to the parish church. The huge tomb rose to the height of a man and half blocked the doorway. The stone slab on top was taken from the saint's desecrated tomb. On this was carved an inscription, invisible except to the birds and those who cared to scramble up the side of the monument. Those who did reported its curiosity and confirmed the belief in Brother Thomas's insanity. To all inquiries about it he replied with one of his vaguest and sweetest smiles.

With the passage of the years the eccentricities of the rector of Croyland grew famous throughout the fens and beyond. By night he could be found keeping his private vespers and mattins, sometimes among the bird droppings in the nave, at others in the cemetery where his old choir-stall had stood in the days when the church had a chancel. By day he was often to be seen swinging his legs on the parapet of the Trinity bridge – first mentioned in the charter of King Eadred in the year 943, as he was pleased to inform visitors, proud that something monastic had survived from the abbey's glorious Saxon days.

He sat there in the centre of the village, not listening to 'bridge talk', as gossip was called in Croyland, but overseeing with glazed eyes the flock he had inherited from the abbot and talking busily to no one visible. He mumbled about people like King Eadred as though they were still alive and argued with himself, using different voices, one of which resembled the abbot's. Children had to be stopped from mimicking him, and their parents whispered to each other memories of the prior and how madness was the way of monks. But most defended him. At least he did not imagine himself to be St Guthlac, and he continued to perform his parish duties capably and could be lucid enough when occasion demanded.

Gervase left after the abbot's death, and Brother Thomas lived alone with Margaret Skelton, which excited further whispering. He loved but would not marry her because, although absolved from his vow of chastity by the king, he had made it to God. She served him with food, otherwise he would have fasted every day. She washed and patched his clothes, otherwise he would have been taken for a vagrant. She shaved him as he had always been shaved, and his monkish tonsure was a sight to be shown to strangers. Any other priest would have been fined and imprisoned for it, but no fensman would let Brother Thomas be harmed, and his tonsured head was said to be the last seen in reformation England.

He lived unmolested through the reign of Henry's son to rejoice in the accession of Mary. When Cardinal Pole came to England at long last – to marry Mary (not himself, as he had once hoped, but to a Catholic king) – Brother Thomas remembered Robert Aske. When God weighed the pair of them in His celestial scales, who could doubt which would be found wanting? The hero 'without consequence or support', as the abbot had judged him, or the coward in the red hat?

During Mary's reign Brother Thomas all but lost his faith. The old religion returned to the seat of power but the monasteries were not restored. Two only were attempted, and both failed. Those who had robbed God were too powerful to be forced to disgorge their loot. How would Queen Mary, the staunch adherent of the Old Faith, behave towards the impious Edward, Lord Clinton, who had bought the site of Croyland Abbey from King Henry's son? Brother Thomas waited confidently for the thunder of her wrath and prepared his petition for the re-forming of the community. But nothing happened. Faith had passed. The age of the hard-faced worshippers of mammon had come to stay. The religious life would never return in his time. He would never see the stones of Croyland reassembled and re-erected to the glory of God.

The end came when Mary died. Confronted with Elizabeth's Acts of Supremacy and Uniformity, Brother Thomas was forced to admit to himself that not only the monasteries had gone, but his Church too. All parish priests had now to conform to the new ways. For him it was an unendurable choice between the cure of Croyland's souls and a final acknowledgment of royal supremacy over the life of the spirit. In all conscience he would not take the oath nor use a prayer-book which was plainly heretical. Neither, in all conscience, could he surrender Croyland to a heretic priest.

There was a third way, and before the dreaded day of decision came God intervened to solve His servant's dilemma.

Towards the close of the first year of the reign of Queen Elizabeth the rector of Croyland collapsed while administering the sacrament at holy communion. At his own request he was carried outside and laid on the site of the shrine of St Guthlac. There the saint's body had been preserved a full year after death without corruption. There, century after century, he had performed miracles for the faithful. From there he had risen to put into Brother Thomas's mind the solution to his historic inquiry.

There Brother Thomas died, in Margaret Skelton's arms. The priest from Spalding arrived in time for him to make his last confession. At the end he recovered enough consciousness to whisper with his last breath: 'God save King Richard the Fourth.'

EPILOGUE

Brother Thomas was buried where he died: in the bosom of his saint. His body lay in peace until another civil war broke out and another Cromwell came to power. This second Cromwell paid Croyland the honour of a visit, in pursuit of royalist soldiers who had taken refuge in the derelict nave. When they would not surrender he blew them out with a cannonade, and the mortal remains of the abbot and Brother Thomas with them.

In the years which followed, the roof of the nave collapsed, the south aisle was taken down, and the skeleton of the great church sagged, stone by stone.

Yet the north aisle has remained a parish church to this day. Beside it one dog-toothed arch strides across the grass to mark the crossing where the central tower stood, and the remains of the west front rise like a giant curtain of stone. Each passing decade erodes still further the statues of the saints and kings and abbots who made the splendour of Croyland. Among them can still be seen St Guthlac holding his whip over a prostrate demon, St Bartholomew his knife, King Ethelbald his charter and Abbot Ingulph his chronicle.

All the monastic buildings have vanished, as though sunk into the soft ground like the piles of oak and alder on which the first abbey was built. In the place of the chancel and cloisters and abbot's lodgings a forest of tombstones has grown. But the triangular bridge, which was old in Brother Thomas's time, is still in the village. The two-armed river it spanned has long gone underground; so now, for old times' sake, it is left to straddle a corner of the market place.

Of the documents which the abbot and Brother Thomas preserved, most have perished, but copies of the charters and parts of the chronicles have survived. Some loving hand, perhaps Margaret Skelton's, has ensured the preservation of the Titulus Regius, unique and incontrovertible evidence that a much maligned king did not usurp his nephew's throne.

Today Croyland is known as Crowland. It lies forgotten a few miles from its triumphant rival, Peterborough. At Westminster and St Alban's, too, the abbey churches remain in the service of God. Glastonbury and Fountains and Bury St Edmunds are remembered and their ruins visited. But Croyland, which stood their equal for more than eight hundred years, lies in the oblivion of what are still remote and sparsely populated fens. The old ballad is no longer sung; its advice no longer heeded:

> In Holland, in the fenny lands
> Be sure to mark where Croyland stands.

Yet the records remain. The abbot and Brother Thomas will be remembered. Their names are in the church: John Wells last on the roll of abbots, Thomas Croyland first on the roll of rectors. With them is one surviving relic: the pierced skull of the martyred Abbot Theodore.

Nothing remains of the last lord abbot's splendid tomb. But in the reign of the first Elizabeth an itinerant antiquarian discovered the strange inscription. 'It puzzled the curious,' he wrote, 'for none could tell whether this mighty edifice contained one man or two, and, if a second there were, why one nobly born should lie unregarded in such rude desolation as here there be; but they do say that he who carved the words was wanting in his wits.'

The head of the stone, so he noted, commemorated 'John of Croyland, last of the abbots', and at the foot was inscribed the name 'Richard of England, last of the Plantagenets'. If this was ambiguous, as the antiquarian complained, the words between were singular enough.

'With him died Faith and Hope, and at his going God wept for England.'

THE PLANTAGENET HOUSES OF YORK AND LANCASTER

(as set out by Brother Thomas)

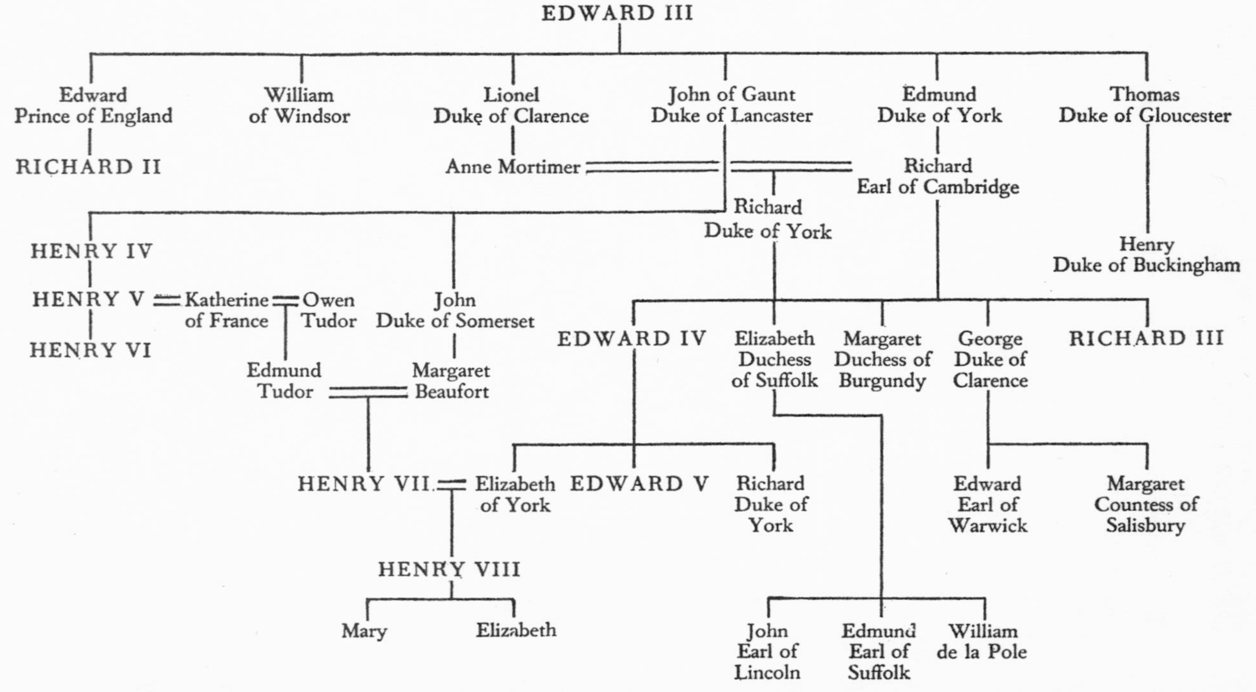